From silver crisis to globe-spanning adventure!

When you're a "bear"
in the big money game,
you'd better know
who your friends are . . .

Books by Paul Erdman

The Billion Dollar Sure Thing
The Crash of '79
The Last Days of America
The Silver Bears

Published by POCKET BOOKS

PAUL E. ERDMAN

THE SILVER BEARS

PUBLISHED BY POCKET BOOKS NEW YORK

POCKET BOOKS, a Simon & Schuster division of
GULF & WESTERN CORPORATION
1230 Avenue of the Americas, New York, N. Y. 10020

Prologue

The southwestern corner of Persia is for the most part a desert. Today it goes under the name of Khuzistan. The region's best known town is Abadan, where Iran's tremendous output of crude oil is refined, and then sent on its way to the world's filling stations.

Three thousand years ago Abadan was just an uninhabited swamp at the mouth of the Tigris and Euphrates rivers. The petroleum resources of the area immediately to the north, instead of fueling car engines, fed superstition, particularly Zoroastrianism. In that religion fire, which magically jetted from the bowels of the earth, was the central feature of worship. This fire was, of course, derived from the gases discharged by underground petroleum deposits. At that time, the province was known as Elam, and its capital was a place called Shushan, or Zusa, or Susa. It was not only the largest town in Persia, but one of the most important cities of the ancient world. It was already inhabited in 4000 B.C., and reached its pinnacle between 600 and 350 B.C., when it served as the capital of a series of empires—under Nebuchadnezzar, Cyrus, Darius, Xerxes, and Artaxerxes. Shushan went into eclipse around 326 B.C. when Alexander the Great captured it. It is recorded by Plutarch that he made a tremendous windfall gain in the process, cleaning up the equivalent of hundreds of millions of dollars worth of treasure, in the form of precious metals, as the spoils of victory. But Alexander did not live to spend it. Just a short time later he got knocked off in Babylon, a few hundred miles to the west.

The Bible keeps fairly close track of Elam, and its capital Shushan. Already in Genesis, chapter 10, it is written that one of Noah's great-grandchildren settled there. A few chapters later, in Genesis 14, it is said that the King of Elam got together with a few of his buddies and made war on Sodom and Gomorrah. Which goes to show that the people of Shushan and surroundings did not go for excessive lasciviousness, false idols, or any other such liberal nonsense. Daniel found this out the hard way. When the Elamite King Nebuchadnezzar discovered Daniel kneeling by a palace window, praying to some god called Jahweh instead of toeing the local Zoroastrian line—whambo, right into Shushan's lion's den. Still, the Book of Esther shows that the rulers of Shushan were not completely adverse to a bit of fun and games, especially with the girls. The king involved this time—with the rather heavy name of Ashasuerus—decided that his wife Vaschti had to go. To choose a successor he staged what must have been the first Miss World contest, with the interesting twist that the judging was based on a series of one night stands in the king's nocturnal chambers. Twelve months later, perhaps more attributable to sheer exhaustion than true love, the king decided on the dark-eyed Jewess Esther, who promptly inherited Vaschti's crown and a permanent place in Ashasuerus's bed.

But enough of queens, beauty contests, and lion's dens. What is interesting is that bed. For according to

Esther, chapter 2, verse 6, in the palace at Shushan "the beds were of gold and silver." Moving along to chapter 5, it is recorded that this same king, Ashasuerus, paid out 10,000 talents of silver to a chap called Hamman, as if the amount involved was just pocket money. Now in those days, a talent of silver equalled 60 minas, a mina equalled 60 shekels, and a shekel equalled 252 ⅔ fine grains of silver. Multiplied out, this means that Hamman carted away 18,840,000 troy ounces of silver. Today that silver would be worth well over $100. million! Which brings one to the conclusion that the province of Elam, and its capital Shushan, not only sat on top of a lot of oil, but was also positively loaded with silver.

But there seemed to be a thing about that silver. While Elam's oil was obviously a gift of the gods, Shushan's silver had the nasty tendency of bringing rather bad luck. Like Alexander, Hamman was given little time to live it up with his new-found riches. The Bible describes it thus: "So they hanged Hamman on the gallows that he had prepared for Mordecai." His alleged crime: conspiracy. Connoisseurs of that fine art of execution may be interested to note that the structure employed was "50 cubits high," which works out to about 75 feet. One cannot help but stop to ponder on how the hell they got him up there. By rope?

Today Shushan, or Susa, is just four huge mounds of earth, barely visible a couple of miles west of the main road—if you can call it a road—leading from Abadan, on the Persian Gulf, to Dizful, at the foot of the Zagros Mountains in central Iran. Knowledge of

Shushan's fabulous silver source died with the city. It was not until the late 1960's that this age-old secret surfaced anew. The consequences were severely felt by tens of thousands of commodity speculators in the United States, in Europe, and throughout the world, who lost their shirts in the biggest market manipulation engineered in the 20th century. Others—a few others—made a fortune. Behind it all was yet another Shushan conspiracy. But to this day, nobody appears to know what really happened. Because the secret of Shushan is still locked up, this time in the vaults of a Swiss bank, and in the heads of the surviving members of that conspiracy.

A few of those people are Americans. Their involvement began in the desert. Not in the desert of southwestern Persia, but rather in the wastelands of the southwestern part of the United States. The time: late March of 1967, A.D.

Part 1

(1967)

The Grand Canyon in late March was a bleak place. Even the rustic lobby of the Big Lodge, on the edge of the southern rim, usually bustling with hordes of tourists and their subhordes of screaming brats, was totally deserted. For it was not only March; it was also a Sunday morning, a time when the God-fearing people of Arizona were either in church or still in bed with a bad conscience.

The total peace was broken around 10:45 when a black Cadillac pulled up. The grey-haired man who emerged was also in black. He pushed through the revolving doors, a strangely incongruous mechanism in this Wild West setting, and approached the reception desk. There was not a soul in sight. But there was a bell. So the man in black banged on it, three times, hard. It was a rather small bell, but it produced one hell of a loud noise, or at least it seemed that way in contrast to the silence which had prevailed prior to the entrance of this intruder. The audible result of the bell-banging was soon replaced by a visible one, in the form of a clerk clad in levis and plaid shirt. After a few words had been exchanged, the clerk handed over a key, in fact, two keys. One of them was for the hotel lounge, just in back of the lobby. It was closed to the general public at this time of year, since there was very little general public requiring its use. The man in black, followed rather meekly by the clerk, unlocked the door, gave the lounge a quick once-over, nodded his O.K., and closed up again. He then disappeared up the staircase, led by the hotelkeeper carrying his only luggage, a small black leather satchel.

Within a few minutes the clerk was back in his lobby, just in time to meet another incoming guest. It was again a single gentleman, also middle-aged, this time in dark blue serge, pink shirt, red tie, and brown cigar. He was without luggage. In fact, it seemed that he was just trying to locate the coffee shop; it was off the lobby to the left, opposite the staircase, and likewise deserted, except for a floozy-looking blonde waitress who took five minutes before she managed to produce the desired cup of coffee. During the next half hour there was a steady uptrend in activity: five more somberly clad men, all but one with cigars, and all wanting a morning coffee. The lone non-smoker was a gum-chewer. The six of them, lined up at the coffee bar, strongly resembled old crows perched on a fence. At least this was the thought of the waitress as she surveyed her silent guests. At 11:45 as if by magic, her flock suddenly deperched, and disappeared into the lobby, leaving behind a cloud of tobacco fumes, six empty cups, a faint touch of juicy fruit in the air, and five tips totalling seventy cents. The man in the black suit with the key was there to greet them. Again without a word he just motioned with his head toward the lounge door. They all entered, the door closed, the lock clicked, and silence returned to the lobby of the Big Lodge on this cold, but sunny, Sunday morning in March.

Inside a murmur of conversation suddenly developed. One by one the men took chairs and grouped them around a low massive table, built from raw timber which had been hacked up and then nailed together by the local purveyor of genuine western lodge furnishings. The man in charge, Joe Fiore, plunked his massive body into the biggest armchair available, and also plunked his highly polished shoes onto the surface of the table, adding another nick to the formidable collection already visible.

"Perfect, ain't it?" he asked.

"Yeah," was the collective and unanimous answer.

"Anybody tailed?" was Joe's next question.

No. Nobody had been tailed. The man from New York had flown into Phoenix and, after a night's sleep, driven up in an Avis. The representative from Chicago had come by way of Albuquerque airport, where he had picked up a Hertz. The Miami man had used Reno as his transfer point. And so it was with the men from Boston, Los Angeles and St. Louis. All had come the prior evening into separate western airports, and then driven themselves hundreds of miles along almost completely deserted high-speed roads to this meeting place on the edge of the Grand Canyon. Except for Joe Fiore; he had come directly from Las Vegas with his own long black Caddie.

"I'm sorry about any inconvenience you might have had getting here. But I think we all agree that one can't be too careful these days."

Everybody agreed that, indeed, one could not be too careful these days, or any other days. Then the man from New York spoke up.

"So all right. We're here. Now what's the big deal?"

"The big deal, Tony, is that I can get us out of our mutual financial predicament. You all know how difficult things have become since the banks have to photostat all evidence of financial transactions over ten thousand dollars. We're hamstrung. All we can do is sit on cash. But no longer. I finally found a foolproof way to put our money to work in legitimate investments without the Feds or anybody else being able to trace it back to us."

"Yeah, how?"

"Gentlemen, through a Swiss bank!"

The muteness which met this revelation was total, except for a disgusted, unidentified, faint, yet distinct, "Jeezus!"

Then the man from Chicago spoke up.

"Ah come on now, Joe, what's so fuckin' great about that? For Chrissake since years everybody claims we've been using Swiss banks to hide our money. Where've you been all that time, for crying out loud?"

"Now hold on one damn minute," interrupted Fiore. "Sure I know everybody's been saying that. But do you know anybody at a Swiss bank?" He pointed his finger at Chicago.

"Or you?" This time the finger swung toward New York. Then Miami.

They all looked at each other. No, nobody had ever dealt with a Swiss bank. Joe Fiore beamed.

"You see," he said triumphantly, "everybody yaks about it, but nobody's ever done it."

"But Joe," said Los Angeles, "after all the phoney propaganda in almost every newspaper in the world

6

about us using Swiss banks, I'm sure no respectable bank in Switzerland would touch our business with a ten foot pole. I mean, they could get into trouble, and then we would get into trouble."

"You are right," replied Fiore. "And I know, gentlemen, I have been to Switzerland. I even opened up a numbered account with a big bank in Zurich. Until, somehow, they must have heard something. Then I got a letter requesting me to transfer my funds elsewhere, and within seven days."

"So then why drag us all the way out to this god-forsaken hole in the ground?" asked Boston.

"Because I've found the perfect solution. I bought us a Swiss bank, lock, stock, and barrel. This way we won't need those Swiss jerks, or anybody else. We run our own show, with our own boys, and our own money."

"And when somebody over there finds out who controls it? Then what?" It was Boston again.

"I've fixed that. I found the perfect front man. A prince. A real one. Him and me got to be real, you know, simpatico. But he also understands our system. So he'll keep his mouth shut. Forever."

Skepticism reigned in the lounge of the Big Lodge. The man from St. Louis, who was known as a very kind and decent man, restricting his activities to gambling and prostitution, adamantly refusing to have anything to do with any of the rougher, though more lucrative lines of business, then interceded.

"Come on, you guys, let's hear Joe out. Maybe he does have something." He turned to Fiore. "How would it work, Joe?"

Joe Fiore looked hurt, deeply hurt, but he continued. "I'll set up a courier service. My boys will pick up your excess cash on a regular basis, and then take it over to our bank in Switzerland via Mexico. It will disappear just like that." He snapped his fingers with a loud crack. "Then we invest it, like the Rothschilds and all those other big guys do over there. The whole world will be open to us. Gentlemen, this could mean the big chance for us to start our sons on sound careers. As we grow, there will be lots of room for our boys to move into the operations over there. I tell you, it's time to think and plan ahead. Sure, we've all done great in our own way. But maybe our way won't be that of our kids. Here's a chance to put both our money and our kids to work, in a high-class legitimate way."

The plea was a passionate one. It would have won admiration especially in the elite financial circles of New York. For as many of the more historically inclined men on Wall Street knew only too well, some of the nation's strongest financial institutions had been built on a heritage no less simple, or shady, than the group of men gathered together on this winter morning in Arizona. Sure, it had been accomplished in many ways. But the quickest and surest method of gaining a foothold in the Establishment was by founding that ultimate symbol of the Establishment: a bank!

Such subtleties of Joe Fiore's vision were beyond the comprehension of his colleagues, as was soon evidenced by the response from New York.

"Yeah," he said, "but although my son is a damn smart kid, he's only thirteen right now. So who's going to run the bank until junior is ready to become senior vice president?" New York had obviously married late.

Joe decided to overlook both New York's sarcasm and the laughter it produced.

"I have put together a small team of men from my organization. They will be leaving this evening for Switzerland to take over operations. Believe me, they're the best I've got. All I'm asking of you is to indicate whether or not you're interested. If so, I'll let you each have a piece of the action, like eight percent of the shares of the bank each. And at my original cost. The only thing I ask in return is that you come through with regular deposits for the bank."

Silence.

"So who wants in?" asked Joe.

Still silence.

Then Tony Regazzoni of New York spoke up. "Listen, Joe. I think we all need some time to think this over. Why don't you go ahead over there in Switzerland, and then let us know how things are working out. I'm sure, after we can see some kind of track record, all of us would like very much to come in. But later, not now."

Everybody else in the room nodded agreement.

So New York continued. "All right. So that's settled. Now as long as we're here, I'd like you all to know that somebody has been running heroin into my territory during the past month and has wrecked the market. I hear it's coming from Montreal. Once something like this gets started, it can spread to . . ."

With a feeling of great relief, the men in the room

got down to a discussion of day-to-day business problems. Joe Fiore listened for a short while, and then slipped out of the room. He went straight to the pay phone box in the lobby.

He had the connection with Vegas immediately.

"This is Joe. Gimme Doc."

A short pause.

"Doc? Right. We're going ahead. I want you to get over to L.A. this afternoon and take that flight as planned. And listen, Doc. Either you guys make a go of that goddammed bank over there, or I'll get you. Personally. And now another thing. If I hear of you trying to pull any funny business—and I mean any—you are going to be in deep deep trouble. Understand? This deal is going to be done 100% straight from the word go. Understand?"

The phone squawked full understanding.

"And take good care of Albert. You hear?"

2

At 9 P.M. Alitalia flight 967 left the Los Angeles International airport bound for Milano, Malpensa. Mathew "Doc" Smythe, Marvin Skinner, and Albert Fiore went directly to the cocktail lounge in the front of the D.C. 8 after the big plane had climbed to cruising height. Smythe ordered beer for everybody. After the drinks had arrived, Marvin took a tentative sip, looked around, and then asked:

"Doc, are you sure we're on the right plane?"

"Look, Marvin," replied Doc Smythe, "if I told you once, I've told you a hundred times: just do what I do, and you'll be fine."

"I know you said that, Doc. But this plane is going to Italy, not Switzerland."

Smythe sighed. "Marvin, I know. But for the very last time, let me explain that Lugano, though in Switzerland, is in the Italian part of Switzerland. They speak Italian there. And why? Because it's right on the border of Italy where, as you may have heard, they also speak Italian."

"What's that got to do with it?"

"Nothing."

"Ah come on, Doc. Don't get sore."

"I'm not sore, and to prove it I will finish. Lugano does not have an airport. Milano does. So, we are . . ."

"I know. You explained that before. But it still doesn't seem right. I mean, let's say we wanted to go to Japan. That doesn't mean that, just because it's close to China and they speak almost the same language, that we would . . ."

"Marvin," interjected Doc, "shut up and leave me alone. If you don't believe me, ask Albert."

"Albert," said Marvin. No response. Albert was reading.

"Albert," yelled Doc, "for Chrissake pay attention. Marvin wants to ask you something."

Albert looked up. "Yes?"

"Marvin wants to know whether we are on the right plane or not."

"Yes, I know."

Doc Smythe's eyes searched for help from above. Then he spoke again.

"Well, Albert, could you give Marvin one of two statements: yes, we are on the right plane, or no, we are not on the right plane."

Albert turned to Marvin. "Marvin, we are on the right plane."

"Oh," said Marvin, "fine."

Doc's eyes again shifted toward heaven.

"Marvin," he asked, "now why all of a sudden do you believe Albert when you've been pestering me to death?"

"Because Albert is never wrong."

The three then lapsed into silence, much to Doc's relief. Actually, he thought, Marvin was right. That Albert was uncanny. The smartest young bastard he'd ever met. And educated. God was he educated! Yet so quiet, so modest. The contrast between him and his old man was incredible. When Joe first introduced him to the boys in Vegas as his son, Albert, everybody had just stared in disbelief: those thick glasses, the pale thin face, the delicate hands, and on top of everything he had blushed like a schoolgirl. So everybody just ignored him. I mean, what could you do with something like that in Vegas? Then the boss had given him that office, and put him to work calculating odds. The results soon became legend. The kid was a teenage Nick the Greek! Well, not exactly teenage, since Albert was, after all, twenty-six. But he looked sixteen. But no matter. If he quoted two to one odds that the St. Louis Cardinals would take the World Series in 1987 in six games, you could order your tickets the next day from Busch Stadium, and will them to your eight-year-old son, in the sure knowledge that a decade hence he would be enjoying hotdogs and beer under an October Missouri sun. If Albert gave you even money that it would rain twice during the last weekend in August in San Diego, only a fool would go to Southern California at that time without an umbrella. How did he do it?

Doc had been dumb enough to ask one time. As Albert had then elucidated, while studying economics under Paul Samuelson at M.I.T. when he was sixteen, he had become fascinated with the probability theories of two foreigners called John von Neumann and Oskar Morganstern. Then he had branched out into something he called "random walk hypotheses" after he'd moved on to graduate studies under Milton Friedman at the University of Chicago, where he had specialized in monetary analysis. Albert explained that by synthesizing these two analytical approaches, he had developed a technique which was universally applicable where situations resembling games of chance were involved, like horse races, stock markets, commodities, football games, elections—the works. Well, that was the last time that Doc had ever put any more dumb questions to Albert. I mean, who the hell could make head or tails of such answers? And Doc was not one to unnecessarily demonstrate lack of intellect. After all, he had built up a reputation which had to be maintained.

Mathew "Doc" Smythe was undoubtedly the smoothest, the most imaginative, the best-looking crook in the entire West. As anybody who has ever

13

lived west of the Mississippi knows, that really means something, since the competition out there is fierce. Smythe exuded an image which demanded confidence and respect; he projected a magnetism which consistently deluded his fellow man into feeling, no, firmly believing, that somehow they knew—and liked—him. Time and time again he was mistaken for other people: a nationwide newscaster; a Welsh Shakespearean actor; a senator from South Dakota. Smythe's full wavy hair, his strong jaw, piercing blue eyes, his magnificent build, his easy walk—together produced a vision which overwhelmed females from sixteen to sixty-six. His deep voice, sometimes echoing memories of Eton, at other times the polish of Harvard, commanded attention whether across a conference table or through the din of a gambling casino. From small beginnings as a con artist in the Midwest, matured by a three year stay in Leavenworth, Doc had risen steadily to the top of America's criminal ranks. Along the line Chuck Synkiewicz of Milwaukee had become Mathew D. Smythe of Boston. And the self-bestowed Ph.D., sometimes accompanied by an equally phoney LL.D., had also become a standard part of his new personality. But, as many people had found out too late, it was a horrible mistake to regard Doc's idiosyncratic attachment to a totally synthetic set of credentials as a sign of weakness. Beneath the smooth external veneer, the man could match any of his colleagues in those attributes necessary for success in his chosen trade: cynicism, cruelty, and a completely detached view of the value of human life, especially the loss thereof. When a contract was taken on by the Fiore group, Doc was not above direct involvement in its execution, even though years ago he had become the one and only lieutenant of the boss himself. His explanation: he enjoyed it! Doc regarded the Swiss bank job as a diversion of his talents, especially because, for some peculiar reason, the boss apparently wanted him to play it straight. But for how long? Certainly having Joe's son along was not going to make things easier, because if the boy ever got into trouble with the law in Europe, or anywhere else, heads would roll. Marvin Skinner was something else. Slow, yes, but as a counterfeiter, one of the best in the Western Hemisphere. And when it came to rough stuff, Marvin could hold his own with the best of the boys. If Joe planned to play it straight all the way, he would hardly have sent Marvin along. Comforted by this thought, Doc fell asleep as the plane droned its way east.

The immense clock overlooking the concourse of Malpensa airport put the time at 6 P.M., as many hours and time zones later the passengers of Alitalia flight 967 passed through immigration and customs control.

The man standing below the clock, tall, slender, in a superbly fitted topcoat, black Homburg, grey gloves, and carrying a walking stick, moved forward when he spotted the group of three men coming toward him.

"Dottore Smeeth?" he inquired, and when the response was positive, caught the good doctor from Las Vegas in the most Italian of embraces.

"Ah, it is so very good to meet you." Having finally released Doc Smythe, he then turned to Albert.

15

"And you must be little Alberto. Your father Giuseppe has told me so much about you." Another hugging session.

Then Marvin, who had been watching all this in stunned awe, got the same treatment.

"Now," said the one-man greeting party, "I would like to ask all of you a favor. My name, given to me at a time when I was not in a position to control my destiny, is Principe Gianfranco Pietro Annunzio di Siracusa. But all my friends from America call me John. I insist that you must also do the same. You agree?"

For the first time Smythe had a chance to speak up.

"With the greatest of pleasure, John," he said. "But then I must also insist that we dispense with the use of any of my academic titles. No more Dottore, please. I would appreciate your addressing me merely as Mathew."

Marvin continued to stand there with his mouth open. Smeeth! Principe! Dottore! John! Maybe the right plane had been the wrong one after all. But "John" left no time for further reflection.

"Gentlemen," he said, "I have reserved a limousine, since I am sure you will all want to proceed to your hotel in Lugano as quickly and easily as possible. Our driver will take care of your luggage."

Darkness was already falling on northern Italy as they moved swiftly along the autostrada toward the Swiss border. Less than an hour later, they entered the outskirts of Lugano. The view was stunning, even at night. The palm trees lining the city's main boulevard; the reflections on the calm waters of the lake; the little islands of light on the mountains which reared up on all sides. It was a twinkling fairy-tale-like scene, which seemed almost unreal to the three Americans, accustomed as they were to the brassy, flashing glare of Las Vegas by night. Even Doc Smythe could not restrain himself.

"I had no idea it would be so beautiful."

"Ah yes, but it is," said the prince. "La bella Svizzera. So much beauty, and so much money."

The limousine was met by three bellboys as it pulled into the courtyard of the hotel. The manager was immediately summoned by Annunzio, and after a respectful bow, personally assumed responsibility for the installation of the Principe and his honored guests from America. The prince did not linger. He felt that all must be tired after the long trip. He would meet them at nine the next morning, in the lobby.

It was only a few minutes after nine when the limousine moved off again, down the Riva Caccia. At the Via Manzoni it turned left, and entered the Piazza della Riforma. The Principe signalled the driver to stop. Then he and the three Americans stepped out into the crowded square.

"Here we are," said Annunzio.

Doc looked up at the massive front of the ten-storey building, at the marble stairs leading to the glass and metal entrance; then at the uniformed doorman, opening and closing the ornate doors as the bank's clients hurried in and out.

"This time we've really hit the jackpot." His choice

of words showed that Doc had not yet fully completed the transition from the Nevada desert and its gambling dens to this garden spot of Europe, and the lofty atmosphere of international banking.

Then Doc continued. "Let's get in there, and start things moving—American style."

He stepped forward, with Albert and Marvin close behind, and moved up the marble stairs.

"Momento," said the prince.

Doc hesitated.

"Oh, is there to be some kind of ceremony?"

"No," answered the prince, "none that I know of."

"Then let's get going." Doc started up the stairs again.

"Momento," repeated the prince. "You are going the wrong way."

"What do you mean, the wrong way?" asked Doc.

"You have the wrong building. Our bank is over there."

Doc, Marvin, and Albert shifted their eyes in the direction indicated by the Italian's outstretched arm. Over there, across the square, was just a restaurant, and a rather crummy one at that. The name, painted in blue letters across the flaked pink brick façade read:

TRATTORIA MONTE SAN SALVATORE

"Prince, old buddy," said Doc in a voice which suddenly had steel in it, "you've just gotta be kidding. That's a fuckin' pizza parlor!"

"Ah yes," replied Gianfranco, "but of course I do

18

not mean the ristorante. We are on the second floor, *above* the ristorante."

Doc just squinted at the prince, as his hands clenched at his side.

"Look, prince. Let's cut the crap. Just show us the bank and shut up."

The building they approached had two adjacent entrances. One was hung with plastic beads on long strings, designed to reduce, if not eliminate, the number of flies per pizza. The other, which had a door, though not closed, led to a dark narrow staircase. Single-file the four stumbled their way up. Apparently the light either did not work, or did not exist.

At the top of the second flight of stairs there was another door, this time closed. A small smudged card had been tacked to it. It read:

BANCA INTERNAZIONALE
DI SICILIA E AMERICA
IN SVIZZERA S.A.

Another card, obviously new, translated:

INTERNATIONAL BANK
OF SICILY AND AMERICA
IN SWITZERLAND INC.

After barely glancing at them, Doc pushed the prince aside, and opened the door.

"Who's in charge here?" he demanded.

A small man, probably sixty-five, rose from a desk where he had been slouched over a ledger book.

"I am, Signore. I am the chief accountant." Then he proceeded hesitantly. "What may I do for you?"

"You must have heard that the ownership of this bank has changed hands."

"Yes, of course. Signor Matteli—he was our general manager—mentioned it before he left last week. But he gave me no details."

"Where is Signor Matteli now?"

"I don't know, sir. He has left the bank and returned to Sicily. He told me the new owners would be appointing new management. That is you, Signor?"

"Correct. That is me. And these are my colleagues." He just waved his hand at the three gathered at his side, but made no attempt at further introductions.

"Is this all there is to the bank premises?"

"Well, Signor, we have three rooms. Normally the girls work out here, but neither came to work this morning. You see, we really have nothing to do. I have the next office, where I do the accounting with my assistant. He is also not here this morning. He is sick. And Signor Matteli had the third office. But as I said, he is . . ."

"I know," interrupted Doc, "he's somewhere in Sicily."

"Are these the books of the bank?" Doc continued, pointing to the ledger books on the desk.

"Yes, Signor."

"I want to borrow them. Albert," he ordered, "you get to work on them right now. Go back to Matteli's office. Take this fellow with you. I'm going downstairs to have a word with the prince. When you get the full picture, come down and join us. Marvin, you stick with me."

Two hours later they—the prince and the two Americans—sat around a table in the pizza parlor below. Doc Smythe, over his third espresso, wearily continued his interrogation of the prince.

"Look," he asked, "I still can't understand it. I mean, you've been at the bank, seen the place."

"Not exactly."

"What do you mean, not exactly? How did you know where it was then?"

"The agent told me."

"What agent?"

"The agent in Palermo."

"And who's he?"

"He is unimportant. He was acting for the former owners."

"And who are they?"

"A very old Palermo family."

"Yeah, a very old family of Palermo crooks."

"Joe Fiore did not think so. I was convinced also that we were dealing with highly honorable people."

"Honorable? Peddling a broken-down outfit like this?"

"But how was I to know?" protested the prince. "I merely provided the introductions, that's all. Then Joe asked me to join the bank as its Chairman—really, just an honorary position. He felt that it would add to its image."

"Christ!" exclaimed Doc. "Tell me just one last thing. How much did you personally make on this screwjob?"

"Absolutely nothing," exclaimed the prince. "I just acted as a go-between for friends."

"No finder's fee? No consultancy arrangement down there in Palermo?"

"Of course not."

Then Doc leaned across the table and grabbed the prince's arm.

"You know what I think? That you're lying." His fingers tightened. "I don't like liars. I especially don't like dago liars. And you're the biggest wop liar I've ever had the misfortune to meet."

At this moment, Albert Fiore entered the restaurant. His face, normally relaxed and cheerful, looked haggard.

Doc released the prince's arm and turned to Albert, as he drew up a chair.

"Well?"

"Bad. Real bad. I could go into all kinds of detail, but there's really no purpose. These guys simply cleaned out the bank before they left. There's about $1,600 worth of assorted currencies in the safe, and that's it."

"What about deposits, and that sort of thing?"

"Nothing. In fact, from what I can determine, the only deposits this bank ever had were from the former owner and his relatives. This place was really nothing more than a front, set up as a vehicle to help the owner's family dodge taxes."

"What did this guy Matteli do?"

"It's impossible to say. All the records are gone. All we have left to go on are the ledger books. The accountant seems to be perfectly honest. He just did as he was told."

"So what do you think we should do now?" asked Doc.

"Get right back on the plane and go home," responded Albert.

"Let's not get too hasty," said Doc. "We're going to have to think on this for a while. But lemme tell you something, if we do go back to the States, then this guy," once again grabbing the prince's arm, "comes with us."

"I simply don't know what to say," stuttered the prince.

"Then keep your mouth shut," suggested Doc.

"Look Albert," he continued, "is there no way we can get your father's money back at least?"

"Doc," replied Albert dryly, "we can hardly go to court, can we?"

"Then can we somehow try to make a go of this thing?"

"Theoretically yes. The bank does have a full charter to do any and all types of banking, both in Switzerland and abroad. It has an office and skeleton staff. But it has no activity whatsoever. Zero. Provided we could generate some business fast—you know—deposits, loans, foreign exchange, securities management —we might be able to get this thing off the ground. But we must also be realistic. We're all total strangers to this part of the world."

"Oh no," responded Doc, "three of us are, but there's a fourth sitting right across this table who is much too much at home here. Right, prince old boy?

Why I'll just bet that you have friends spread all over Europe who would love to do business with our bank. And I'll bet something else. If you don't come up with something good—quick—you are going to be a dead man."

These last words were spoken softly and slowly.

Doc then rose. "Come on Albert, Marvin. We're going back to the hotel. Prince, you have exactly twenty-four hours to deliver. Don't try to run. Because if you do, I'll get you."

The three Americans left, leaving the Sicilian slumped over the table in the now empty restaurant.

At noon the next day, there was a knock on the door of Doc's hotel room.

"Marvin," he said, "open it."

It was the prince. He looked bad. But there was strength in his grip as he shook hands with each American in turn.

"O.K." said Doc, "let's hear it. And forget the bullshit."

The prince looked around the suite, picked out a chair, sat down, and crossed his legs.

"First," he said, looking directly at Doc, "from now on I expect everyone here to behave in a civilized manner, and to use civilized language."

Then he lit a cigarette.

"Good," he proceeded, "now to the matter at hand. I believe I have—successfully—arranged for our bank to get some business. Big business. During my explanation, I expect all of you to keep quiet."

He looked around the room.

"Have we nothing to drink?"

No answer until finally Albert responded: "No. Would you care for something?"

"Perhaps some wine." He turned to Doc. "You might make the arrangements. The telephone is right beside you."

The puzzled look on Doc's face deepened, but without any comment he picked up the phone on the small table beside his bed, where he lay stretched out, and did as requested.

"Thank you," said Annunzio. Then he spoke again.

"The deal I've arranged involves Iran—Persia, if you prefer. My family has had ties with Iran for many years. In fact, in the past there have been a number of cases of intermarriage with the aristocracy of that country. This may appear strange to you, but you must remember that relations between Sicily and the Near East have been close for many centuries, going back to the Saracens. That is why some of the nouveaux riches in Milan or Turin think they are so clever when they call us Sicilians the Arabs of Europe. Be that as it may. The family I have contacted is very rich. They have enormous landholdings in the southwestern part of Iran, in Khuzistan. For generations these holdings were worthless. The area was a desert. But just a few years ago, an enormous dam was constructed in the mountains immediately to the north. It was named after one of their relatives: Shah Mohammed Reza Pahlavi. The result was water for irrigation. My relatives' desert has been turned into one of the most productive agricultural areas on earth."

"Interesting," interjected Doc, "but not very. We've

been doing the same in the central valley in California for years. Just exactly what has your story got to do with us?"

The prince continued as if Doc did not exist.

"During the past few years, my friends have accumulated large profits, and, being cautious people, they have kept it mostly in cash. In rials, the currency of Iran. But they would like to get this money out. Their memories of people like Mossedegh, who almost succeeded in forcing Iran into the Socialist camp in the early 1950's, are still vivid. They strongly desire to establish a nestegg abroad—something upon which they can fall back if bad times return to their homeland."

He paused and looked at Doc, but this time not a word came from the American.

"But Iran has very stringent laws which prevent any Iranian resident from sending rials abroad, or even converting them into dollars at home. The penalties are severe for breaking this law: as much as ten years incarceration. This may appear overly severe, but I remind you that Iran is a country which punishes people involved in the drug trade with death by firing squad—after a summary hearing before a military court. No appeal possible."

The prince again paused. The lesson on Iranian justice was apparently to be given time to sink in. Doc disappointed him by not appearing at all impressed.

"So," he said, "your relatives want us to bring their money out for them, because they're too scared to do so themselves."

"Exactly."

"How much is it?"

"About four hundred million rials."

"How much is that in dollars?"

"Around five million."

"Well," said Doc, "it would be a start. What would we get out of it for the bank?"

"First, they would be willing to pay a five percent transportation fee. Then they would agree to keep the funds in our bank for an indefinite period, provided, of course, that we give them normal conditions."

"That sounds fair enough," responded Doc. "When do we leave?"

The prince lost just a touch of his former poise. "Are you sure you understand everything I've just told you?"

"Sure. Why? Something bothering you?"

"I thought I quite clearly outlined how severe the law operates in Iran."

"You did."

"Under such conditions, I see no reason why any of us should get personally involved. The risks are . . ."

"Who do you want to send? Our bookkeeper?"

"No, but I do have friends in Sicily who are quite used to this type of thing."

"I'm sure you do, prince old boy. But we have had enough of your Sicilian friends. Oh, no. No more of that stuff. I think your project is just great. And I think you and I—personally—are going to take care of it."

"Can't I come along?" pleaded Marvin.

Doc looked at him for a moment. "No. Both you and Albert stay here."

"Why?" asked Albert.

"Because, dammit, somebody has to. And furthermore, your old man would kill me if anything happened to you, especially where the law's concerned. So Albert, you stay here. And Marvin, you take care of Albert. Maybe while we're gone you two can think up some ways of improving the setup here. Although I doubt it."

At this point there was a knock on the door. The wine had arrived. Doc just motioned toward the table beside the bed, and tossed the waiter a dollar bill after the tray had been deposited.

"Prince," he said, "it's your party, so why don't you do the pouring?"

He did.

With brimming glass in hand, Doc carefully unwound himself from the bed.

"Gentlemen," he said, "I think we have underestimated our friend from Sicily. I propose that, for the time being, we forget the past and get on with the job." He walked up to Annunzio. "John, here's to success in Persia!"

Gianfranco beamed. "Mathew," he said, "I'm sure we are going to be good friends."

"Great," replied Doc, "let's drink to that."

Which they did. Whereupon the prince nimbly filled the glasses once more. Fifteen minutes later the foursome left for the dining room. Three days later, on April 3, 1967, Doc and the prince left for Abadan on an Air India flight from Malpensa. Albert and Marvin waved from the spectators' terrace as they disappeared into the 707.

3

The Persian Gulf is no match for the Mediterranean or the Caribbean. This is especially true at the point on its northern coast where the combined waters of the Tigris and Euphrates rivers flow into it, forming a dark brown corridor in the already murky sea. The Air India 707 came in very low over these waters, and just skimmed the long line of majestic palms lining the Iraqi bank of the river. The illusion of a desert paradise created by such lush trees was immediately destroyed as the plane slowed to a stop on the runway at Abadan. The reversing thrust of the engines created whirlpools of sand and dust on both sides of the concrete strip. Beyond there was nothing but perfectly flat, barren bleakness.

The airport terminal, a small wooden barracks-type structure, appeared deserted as the two men from Lugano approached. All but a few of the other passengers had opted to stay on the plane as it was quickly refueled for the next lag to Delhi. Nobody from Air India seemed to mind. As they entered the building, the first people to meet them were four soldiers, all with submachine guns slung over their shoulders.

Beyond them stood two other officials, also dressed in khaki, waiting behind three low tables. Almost immediately their baggage came in through another door, carried by two small Arabs. The suitcases were deposited on the tables.

"Passports," demanded one of the men.

"Open," said the other. Two of the four soldiers moved up behind them, while the other two stood sentry at the door leading to the tarmac.

"Real friendly atmosphere," muttered Doc, as he handed over his documents, and began to fumble at the locks on his suitcase.

"What you want in Iran?" asked the passport man, as the other began to dump the contents of Doc's suitcase onto the dirty table.

"Hey, what're you trying to do?" exclaimed Doc, with no effect, as the customs man proceeded to unscrew a pocket whiskey flask and sniff at the top.

"Why have you come to Iran?" said his partner, in an even surlier voice.

The prince then intervened. "We are here on a visit. At the invitation of the Firdausi family. I believe they have a car waiting for us outside."

"Firdausi?"

"Yes."

Both passports were returned immediately, and the Iranians hurriedly began to replace the contents of Doc's suitcase.

"Many pardons," said the passport man. "I was not told, you see. If you would please come this way. I will arrange that your baggage follows immediately." He bowed ever so slightly, and then motioned that they should follow him through the building and out the opposite door. A solitary vehicle stood there, a yellow Range Rover. The chauffeur, who had been leaning against its side, smoking, sprang to attention as they approached.

"Prince Annunzio?" he asked, with great difficulty.

"Yes," was the reply. That did it. Now the immigration official insisted on personally stowing their baggage in the back, while the customs man solicitously held open the doors. Both officials saluted smartly as, with a jerk, they moved off.

"Prince," said Doc, "I've got to hand it to you. Your relatives pack a lot of wallop in these parts. I've got a feeling this is going to be a walkover. I'm just going to sit back and enjoy it."

The scenery outside provided very little in the way of entertainment. Instead of going into the town of Abadan, the driver took a left at the main intersection just outside the airport gates, guarded by another army foursome, again with automatic weapons. Almost immediately they found themselves in the middle of row after row of huge oil storage tanks, followed by a series of refining installations, all pipes and belching fumes.

"Looks like Pittsburgh," commented Doc, "and smells like East St. Louis."

"Doc, do they have camels in East St. Louis?" questioned the prince, innocently. And sure enough, five camels with clanging bells, followed by a half dozen mangy donkeys, attended by two even mangier Arabs, blocked the road ahead.

"John," laughed Doc, "you are slowly starting to grow on me."

The driver just leaned on the horn, and, grudgingly, the menagerie was cleared from the road. All signs of civilization disappeared as the Range Rover sped up a perfectly flat and straight road into the desert. Only one half of the road was paved, the left half, and it was there that the driver stayed, in the obvious knowledge that the odds were very low indeed that they would meet anyone coming from the opposite direction. The hum of the tires on the hot asphalt and the dry desert air streaming through the open windows soon took their toll as the heads of both passengers slumped in a fitful sleep.

The route took them through Khurramshahr and Ahwaz, across the bone-dry bed of the Karun river, then straight north. The desolation was complete, and the country devoid of human life except for occasional groupings of black tents visible well in the distance on both sides of the semi-highway. After two hundred kilometers, mountains began to emerge on the horizon to the right. On some of the peaks the whiteness of what must have been snow reflected the late afternoon sun. Thin, isolated patches of grass began to appear in the open land, and with darkness rapidly falling, for the first time they met traffic: horse and donkey-drawn carts; small herds of goats attended by small boys; even trucks of unknown vintage, packed full of people and animals. As they came to an ancient bridge, the driver was forced to cope with a desert traffic jam: hordes of people on foot—black-veiled women, barefoot children, men in those dirty-grey robes so common to the Arab world. The continuing honking of the Range Rover's horn soon had everyone inside fully awake.

Across the bridge, the vehicle was forced to a creep as they pushed their way through the town of Dizful. Its narrow streets now took on the form of an oriental bazaar—food shops with cadavers of unidentifiable fowl hanging from the ceilings; a hardware niche with its disarray of misshaped pots and utensils; then the shoemaker, the rugs, the inevitable donkey supporting brass urns surrounded by customers sipping tea and gossiping; the garbage, the spices, the dust.

Suddenly the Range Rover swung left into an alley, and after fifty meters turned again onto a wide boulevard which ended abruptly at tall iron gates. They were open. As they drove through they moved into a different world, one of water in the desert. Green lawn, hibiscus shrubs, palm trees, flowers—all softly lit by invisible lamps. Then the villa, which would have been quite at home on the Bay of Naples. Two fountains, also dancing in light, framed the wide staircase which led up to the entrance. The car stopped, the doors opened, and the two bankers from Switzerland stepped out into the warm Asiatic night of southern Iran.

Simultaneously, two figures emerged from the villa, and descended the steps toward them.

"Gianfranco," said the approaching man. "It has been so long. We are honored by your visit."

The girl was a beauty. All of her. Her voice was husky and low as she caught both of Annunzio's hands in a happy embrace.

"Oh, how we have looked forward to this since your phone call, Gianfranco. You have always been our favorite cousin."

Gianfranco gallantly kissed her hand, and then embraced her.

"Shireen! How wonderful you look! And how glorious this all is. I had no idea. But first I must introduce my friend from America. This is Doctor Mathew Smythe. We are associates in the bank in Lugano. Mathew, my cousins Agha and Shireen Firdausi."

It was Doc who stepped forward and bestowed a kiss on the Iranian girl's hand with movements which were fully as elegant as those of his Italian companion. After a handshake with her brother, they all moved up the stairs and into the villa. Within minutes the foursome were seated in the vast reception room which was furnished in Western style, except, perhaps, for an overabundance of rugs and tapestries. The drinks were served by a silent, almost black man, in a white jacket and sandals. The dinner that followed was equally Western, the wine definitely French, and the ice cream apparently American. No business was discussed. All retired to separate bedrooms shortly after eleven. Their host suggested the men plan on rising fairly early the next morning. He had scheduled the grand tour.

At nine, Agha Firdausi, the American, and the Italian nobleman, all clad in sportsclothes, left the grounds of the estate in the Range Rover. The temperature was already in the high 80's.

At first it was just sand and dust again. But then a vast area of shimmering green came into sight, and soon they were surrounded by rich vegetation on all sides.

"Let me explain," said Agha, his hand sweeping from left to right, as he sat beside the driver in the front seat. "Until five years ago this was a desert. But with the water from the high dam in the mountains on the horizon in front of us, we are turning it into one of the most fertile areas on earth. Or should I say, returning it. Three thousand years ago this entire area was crisscrossed with irrigation channels, fed from dams which probably numbered in the hundreds. I will show you one later. It has survived almost three millennia. It's six hundred meters long, twenty-two wide, and was capable of raising the water level of the nearby Nan-i-Darayan River by two meters. Two meters does not sound like much. But in an area like this which is utterly flat, as you can see, it allows for a tremendous dispersal of water through completely natural irrigation methods. We have learned from our past. You will see practically no pumps here. We are reviving this desert in the same manner as that employed by Darius or Xerxes: with the help of gravity."

"Does all this belong to you?" asked Doc.

"To my family, yes. For many generations. It was totally useless and barren, even in my father's time. But our Shah changed all that. He took the income from our petroleum resources, and put it back into the country—into roads, steel works, and into dams. Here in Khuzistan, which is the source of Iran's oil, he built the greatest dam of all, and named it after himself."

"What does the water cost?" asked Doc.

"For the first twenty years, nothing," replied Agha. "Because we are using it for the good of the Iranian people. You see over there? Tomatoes. Millions of them. And that? Strawberries. We fly two planeloads every week into Teheran. Now we are coming to alfalfa. We get four crops a year and make high protein cattle feed out of it. You see those trees? They are not very big yet. But in a few years we will have some of the largest orange groves in the Near East. Even more productive than those of Israel. In fact, it was Israeli agricultural engineers who helped us with much of the planning and implementation of this project. They are quite used to turning deserts into gardens of Eden."

"But don't you people have problems with the Israelis?" queried Doc again.

"No. We are Mohammedans in Iran, yes. But remember. Although some Arabs live here, especially in Khuzistan as you must have already noticed, we ourselves are not Arabs. Our culture and heritage are radically differ... We Iranians have no quarrel with Israel. In fact, we have no quarrels with anyone at present, except for Iraq. They continually try to claim territory of ours on the Gulf. They are a primitive people. But I do not involve myself with politics. Look at what comes."

The Range Rover bumped over a series of simple bridges spanning irrigation ditches, and suddenly they found themselves in the middle of the lushest vegetation thus far.

"What is it?"

"Sugar cane, and we have built one of the most

modern sugar mills in the world. You can see it over there."

"How much land do you have?" asked Doc.

"Well, it goes from here to the foothills. And it is about the same width, or length, depending upon how you want to describe it."

"Don't you have fences?" asked Doc.

"No. At least, not yet. This land has always been open to our people. The nomads. We still have hundreds of thousands in this region. They spend their summers high in the mountains, here and in Luristan further north, where they graze their livestock. In the winters they come down into the valleys and plains. To your eye, most of this area looks like useless desert. But if you look closely, it is not. There is grass. True it is very thin. But it is there. Enough to satisfy the nomads in any case. So they leave our irrigated areas alone."

As the sugar cane fields began to end, they pulled up in front of what appeared to be a vast construction site. Large Caterpillar tractors, towering shafts, cranes, trucks, a huge corrugated metal shed, even a narrow gauge railroad spur.

"Is this to be another sugar mill?" asked the prince.

"No, no. This is Choga Zambil."

"What does that mean?"

"Come. I will show you."

As they walked into the site, it suddenly began to take on contours. It was not a construction project, but rather one of reconstruction: a huge archeological dig.

A bewildering number of walls and broken walls,

some extending hundreds of yards, indicated that once this had been a vast complex of civilization. But almost immediately all eyes were drawn to a towering structure of massive stone. It rose a good hundred feet above the ground, and distinctly resembled a pyramid.

"It's enormous," exclaimed the prince. "What is it?"

"A ziggurat. The largest and best preserved in all of Persia."

"How old is it?"

"Three thousand years, give or take a century or two."

"What was it used for?"

"Religion. All ancient Persian cities' religious life centered around such sacred temples. But, of course, very few have survived centuries of pillage, and the simple ravage of time."

"When was this one discovered?"

"Four years ago. We were pushing a main channel irrigation ditch through here, and the bulldozers suddenly began to uncover this buried city. We have managed to dig up, and then restore, all of what you see here in the time since."

"You mean the government?"

"No, we. The Firdausi family."

"But," said Doc, "surely such an undertaking must be expensive. Why do you do it?"

"My family has an obligation not only to present-day Iran, but also to the Persia of the past. We have always had great civilizations here. We are a people who have always been master of this part of Asia. Today we are gradually reassuming that role. It is good to remind our people that they are part of a great heritage, and that they—we—are destined to continue to play a major role in world history."

"But still," said Doc, "surely the government has the primary responsibility in that regard. They can hardly expect private people to . . ."

For the first time Firdausi interrupted. "There is another reason. But we shall speak of that later. Now we must go." He turned abruptly, and the rest of the party had no choice but to follow him back to the Range Rover.

"I have just one more thing to show you," continued Agha, as the vehicle moved off. "Then we must return to our home for more serious talks."

After seven miles, they came to a main road and approached what appeared to be a structure transplanted from medieval Europe.

"That looks like a German castle!" exclaimed the prince.

"No, French," replied Agha.

"But who in the world did such a crazy thing, here in the middle of nowhere?"

"The French, as I said. A certain Monsieur de Morgan, around the turn of the century. He was the leader of the French archeological mission. He built it for a very practical reason: to protect himself, and the treasures he unearthed here, from the marauding Arabs coming from the west, and the nomads from the north. It turned out to be an excellent solution. Both he and his treasures survived. You must remember that until the 1920's this part of the world was completely hostile to any outsiders. In fact, it is only since the late 1940's, when the army tightened its control, that Khuzistan has been relatively safe for visitors."

"What is the name of this place?"

"Susa. Or, as it was known in the Bible, Shushan."

"Never heard of it," commented Doc.

"But you have heard of Daniel and the lion's den."

"Of course."

"Here is where it happened. In Shushan."

"Yeah?"

"Yes. When we get back to our home, I will tell you more. For the moment, let me simply say that we are standing literally on top of what was Persia's most glorious ancient city. A city of enormous riches. And Choga Zambil, which we the Firdausi family have rediscovered, was the source of most of those riches."

Doc looked puzzled, but asked no more. The party got out and walked through the excavations behind the fortress. Part of the foundation of a huge palace had been uncovered. Yet, unlike Choga Zambil, there was not much to see—just a few large blocks of granite, a number of columns lying on their sides, the remains of mosaics of either the palace floor, or that of its courtyard. It was only with a great deal of imagination that one could visualize the immenseness of the structure which stood here many centuries before Christ was born. Agha was not particularly helpful. After five minutes, he suggested they return home. On the way they again crossed that narrow bridge, but this time it was in daylight. Agha pointed to a massive pile of rubble, partially blocking the river upstream.

"That is Bankd-i-Quisar, the ancient dam I was

talking about. But I think we have all had enough of this sort of thing. It's time for lunch."

Both Shireen and lunch were waiting for them when they returned to the villa. Salads, fruit, yoghurt, tea. Conversation was restrained—just small talk, dominated, of course, by Gianfranco who had fully mastered that art, in various languages. Agha Firdausi appeared increasingly impatient, and before long he suggested they move outside. It was warm, but the palms provided ample shade. The pool looked inviting, but that was obviously not on. No sooner were they settled in a circle of lounging chairs than Agha turned to business.

"I do not wish to appear impolite, but still, I would like to come immediately to the purpose of your visit."

He turned to his cousin. "Gianfranco, as you know, I did not care to go into detail on the telephone. One never knows. But I must say, your call could not have come at a more opportune time. You and your bank in Switzerland are exactly, but exactly, what we have been praying for. First, the rials, I have them here at home in the safe, in fact in two safes. They will fill two large suitcases. I also have the suitcases ready."

"Two large suitcases?" interjected Doc.

"Yes. Unfortunately, I could only manage to accumulate a very mixed assortment of bills, and I could hardly exchange them at the bank for larger denominations. So I'm afraid you will have to cope with a rather substantial volume of paper. This presents a problem?"

"Frankly, yes," said Doc, "I had hoped we were dealing with a relatively small package. To get two suitcases through, unopened—it's going to mean running a risk. You know as well as I do that every airline on earth has started to make spot checks of baggage as a result of hijacks. Especially large heavy suitcases."

"Ah," interrupted Firdausi, "that must not worry you. I have taken care of that problem. My friends at the Iranian Oil Company have agreed to take you back to Europe as their guests. They have their own Lear jets which regularly fly Abadan-London. Once in London, there should be no problem. There is no law against bringing rials in and out of London airport."

"But what about the controls at *your* airport?"

"Iranian Oil people are not subjected to controls at Abadan. They own Abadan. On this you have my guarantee."

"Then everything seems already settled," said the prince.

"Yes."

"Then you already know when we shall be leaving?"

"Yes. Tonight. Takeoff is scheduled for eight P.M. This means we shall be leaving here in about two hours. I will bring you to the aircraft."

This statement surprised both the prince and Doc.

"How would you like us to settle the technical arrangements?" asked Doc, hesitantly, disturbed by such fast moving events.

"What technical arrangements?"

"You know, the deposit arrangements in Switzerland. We have brought the basic bank forms with us, and . . ."

"Wait a minute. I'm afraid that I have not made my position entirely clear. There can be no connection whatsoever between my person and these funds. When I come to Switzerland at a later date, we can make any arrangements you suggest. But there can be nothing—nothing—in writing in this country. Either now or later. I want this understood. And I suggest you leave those forms with me. I'll burn them."

"But of course," replied Doc, flustered. "I just wanted to make sure."

"Still," interrupted the prince, "you must tell us how you desire that we employ these funds, Agha. I give you my assurance that your wishes will be carried out immediately and exactly."

"Gianfranco, that goes without saying. At first I was thinking in terms of a simple bank deposit, probably a time deposit. In dollars or Swiss francs. It would not really matter. Just so the funds are taken out of Iran and put into a freely convertible currency. I still want this done. But after a lot of thinking, I have decided that our relationship could go well beyond this." He paused. "Before I go further I must have an absolute pledge from both of you that what I tell you will remain secret. The fate of my family, that of my sister and myself, will depend upon your keeping this pledge."

With that, Agha turned directly to Doc: "Sir, can you give me your solemn word?"

"You have it," replied Doc simply.

"And from me, Agha," said the prince, now observing his cousin with a great deal of curiosity.

Agha glanced at his sister. She nodded ever so slightly.

"Good. Then I will proceed, and quite bluntly. I have discovered on my land, our land, a silver mine. It will be, beyond any doubt, the richest source of silver existing in the world today."

Silence.

"Where?"

"At Choga Zambil. You remember—the excavations, the ziggurat."

"Aha. That's why those shafts, the drilling rigs."

"Exactly."

"But," asked the prince, "why the secret? There can hardly be anything illegal about finding a silver mine. You said it is on your property."

"It is, of course, not illegal. But you forget about taxes. They are nothing short of confiscatory in Iran. The government would take 60%, maybe 70% of all the profit. In the end, they could very well nationalize the mine—just as they are doing with the oil fields. Why should I run such a risk? Especially if there is no necessity—and there is none. This thing is secret, and it can be kept secret. All the people I use at Choga Zambil have been working for the Firdausi family all their lives. They have complete loyalty to us, not to the government in far-off Teheran. Anyway, at least thus far, they have no idea what Choga Zambil is really all about. They are an uneducated people."

"Yes," said Doc, "but surely you require the help

of engineers in such an undertaking. They cannot be that ignorant."

"You are right, of course. But so far I have also been able to cope with that problem. The entire project has been managed by an Englishman. His name is Ron Howard. He was with Rio Tinto in Africa for many years. Apparently ran into some trouble, I don't know the details. I do know he is extraordinarily competent. He couldn't care less about the interests of the Iranian government. He's worried only about himself. He knows what we're onto here, and he also knows that when this venture succeeds he can settle down wherever he chooses as a wealthy man. His loyalty is further guaranteed by the fact that he is working in Iran illegally."

"But can one man manage such a thing? You intimated you have struck something enormously rich. To get it out, to refine it, is going to require more than just an Englishman."

"You are right again," replied Agha, "and it is not just going to require more men. It will require much more equipment."

"Then how do you propose to continue?" asked Doc.

"With your help."

"But we know nothing about mining," said the prince.

"Neither do I," said Agha, "but that's not the point. You know everything about money, and how to finance a potentially vast operation like this."

"What kind of financing?"

"Initially, loans to buy the needed equipment.

45

Later, if we need more capital, we may want to sell shares to other investors. But for now, all we need is a modern metal refining facility, and the technicians to go with it. We know exactly what is required, and where to get it."

"Where?"

"Rhodesia. That's where Howard came from. When he was with Rio Tinto, they bought a lot of equipment from a company in Salisbury which specializes in that sort of thing. Almost all their sales are today restricted to South Africa, since most nations of the world have put a total embargo on trade with Rhodesia because of their racial policies. So they've got both the knowhow we need, and the spare capacity to do a quick turnkey job. And in Rhodesia, since the embargo, they have learned how to keep such matters secret."

"And the technicians?"

"From the same country. Rhodesia attracts the type of roustabouts we need. Howard says it would take him no more than a week to find the men he requires. So all we need now is the necessary banking arrangements, but they—as you must now appreciate—have to be set up outside of Iran."

"But wait a minute. It seems to me that there is still a big hooker in this whole deal."

"That is?"

"How would you get those people and equipment in? Smuggling in an Englishman like Howard is one thing; to bring in a gang of technicians from Rhodesia, and tons of equipment is another."

"It's an easy run by ship from the east coast of

Africa to Dubai. We are only a few hundred kilometers from the Persian Gulf. The biggest, in fact the only, major business on the Gulf, except for oil, is smuggling. Gold, watches, cattle, even what closely approximate slaves—the list never ends. All of this type of trade is based in either Abu Dhabi or Dubai. From there, the needs of Iran, of Saudi Arabia, of Pakistan, of India are served. It will be in Dubai where our cargo will be trans-shipped. From there, the goods are usually run in djerbas, hundreds, probably thousands of them. But of late, large modern craft, equipped with powerful twin engines and radar, are becoming more and more common. We also have enough large trucks of our own to bring everything across land from the Gulf to our place. I assure you, we will have no problems."

"But what about when everything arrives here?"

"This morning I showed you the extent of our land holdings. It is private property, the property of the Firdausi family. I can, and will, insist that this privacy be respected. I shall hire people to enforce it, on the pretext of protecting both our crops and our archeological findings. The town people, and the few government officials living in these parts, will respect this. The only exceptions will be the nomads. But they will cause no trouble. It is preferable that we maintain our peace with them. So you see, this whole venture has been carefully thought through."

"I have yet another question," said the prince. "How will you get the silver out?"

"The same way we get the equipment and people in: by truck to the coast, then by djerba, or preferably something faster, via the Gulf, to either Abu Dhabi or Dubai. Finally by plane to wherever we choose."

"Without anybody knowing?" was the skeptical response.

"Gianfranco, I see you know very little of this area of the world. Let me briefly explain. Dubai is the center of an immense trade in bullion—all illegal. The focal point is the Indian subcontinent. There it is forbidden to import gold. Yet for time immemorial both the Indian and Pakistani people have revered gold. They have also found it a safe investment. So there is a constant high demand for the metal. The merchants of Dubai, many of them expatriate Indians, meet that demand by djerba. They charge a premium over world prices, but they deliver c.i.f. And they keep their mouths shut, regarding both their 'clients' and their bullion sources, for obvious reasons."

"What has all that to do with silver?" was Doc's dry comment.

"This. With what do you suppose the Indians pay for this gold? I'll tell you: silver. Tons and tons of silver. India has been hoarding silver for millennia. Literally every household of any means has countless silver objects—bars of bullion, ornaments, jewelry, coins. Collectively, the Indians have the largest hoard of silver existing on this earth today. They trade it for gold, using those same djerbas operating out of Dubai. From there, it goes to Europe by air. I intend only to use a smuggling system which already exists, and already manages to cope with a high volume of bullion trade."

These last words created a long lull.

"What more is there to say?" suggested Doc, finally. "It's perfect. At least from the standpoint of logistics. But—and I'm afraid I must again use that word— how can you *really* be sure you have that much silver in the ground underneath Choga Zambil?"

"I shall prove it. Excuse me for a moment."

In less than five minutes Firdausi returned. He carried an object about eighteen inches high. With great care he placed it upright on the table in the middle of their sitting group. It was an alabaster statue, depicting the stylized figure of an ancient queen or princess. Her features, her dress, closely resembled those pictured in some of the ancient tombs of Egypt. But this figure was three dimensional, and in a state of perfect preservation. Astoundingly, the figurine's jewelry was also intact. No less than seven rows of necklaces; a diadem; long, hanging ear rings composed of a series of interconnected spheres; even bangles fastened well up on each arm, probably a dozen in all. All were made of silver, even the massive metal base.

"Agha," exclaimed the prince, "it is unbelievable!"

"But it is true," replied his Persian host, "and it is almost four thousand years old. Yet still perfect. It came from Shushan, our ancient capital—the place we visited this morning just before lunch. You note the jewelry—all perfect miniatures. In our vault at a bank in Teheran we have some of the counterparts in their original size. They are also made of silver, and the diadem contains many small, but perfect, gems. The Louvre has something very similar to the statue, but devoid of the jewelry. The British Museum has many counterparts to the bracelets and earrings. Only we have such a perfect diadem, and this unique figurine, completely intact. My father collected all this."

"And the connection with your silver mine?" asked Doc.

Again Agha rose. "Excuse me once more."

Again within a matter of minutes he returned, this time carrying a large metal box. He opened it and removed a gleaming block of metal. Holding it up in both hands he said, "This is a silver ingot. I have a dozen more in the house. We found them all at Choga Zambil."

A low whistle came from Doc's lips.

"Now listen," Firdausi continued, "what follows is of key importance." He again reached into the container, this time removing some documents.

He handed one bound set to the other men.

"That," he said, "is an assay, done by a metallurgist in London for me. It gives the makeup of selected pieces of ancient jewelry taken from my father's collection. Now listen carefully: no two pieces were chosen from the same source. One was found at Ur, Abraham's birthplace, which lies about three hundred kilometers southwest; a second from Shushan; the third from Ashur, then from Tell Asmar, even Uruk. All in all it was a random selection of ancient Mesopotamian jewelry and religious objects—all made of silver. Now compare the *makeup* of the metal. It was the *same* in each case."

What followed was a slightly awkward moment, since obviously neither Doc nor the prince could make head or tails out of the print in front of them. Doc finally admitted it.

"O.K.," said Firdausi, "you will understand in a minute. Both of you look at the last page. There you can read a summary of the assay results: Silver 93.5%; Copper 6.10%; Gold 0.08%; Zinc 0.15%. Each object assayed out exactly the same way. Right?"

"You're right."

"Now compare the last page of *this* document. It is an analysis of our silver ingots, the ones we uncovered at Choga Zambil."

They did.

"Don't you see?" asked Firdausi, now visibly excited. "All of these silver objects had their origin in similar silver ingots. These ingots must have come from a single source, *and that source had to be Choga Zambil*. Because everything matches!"

A pause, a long one.

Then Doc: "No one could possibly argue with evidence like this. You've made your point, Agha. But," he continued, "that still leaves the million dollar question open. Is any of that silver still left in the earth today?"

"I'll make the answer short. We have driven a shaft, and made several hundred borings. All have proven positive. There are two major silver veins, both less than a hundred feet below the surface. The seams are of an immense size and extraordinarily rich. When processed, the silver has exactly the same assay as that of both the ancient ingots and the jewelry. The circle has been closed. And one of the puzzles of ancient Persia has been solved." Agha Firdausi now rose to his feet. "This," he continued, "is Elam, and Shushan," his arm pointed to the south, "was the most powerful city in Elam. Because it was by far the most wealthy city in all of ancient Asia, since for many centuries it seemed to possess an almost inexhaustible source of silver. To this day, no one has discovered where. It certainly wasn't in Shushan itself. Nobody even thought of Choga Zambil, since no one knew it existed, just ten kilometers east of Shushan. Today everybody knows about the ziggurat, but only we know of Choga Zambil's ancient silver refinery, and of the silver deposits beneath."

Abruptly he sat down.

"Well I'll be goddammed," exclaimed Doc. "Obviously the guys who ran Shushan knew how to keep their mouths shut too."

Firdausi glanced at his watch. "Our time is running out. We must come to specifics. My proposal is this: between us we should work out some kind of joint venture. You would be responsible for the financial arrangements. I will take care of everything else."

"How much financing are we talking about?" asked Doc.

"Around five million dollars."

"Which we have, except that it's still in rials," answered Doc.

"Not exactly," said Firdausi. "My rials are, after all, meant to be a deposit in your bank. I am sure you have many other depositors, as well as a great deal of capital of your own. I can hardly be expected to bear the entire risk in this venture. Otherwise I would hardly need a partner, would I?"

"Maybe not," replied Doc, "but you need somebody to take your rials out for you, don't you?"

"To be sure, but as Gianfranco has no doubt told you, I am also prepared to pay a handsome fee for that service. I am talking here about a partnership, in the true sense of the word. I think that when you've heard me out, you will agree that what I propose is fair."

"O.K., go ahead. How would the financial side work, technically?"

"I always feel the simpler, the better. We would just set up a special joint numbered account in the bank, and your bank would put the necessary funds into it —as an investment. For my part, I would assign our family rights to the mine, in fact to this entire property, to that account. Your bank would then transfer the funds to a bank in Kuwait, and against them I could get the necessary letter of credit. I would probably use the Bank of London and the Near East. I know them, and they know me. They are well established in both Kuwait and Rhodesia. Unless, of course, you would rather issue the letter of credit directly?"

"No, no," replied Doc, quickly, his knowledge of letters of credit being something less than encyclopedic, "what you suggest sounds quite reasonable. What about sales? Who would handle them?"

"I have all the necessary contacts in Dubai."

"All the better." Then Doc added, "What is your concept of how we will split the profits?"

"Fifty-fifty. All profits would accrue to our joint account, and we would share them equally."

"Who will control your expenditures here in Iran?"

"No one. You will have to trust me just as I will have to trust you to protect my secret."

"That sounds reasonable. I think we've got a deal. Do you agree, John?"

The prince nodded his head vigorously.

"O.K., what about timing?"

"First," said Firdausi, "I need your money, and the transfer of the funds to my bank in Kuwait. When I have their letter of credit, Howard and I will fly down to Rhodesia. We should be able to conclude the arrangements there within a fortnight."

"Assuming everything works out, when will the silver start to arrive in Dubai?"

"Perhaps in six months. More probably it will take a bit longer. Let's say shipments will start no later than January 1, 1968."

"Do you have any forecasts of probable volume?"

"Yes. Howard estimates we can do as much as fifty million ounces the first year, provided the equipment works at 100% capacity."

"That would be worth how much?"

"About $65. million. The current price is $1.29 an ounce."

"And your costs?"

"Probably fifty cents an ounce. But it should be obvious that as the project develops, we will need progressively more working capital. Loans from the bank. Of course, by that time such loans could be fully collateralized by silver bullion in the Dubai warehouse. I must have your assurance on this."

"I am sure all that can be arranged. Now one final

matter. I know you don't like documents, but you do realize that we can't avoid them when we set up the joint account, assign the ownership of your property to it, make the loans, etc. At some time, probably fairly soon, we'll have to get together again and finalize these matters—on paper."

"I agree. But I'm sure that lawyers in Switzerland work just as slowly as those in Iran. When everything's ready, I'll come to Switzerland. But I can see no reason why we must hold anything up because of the paperwork. I think it logical we move forward on the equipment right away."

"Sure. In fact, we'll be right on top of that when we get back to Switzerland."

"Good. I imagine that in the meantime you can hold my cash deposit as a performance guarantee. Isn't that the way you people usually handle these things?"

"That's right," replied Doc, now on very uncertain ground indeed.

Again Firdausi glanced at his watch, and then turned to his sister.

"Shireen, you say nothing. Does something disturb you?"

At first there was no answer. Then, "Agha, it is all too big and complicated for me to really follow. You know that. It is just . . ."

"What?"

"Nothing really. Certainly nothing to do with you and your friends. I am sure everything you have discussed and planned will work out. It is only . . ."

"Now Shireen, you don't mean those old fairy tales!"

"They are not just fairy tales! You know what father always said."

"Ach, that was pure superstition. Forget it once and for all. Otherwise do you agree?"

"Yes, Agha."

"Good. Then we must put these things back into the house. And you, gentlemen, must pack. We shall be leaving in half an hour."

This time it was not the Range Rover that was used for transportation. Instead, a long dark blue Cadillac Brougham waited outside the villa. Agha Firdausi himself took the wheel, accompanied by his cousin, the prince, in the front seat. Doc and Shireen sat silently in back, as they moved through Dizful and south into the desert. Agha and Gianfranco maintained a steady chatter, in French, a language in which both seemed to be more at home than in English. Occasionally Agha laughed aloud in appreciation of some of the anecdotes which Gianfranco was relating nonstop, with obvious relish.

Doc felt increasingly embarrassed as the silence continued in the back seat, but Shireen seemed unapproachable as she sat stiffly in her corner. Then, suddenly, she turned to him:

"Mathew," she said, "I am so sorry. I was, I mean my thoughts were elsewhere. I have been a terrible hostess. We have hardly spoken ten words to each other since you have been here."

"Oh," said Doc, "I understand that. After all, this does involve serious matters, and I'm sure they must worry you at times, Miss Firdausi."

"Please don't call me that. I'm Shireen to my friends, and I hope you will regard me as your friend."

Doc smiled.

"You know," he said, "I'm glad to hear you say that. For a while I thought you had something against me. Because I'm American, or something."

"No, no," was Shireen's forceful reply. "But you must understand. We have so few guests at our home. We are quite cut off from the world, even Teheran. And so, probably, I require a little time to adjust when people like you suddenly fall upon us, out of the heaven."

"But don't you ever go to Europe?"

"We did for a while. But not since 1965. I would so much like to again. But Agha says our duty lies here, at present."

"I will talk to Agha. You must come with him to visit us in Lugano. After all, we are now business partners, aren't we?"

"Yes. I will come. Agha will certainly agree now. Oh, how I already look forward to it."

As dusk began to fall, the interior of the car slipped into darkness, and it was with pleasure that Doc noticed that the Persian girl no longer remained stiffly sitting in her corner. First, there was just the hint of her arm brushing his. Then, as the car jostled over yet another pothole, their bodies came suddenly together, and Doc felt the firmness of her breasts. She made no effort either to say anything or move away.

"Shireen," said Doc after what seemed an hour of satisfied silence. "What was that you were referring to back at the house?"

"You mean my uneasiness?"

"Yes."

"Oh, it is like Agha said. Just old wives' tales and local superstition."

"About what?"

"It relates to some of our ancient myths. Persia, you know, is full of myths. Quite often it is impossible for us to tell the difference between the true history of our country, and mythology."

"And this particular myth?"

"It involves silver. Our father often came back to it when he showed us the ancient jewelry which he collected with a passion all his life. It is said that there is evil connected with the silver of Elam. Outsiders who tried to exploit the riches of Shushan usually met violent deaths, or faced other personal tragedies."

"Come on, Shireen. Metal is just metal."

"Of course I realize that. But our father was a rather strange man. He was not even a good Moslem. All his life he felt a peculiar attraction to the old religions of our country, especially Zoroastrianism. In those times, gold and silver were regarded as possessing specific properties. Gold was associated with the sun, and silver with the moon. The god Ninurta endowed both metals with magical powers, both to protect and to harm. My father believed these things, and he always said that it was good that Elam's silver was gone. You must think, Mathew, when you grow up with such legends, they are impossible to forget. And my father was not alone in these beliefs. Many thousands of people in this region still actively practice that religion."

"Sure, and many people in America believe in astrology."

"Mathew, let's change the subject. I'm being silly and emotional. Agha was right and you are right. I will never bring it up again. Anyway, it makes me shiver."

The conversation shifted to the subject of America, of Las Vegas, the Kennedys, even Hollywood and Frank Sinatra. At 7:30 they approached the outer perimeter of Abadan airport. A car marked with the letters of the Iranian Oil Company was waiting at the gate. Its driver exchanged just a few words with Firdausi in Parsee. Then both vehicles passed through the gates unchallenged and seemingly unnoticed by the guards standing there. Ten minutes later, the four suitcases of the two passengers were stowed in the hold, and the doors of the Lear jet closed. With whining engines, the plane taxied onto the runway and, without stopping, turned and plunged forward. A half minute later it had disappeared into the night sky.

4

"Comfortable, isn't it?"

"Yeah."

"Have you ever been in one of these before?"

"Yes."

"It's the first time for me."

"Yeah, I gathered as much."

"Something bothering you, Doc?"

"No."

"Then why so quiet?"

"I'm thinking."

"Should I be quiet?"

"No, John. I'm sorry. I get this way sometimes."

"I understand. So do I. But usually I talk quite a bit. Especially when I'm nervous. And I'm nervous. Are you, Doc?"

"Yes."

"I'm relieved to hear that. Do you think we will have any trouble?"

"I hope not. But you can never be sure."

"Doc, let me ask you something."

"Sure, shoot."

"Does all this make sense?"

"What do you mean?"

"I mean, this whole thing. Risking our necks. Or at least our freedom. And reputations."

"Well, you don't make money sitting at home and knitting."

"Yes, but there are more accepted ways."

"You're looking at it all wrong. What we're doing might be illegal for Iranians in Iran. But we're not Iranians. And in just a few minutes we will no longer even be over Iran, I hope. Prince, you and I are just plain businessmen. And from all I heard today, we are well on our way to becoming big businessmen. Look. This thing was *your* idea, not mine."

"I know. It's just that all of a sudden, now that we're up here alone, I got to thinking. You know how it is."

"I know, John. But forget it. I got over such stuff when I was about sixteen years old. Either you look out for yourself, or you get hurt. We're just taking care of what's nearest and dearest to both of us—our own interests. Who are we hurting? Nobody. And we're helping your cousins in Iran."

The door leading from the small, though luxurious, cabin to the flight deck opened, and one of the crew ambled back to them.

"Comfortable?"

"Yes. Where are we?"

"Almost at the Iranian-Turkish border. We came straight north from Abadan. It's our usual flight pattern. We have strict orders to keep out of Iraqi air space. They don't like Iran, and the guys that fly their MIG's are triggerhappy as hell. They can't hit anything. But why take chances? So we always follow this route to Europe, weather allowing."

"Any problems with the weather?" asked the prince, now concerned.

"No. None really. Some thunderheads are building up just ahead of us on top of the mountains. But we're at 35,000 feet and should clear them all right. After that Istanbul, Athens, Rome—they're all clear. We'll refuel at Rome and get a new weather reading there. So relax. You fellows want some coffee?"

"Please," replied both passengers simultaneously. After some time two cups of coffee arrived.

"It's not very good, or even very hot. But it's coffee," commented the copilot.

"You English?" asked Doc.

"No, Australian."

"What are you doing in Iran?"

"I fly for money. There are lots of us Aussies in Europe doing the same thing. Usually with the scheduled airlines. I spent a couple of years with KLM. Then got an offer from these oil guys. They pay more, and work shorter hours."

The plane lurched slightly, and then appeared to veer. The Australian cocked his head quizzically. Then another lurch.

"Excuse me."

Doc glanced at the prince who now sat with his coffee cup clenched in both hands.

"John, I can see we are of one mind."

Ever so slightly the plane tilted forward. Slowly the turbulence began. Again the door up front opened. This time the copilot just stuck his head out.

"Heh, you guys. Buckle up. And get rid of that coffee. We're about to run into some real shit."

"What's wrong?" shouted Doc.

"Starboard engine's losing power. So we're taking her down. Ankara's socked in. So it's Istanbul—after we get through these fucking thunderheads. Just take it easy. Everything's under control. It'll just be a little bumpy for a while."

He grinned widely, and disappeared, this time leaving the door open.

The storm outside soon took on awesome dimensions. The murky blackness was increasingly interrupted by flashes of lightning. The rush of air against the fuselage seemed to come in gusts, from both front and sides. For a split second the cabin lights went out, then flickered back to full power.

Then they entered what appeared to be a vacuum in the sky. The aircraft plunged. And plunged.

"Uhh," grunted the prince as they hit bottom, and rebounded off an invisible layer of air, skidding sideways in the process. "Santa Madonna mia, fammi la grazia!"

The cabin's interior again flared, reflecting lightning which must have glanced off the near wingtip.

"Maybe Shireen's old man had something," muttered Doc, when the entire plane appeared to groan, as it twisted and screwed its way through the hostile and conflicting streams of air.

Then, abruptly, calm. Total peace. Except for the reassuring steady hum of the engines—or was it now engine? Once more, a series of minor shudders. But not worrisome. For the plane regained its self-confidence, having again proven the superiority of modern technology over the primitive brutality of nature.

"I think we've made it," said Doc, softly.

Gianfranco Annunzio di Siracusa refrained from comment.

Doc spoke again, "John you've got the window. See anything out there?"

"Many lights."

"Then we must be approaching Istanbul."

"Thank God!"

"Yes and no."

"What do you mean?" asked Annunzio. "Are you not thankful for our deliverance?"

"Of course," replied Doc, "but I'm not sure to whom we're being delivered."

The prince just shook his head in dismay.

"John," continued Doc, "don't you remember what this little trip is all about? We've got five million dollars in hot money with us."

"But you said our only problem was in Iran. We're out of Iran. So we surely have nothing to worry about."

"Maybe."

The landing itself was a nonevent. The plane was not even brought to a full stop on the main runway, but veered onto another concrete strip and proceeded directly to a hangar well away from the main terminal building. The engine noise subsided with a lazy whine, the lights flickered again, and the copilot reappeared, struggling into his jacket.

"Sorry about that," was his comment. "I'm afraid that this will be the end of the line for a while."

"What do you mean?" asked Doc.

"We've been talking to these people on the way in. No spare engines here, and nobody capable of repairing the one we've got. So we're grounded until they fly in a new one from Abadan."

"How long will that take?"

"Three, four days."

"And then?"

"Depends."

"On what?"

"What Abadan tells us. Maybe we go on to London. Maybe we'll have to go back. Probably back. My guess is that the people we were supposed to pick up in England will find another way to get down. Then we just wash out the whole thing."

"What about us?"

64

"Well, my best advice to you would be to buy yourself an airplane ticket."

"Right," said Doc, without hesitation. "But first, both of us will want to shake off this little trip. Where would you suggest we stay in Istanbul tonight?"

"Hilton. That's where we always go. Why don't you just stick around. We'll take you into town and fix everything up."

"Fine. What about our suitcases?"

"We'll also take care of them. I'll put crew tags on them. Then, maybe, we won't have to screw around with customs all night. They've gone wacky here lately. Think everybody's got a ton or two of hashish on them."

"And going out?"

"Same thing. Only then they're looking for bombs too. Believe me, the best policy in Turkey is to steer clear of border officials. They're nothing but trouble. Hell, they once delayed us for six hours because they found a few thousand dollars on me. And I'm crew! They claimed I was smuggling out currency. Dumb bastards. All I was doing was taking money to London to put in the bank. From Iran, not Turkey. But that was too easy an explanation for these knuckleheads." He glanced at his watch. "Look, it's getting late. There's a little office in the hangar. Come on in with me. We'll take care of the rest."

The Australian led them across the tarmac and into the huge building. The office was dirty and bleak. As soon as they were alone, the prince spoke: "Doc, what are we going to do? Did you hear what he said?"

"I don't know. I need a drink, and then some time to think. Anyway, let's not talk about it here."

Within a short time, the copilot returned, accompanied by the pilot—another Australian. They had somehow rounded up a car, a brown Chevrolet.

"Our luggage?" asked Doc, as he and the prince climbed into the back.

"In the trunk."

They sped away from the hangar, through some open gates, and onto a divided expressway. Despite what the copilot had said, nobody challenged them. The pilot, at the wheel, was apparently also in a hurry to get a drink. In less than half an hour they wheeled into a large park, ringed with palm trees, flooded with an eery green light from the lamps below. A little bit of Las Vegas in Turkey. Doc perked up.

"Say," he commented, "this looks all right."

From the inside, the Hilton in Istanbul was not immediately recognizable as such. The entrance, the lobby, the restaurants—all were well appointed, spacious, and even reflected some truly original design. The sunken lounge, the elaborate terraces overlooking the Bosphorus, indicated that somewhere along the line the cost accountants had slipped, or been cleverly misled by a mad architect who felt that hotels did not necessarily have to be totally devoid of aesthetics. Even the prince cast an admiring eye at the marble floors and pillars as Doc, in charge as usual, arranged for their check-in. The two-bedroom suite on the eleventh floor was also surprisingly large, and not very expensive—thirty-seven dollars a night. The two men did not bother to change, but returned immediately to the elevators after having, between them, found an appropriate number of foreign coins for the bellhop. They left the suitcases with the four hundred million rials sitting in the middle of the living room rug.

Back downstairs they had the choice of the night club or the American bar. Neither was in the mood for belly dancers, Hilton style, so the bar it was. Not surprisingly, the Australian pilots were in charge. Somehow they had already rounded up two Pan Am stewardesses.

"Come on, join us," said their ex-copilot. "We owe you a drink after giving you a ride like that."

This was followed by introductions all around. He was Jack, his mate was Frank, the two virgins of the airways went under the names of Billy-Jean and Sue. Scotch with water was the in drink. Dimple. Because, as Billy-Jean pointed out, the bottle was so cute. Billy-Jean also found the prince cute. Frank, who appeared already to have established preemptive rights where she was concerned, didn't seem to mind the new turn of events. The novelty of being able to drink uninterrupted well into the night, unimpeded by Australian laws, obviously took constant priority over women. Doc's expression indicated that he considered the whole business a pain. Three rounds later, Jack had a firm hold on Sue's left tit, while Billy-Jean was fondling the prince's ass. She was a big girl, and had managed to wedge Gianfranco firmly between herself and the bar; this way she could do her little thing with a modicum of privacy. Doc and Frank just drank, more or less in silence. Then Doc's face brightened.

"Frank, where did you get that car?"

"One of the guys out at the airport."

"Think your friend would like to sell it?"

"What would you do with a car in Turkey?"

"I don't know. But it just occurred to me. As long as we're here, we might as well see some of the country."

"So why don't you rent a car?"

"I figure if I could get something like that Chevy— cheap—and resell it, I'd make out about the same. And probably the rental agencies only have those little European cars. I prefer something I'm used to."

"Maybe you're right. But I doubt it."

"That would be my funeral. O.K.?"

"Sure. How much would you be willing to pay?"

"A thousand."

"A thousand what?"

"Dollars. Cash."

"Hey, that's crazy. I can get it for five hundred. They like cash dollars here."

"O.K., get it. Keep the other five hundred for yourself. Just make sure all the papers are in order. We might want to cross a border or two."

"Buddy, you've got a deal. Where's the money?"

"Here." Doc pulled out his wallet, and quickly extracted the necessary bills.

"By when do you need it?"

"Noon tomorrow."

"My friend, you've just bought yourself a 1961 Chevrolet. Congratulations! Another drinkie to celebrate?"

At 2:30 the party broke up. Billy-Jean was so sloshed they barely got her to the elevator. Sue and

Jack promised to put her to bed. The prince did not look in the least put out. Frank announced he was staying for just one more. Doc said he'd had enough. The prince concurred. As they entered their suite on the eleventh floor, both men's attention went immediately to the center of the room. Both suitcases were still there, and apparently untouched. Doc checked to be sure. They mumbled their goodnights, and that was the end of what had turned out to be a rather complicated day.

It was already 10:30 in the morning before the maid's persistent opening and closing of doors finally roused Doc. He immediately went into the living room to check. Yes, both suitcases were still there. There was a small terrace off the living room. Outside it was slightly chilly, but the bright sun and blue sky held promise of a warm spring day. Doc appeared satisfied. Back inside, he made three phone calls with the assistance of an extremely helpful hotel operator. The fourth call was to room service. Only after breakfast had arrived did he wake the prince. Five minutes later, freshly shaven and garbed in a dark red robe, Gianfranco sat down to coffee.

"Say, John," remarked Doc, "You look your old optimistic self."

Annunzio actually grinned. "Everything looks brighter by the light of a new day. Old Sicilian saying."

"I think they had something there."

The toast was just right, but the butter had a rancid taste. Maybe they used goat's milk. The coffee came in the form of tiny packages of Nescafe and a large pot of hot water.

"Well, Doc," said the prince, "what now?"

"We leave at just after noon."

"But you heard what those Australians said about the customs people at the airport last night. I'm not going to . . ."

"We're not going to any airport. We're leaving by car. I bought us one last night."

The prince actually sputtered in his coffee cup, and then broke into a series of violent coughs.

"Take it easy, old man," suggested Doc.

"I cannot," replied the prince, after he had settled down. "Do you realize what's on the other side of the Turkish border? A choice of Bulgaria or Greece. Communists or dictators. Do you think *they* are going to just shrug their shoulders when they spot our four hundred million rials? Doc, you must have had too much to drink?"

"We're not going to Greece or Bulgaria. We're headed south."

"South? I'm not even sure what's down there. Syria, I think. Whether there's a road all the way is another thing. Still, that's at least a better idea. Provided we can make some sort of arrangement at the border. Which I somehow doubt, considering that I know neither Turkish nor Arabic, and I strongly suspect that you don't either."

"John, could you stop talking for just a minute? I would like to explain."

"All right," he said grudgingly.

"Good. We are leaving by ship. We and our car."

"By ship?"

"Yes. I'm convinced it's by far the safest way. There's always enormous confusion at ports. And the people who take cruise ships are perhaps the least suspect of all types of international travelers. In addition, the cars and the passengers are loaded separately and at different times. Nobody really cares about the cars. They're more of a nuisance than anything else. I noticed that on a trip around the Caribbean a few years ago. Then there's another thing. They hardly need to check for bombs or weapons like they do at airports. Nobody's ever tried to hijack a cruise ship. Well, once I think. Some Portuguese revolutionaries, if I recall correctly. But that was years ago." He paused. "Now do you understand?"

"Doc," exclaimed the prince, "You are a genius. You've got it!" He got up from the breakfast table, and insisted on shaking Doc's hand.

"Now," continued the prince, starting to pace around the room, "what ship?"

"Well, that's still not completely clear. The hotel operator put me onto three shipping lines here in Istanbul. None of them has any cruise ships calling here for at least ten days. It's still too early in the season. But they all said we should be able to get one in Izmir. That's down the coast of the Mediterranean, about a day's drive they claim. Apparently about the only cruises running right now are those from Europe to Egypt. They usually call at Izmir on the way back. Because of Ephesus. Archaeology. Ephesus is just the other side of Izmir, it seems. So that's where we catch our boat."

71

Within the hour their luggage was already outside the main entrance of the hotel, with the prince standing loyal, though nervous, watch. Inside Doc, having taken care of the bill and bought a fistful of Turkish lire, was working on the hall porter. A small bribe, in dollars, produced the desired result: a reasonably up-to-date road map, upon which the man behind the counter had drawn a thick red line indicating the Istanbul-Izmir route. At noon on the dot, the Chevy arrived. Somebody had even washed it. The Australian obviously thought that all this was great fun, and wanted to offer a farewell round of drinks. But Doc put a quick stop to that.

"Frank," he said, "some other time. Just point the way to Izmir."

"It's easy. Take a right outside the hotel grounds. Then take another right at the first main intersection, and down the hill. That'll take you to the Bosphorus. You can't miss it, as you Yanks say. Right there at the bottom of the hill is where the car ferry lands. It runs every half hour. The trip across takes about fifteen minutes. So you can figure that you'll be back in Asia before one o'clock."

"You got gas in this jalopy?"

"Full tank. By the way, you'd better check the oil now and then. She ain't as young as she used to be."

"Thanks, Frank. If you're ever in Lugano, look us up."

"Sure."

The Bosphorus turned out to be exactly where Frank said it was. Getting onto the ferry was another thing. Cars of many types and vintages were haphazardly assembled like a group of unruly and battle-scarred greyhounds, waiting for the rabbit to appear. In this case, the rabbit took the form of a small man who blew a whistle. With an explosion of engine noise, everybody tried to drive onto the ramp and into the ship at the same time. Doc got aced out completely, until he caught the spirit of the game, and by almost faking a Renault Dauphin into the water, got the second last place.

"Phew," he exclaimed, "this is going to be fun."

They disembarked at Yalova, and headed southwest. The road was broad, and in relatively good shape. Soon after they left the Bosphorus, the traffic thinned out to just an occasional truck. The country was a series of low rolling hills which the Chevy barely took notice of. There were no road signs or directions, but neither man worried. There was obviously just one main road in these parts and they were on it. The sun was starting to sink as they approached the first big city since Istanbul—Bursa. One could see it from a great distance, since it was situated on a series of hills. On top of the highest was a spectacular mosque, its dome a gleaming green, its minarets a pure contrasting white. In the main square there was a large crowd of men standing outside yet another mosque, one of huge proportions.

"Say, Doc," said the prince, "maybe we should stop and take a look. That mosque looks interesting."

"We stop, yes. But for gas."

The man at the Shell station, incongruously situated vis-à-vis the mosque, spoke English of a sort. He strongly advised against their proceeding to Izmir.

There were no hotels on route, and no gas stations open after dark. He was sure they could not make it on one tank. In Bursa? The Anatole Palace. The most luxurious hotel in all of Asia. It turned out to be a large, rambling place, but its luxury was that of a nineteenth century English seaside resort.

The next morning shortly after dawn they took to the road again. Now the landscape changed into a series of huge mounded hills, covered by endless brown grass. Don Quixote country, ex-windmills. During hundreds of miles they met perhaps a dozen trucks, three mini camel caravans plodding alongside the road, and passed through no more than a half dozen villages, all extremely primitive. It was mid-morning before they spotted the first gas station at Balikesir. The Shell man in Bursa had been right. By noon they were already in the outskirts of Izmir. What a contrast! It looked like Liverpool. A dirty, crowded, rundown, port city. The main drag led directly to the port itself, where they were greeted by a scene of turbulent confusion. Cargo lay haphazardly about; trucks pushed their way aggressively through crowds of talking men. At pierside, there were rusty old tramp steamers, stained oil tankers, evil-smelling fishing boats. But not a sign of anything even remotely resembling a cruise ship. Yet in the middle of all this lay salvation: Italian Lines! Spelt out in foothigh letters in front of the only respectable building in sight.

"Benissimo," exclaimed the prince, "exactly what we want."

"I agree," said Doc. "Why don't you go in, John.

You speak the lingo. I'll stay out here and guard the goodies."

After just fifteen minutes, the prince returned, followed by a man with a huge moustache clad in impeccable white. Gianfranco leaned down to Doc through the car's open window.

"Well?"

"The news is not perfect, but also not too bad."

"Go on."

"First, there are no cruise ships calling in Izmir this week."

"That's not bad news?"

"Wait a minute, Doc. There is an Italian ship, bound for Venice, that will be leaving Rhodes the day after tomorrow."

"And where's Rhodes?"

"It's an island."

"Where?"

"In the Mediterranean."

"Now that much I guessed," replied Doc in disgust. "I mean where in relation to where you are now standing?"

"It's off the Turkish coast, about another two hundred miles south."

"And how do we get there?"

"There's a ferry from a place called Marmaris."

"None from Izmir?"

"Not at this time of year."

"Great."

"But listen. My friend here said he can work it all out. He will book us and our car on the *San Christofer*, and will telephone a friend of his in Marmaris to make the ferry arrangements. His friend runs a hotel down there. We can stay with him tonight, cross over to Rhodes tomorrow, and sail for Europe the next day."

Doc nodded, and then spoke softly. "Did you, uh, somehow figure out how we will get around our little problem?"

"Little problem?"

"In the trunk, stupid. And not so loud!"

"Don't worry. He doesn't speak English. Momento."

The prince and the man from Italian Lines entered into a spirited exchange.

"He says that our man in Marmaris can take care of anything. He is an important man, and Marmaris only has about a thousand inhabitants."

"Sounds all right."

When all was done, both Italians appeared again. Success demanded that everyone have an apéritif. A clerk would guard the car. So campari and soda it was outside a small café right around the corner. Doc made no attempt to communicate with his host. But the prince more than made up for this with his usual non-stop patter. He only paused once to announce in English that they had decided that next on the agenda was lunch. That idea Doc vetoed. He did not want to miss any ferries or ships, and Marmaris was still a long way off.

As it turned out, he was right. After passing Ephesus about thirty miles south of Izmir, the road narrowed and became rougher and rougher. They could have been back in Iran. The farther south they went, the higher the mountains became. The last one must have been well over a thousand meters. From what seemed to be the top of it, they began a hair-raising descent along a dirt road, barely wide enough for one car. No guard rail, no nothing, stood between them and the precipice that fell off to the deep valley below. By six in the evening they were on its floor: flat, well watered, and covered with thick green vegetation. Suddenly the valley swung to the west, the river in its middle widened, and there it was! A marvelous blue sea, perfectly calm, and invitingly cool. Next came the first main intersection for hours; this time there was a sign: Marmaris Lido Hotel 100 meters. The building was really nothing more than a large bungalow, completely surrounded by a wooden-railed porch. Doc braked the Chevrolet to a halt, and honked the horn. It produced a gaily dressed man, with arms waving high in the air. When they stepped out of the car, it was to the Italian that the hotelkeeper rushed in a direct beeline, proving once again that it takes one to know one.

"Principe!" he exclaimed, "we have been awaiting your arrival eagerly. Come. We will take care of everything. Just leave the keys in the car. I have drinks ready. No, no," to Doc, as he started to open the trunk, "let us do that."

He left no option. The gin and tonic, with real Schweppes, not the local non-fizzy imitation, disappeared promptly. It had been hot and dusty in those Turkish hills. It was just as promptly replaced by a second. Then a third. Loud Italian filled the air, especially after the hotelkeeper was joined by his dark, well-rounded, shrill-voiced wife, and their thickset teenage daughter. She hesitantly tried out her school English on Doc, looking painfully embarrassed at the fuss her parents were making over the visiting royalty. The dinner that followed was sumptuous and excellent. The pasta was perfect; the fish was fresh from the sea. The wine, a Frascati, was cool and delicious. Three bottles disappeared before the cognac was brought out. It was Italian cognac, and thus a bit on the sweet side. Everytime Doc started to talk about schedule, ferries, ships, and the like, he was silenced with the waving of many arms. All was taken care of. And so all retired to bed shortly before midnight satisfied with themselves; the Principe, the Americano, and the Italian expatriates of Marmaris.

The dawn of the next day, April 7, 1967, was glorious. The Asiatic coast of the Mediterranean glistened in the warm sun. There was not even the hint of a breeze. Breakfast was taken just after nine on the terrace behind the hotel. It bordered directly on what could only be described as a lagoon, a large pool of crystal-clear water, almost completely protected from the sea beyond by a series of upcropping rocks. Even from the terrace the myriad of small fish which had come to feed in its lush waters was visible. At ten, they loaded the car and headed for the port. The prince had already settled all money matters, discreetly.

Then the trouble began.

First, the ferry. There was none. That must have been a misunderstanding. Yes, there was a ferry. But no, the ferry could not take cars. It only took people. And it only ran on Sunday. How was such a misunderstanding possible? The phones in Turkey are very bad. So what now? No problem. Everything was being arranged. Just pull the car onto the pier. Pier? That narrow concrete slab over there, about fifty meters long. And then what? Just wait. So they waited.

The waterfront was deserted. Until 10:30 when the uniforms appeared, three of them. Customs and immigration. Not to worry. But why then all the talk? First in Turkish, then in Italian, then in both. Doc deliberately moved away from the group, calculating correctly that all this was beyond him. He still stood there, silently smoking, when the five other men moved off, and disappeared down an alley beside a building which must have been the center of local government if the huge Turkish flag which hung from a rather bent pole outside its entrance was any indication of function. When the group reemerged, it had grown to six men, a donkey, and a cart. The cart was laden with long two-by-four planks. All this was paraded to the end of the pier. The agitation among the men was, if anything, increasing. Doc and the car were ignored. But that also changed. As if by signal, the whole shouting clan moved at him, and surrounded the car. Two of the uniformed men even kneeled down in front of the Chevy, and took measure of the car's underside and wheels.

"Christ!" thought Doc, "he's blown it!"

But then came a shout, and a renewed mass movement back to the end of the pier. Because it was arriving. Their ship. Their ferry. Except that it resembled neither. It was a very old boat, and a very small one. The chugging of an ancient diesel engine and the smoke that rose from a pipe above the solitary super-structure—a cabin about the size of an outhouse—at least attested to the fact that it could move without sails. Slowly it approached the pier, and a dark, heavy-set man, threw a line to the waiting men. They scrambled like children for the honor of assisting in the docking procedures. Doc slowly moved out to join them. The boat was even more disappointing at near distance. It did not have a deck; just a huge gaping hole obviously designed to be filled with some unknown type of bulk cargo. In the front was a small platform, perhaps three meters square, one at the back upon which the outhouse was mounted, and narrow ledges along the sides connecting them. The boat rode high in the water. Its sides were at least three feet above the level of the concrete pier.

"Well," said the prince, having caught sight of Doc staring at this creature of the sea, "here is our ferry."

"Of course," replied Doc, calmly, "what else?"

"Now we must prepare it to take our automobile."

"Sure," replied Doc, "go right ahead. What, exactly, will that involve?"

"We just run a few planks across the boat from side to side, to match the width of the car's wheels. You know, like those hydraulic lifts they have in garages when they change the oil. You just drive on!"

"Onto a couple of planks?"

"Why more?"

"Because, you meathead, if the car doesn't hit those planks exactly, it's going to go right down into that hold, and then right down through the bottom of that hold. With me! Anyway, it's impossible. Look. The sides of that boat are at least a yard higher than the surface of this pier. What do you expect that Chevy to do—jump on?"

The logic of these last words struck home. The prince turned and launched into a violent tirade directed at his Italian compatriot. The latter repeated the performance in Turkish. The crowd of Turks on the receiving end was steadily growing. The three customs men and the donkey driver had been joined by the crew of the ship, both of them. Before the shouting had begun to even reach peak volume, the man who appeared to be the captain jumped nimbly back onto his boat, and then swung down into the hold. His number two followed. Soon came a new sound, one that more aptly should have come from a quarry, than a boat.

"What the hell's going on?" asked Doc.

"They have found a solution," answered his partner. "It is actually quite simple. All they must do is shift the ballast from one side to the other. That will tip the ship. This side will gradually sink to the level of the pier. Then you just drive on."

"Uphill?"

The ballast was in the form of large smooth rocks, which explained the strange noise. It lasted for about twenty minutes, and, miraculously, produced the predicted result. Quickly all of the assembled Turks pitched in with the planks. After much ado, they decided that two sets of two were enough: one pair for the left wheels and another for the right. One set led from the pier to the edge of the boat; the second straddled the vessel from side to side. Simple. All that was required now was a bit of reasonably precise driving.

That was up to Doc. He walked back to the car, started it, and in one unhesitating go, drove off the pier and onto the frail scaffolding spanning the hold of that ancient sloop. With almost scornful bravado he jerked the car to an abrupt halt just a split second before it seemed doomed to plunge over the side of the now violently rocking craft. Circus act completed, he squeezed out of the car through the half-opened door, inched his way back along the edge of the planks, stepped back onto the pier, lit a cigarette, and said:

"Let's get the hell out of here."

The car was quickly lashed to the boat, the diesel started, passports stamped, hands shaken, and within ten minutes the Pride of Marmaris, with its strange cargo, moved off into the waters of the Aegean Sea.

The Turks kept to themselves to the aft. Doc and the prince settled down at the opposite end of the boat, saying little, watching the world go by. The coast itself was a series of tiny coves—jagged and for the most part rocky. They stayed perhaps three hundred meters offshore as they chugged their way north. Both land and sea remained totally devoid of any human presence. Almost exactly on schedule, after three and a half hours, the boat swung west, out into the open sea separating Turkey from the island of Rhodes.

At first, the rising swell of the sea seemed logical. After all, they had lost the protection of the mainland.

But then came the first hint of a wind from the north, bringing with it streaks of white vapor high in the sky. The slow chug of the engine increased in tempo. The wind picked up in velocity. The white wisps became black scudding clouds. The inevitability of a storm became apparent.

"Maltempe!" shouted the prince, between gusts of wind.

"What?"

"Maltempe. The evil wind."

The bow of the ship rose and fell with increasing violence. But it was the roll that became worrisome. For they were passengers on a vehicle which was, by any standards, inherently unstable. Both the front and rear bumpers of the two ton automobile extended well over the railings of the boat. In fact, the trunk of the car was awash with disturbing regularity as the forces of both wind and water, coming from the northwest, bashed the boat over on its side. The whole motion topside began to resemble that of a monstrous seesaw, one which had somehow begun to gradually defy the laws of gravity. After the assault of what must have been the seventh wave, the threat of capsizing even signalled itself to the Turkish crew. Number two emerged from the cover of the wheelhouse and descended once again into the hold, down a makeshift type of ladder. Accompanied by the renewed sound of crashing stones, audible even above the wind and water, he went to work readjusting the ballast, trying to bring the ship back into balance. Within less than five minutes it started to work. The oscillations became less acute; the entire boat seemed to regain a new sense of stability. But for its passengers up front, this improvement meant little more than moving from worse to bad.

Then it was Doc's turn to sense a need for action.

"Hey," he yelled to Gianfranco, "our rials are in that trunk!"

The prince appeared to neither hear nor understand what Doc was saying, as he crouched in a huddle. So the American moved closer and shouted directly in his ear.

"Listen," he screamed, "I'm going to get those two suitcases full of money out of the trunk. Understand?"

This time the prince nodded.

"Right," Doc continued, "when I've got them, I'll hand them to you. Then you stow them. Here." He pointed repeatedly to the space under the ledge at the bow of the boat.

Again the prince indicated his understanding.

"So come on!"

Both grappled their way along the side of the plunging vessel. What Doc then proceeded to attempt was not an easy task. Tenuously propped, with both feet on the outside rail, left hand gripping the underside edge of the steel frame above the rear wheel, stomach braced against the tailfin, he blindly searched with his right hand for the keyhole of the trunk. Three times he was drenched as the boat, and the rear end of the Chevrolet, dipped into the foaming crests of the waves.

Then he succeeded. With a lurch, the lid sprang open. Doc scrambled up and over, until he was half in, half out, of the car's trunk.

"John," he yelled. "Quick!"

John was there, quick. He caught the first suitcase which Doc thrust down to him. Almost between waves he managed to scamper back to the bow of the boat, stow it, and return for the second. He tugged at Doc's trouser leg, indicating his readiness. Carefully twisting his body, Doc swung the second load of rials, worth two and a half million dollars, into the outstretched arms of his partner.

Almost. But not quite.

At first, the suitcase seemed destined for the bottom of the Aegean Sea. But at the very last moment, with a frantic movement of hands and arms, Gianfranco managed to tip it the other way—right down into the hold of the boat.

"Jesuz," exclaimed Doc, who had witnessed this traumatic operation from his perch above.

"God we were lucky," he said, after both men had safely returned to their little piece of deck at the front of the boat. "That money was within one inch of being lost and gone forever."

The prince just smiled weakly. He was not sure whether it had been his fault or not.

"Don't worry," consoled the American, "the money's safe, and it looks like the storm's almost over." Indeed it was. The sea was calming almost as abruptly as it had erupted less than a half hour earlier. The sun was already starting to break through the clouds.

"John, you just stay here. I'll go down there and retrieve the other half of your cousin's life savings."

But when Doc peered into the bowels of this peculiar vessel, he discovered that his idea was not entirely original. The captain's mate was already busy, gathering in the sheaves which had fallen, if not from heaven, at least from the chariot of some visiting foreign gods. The locks of the suitcase had obviously been sprung as a result of the fall. Two hundred million rials lay scattered across the entire bottom of the boat. They represented a lot of paper. Slowly the Turk appeared to reach the same conclusion. This was beyond the capacity of pockets. He scampered up the ladder, and disappeared behind the wheelhouse. Seconds later the captain himself appeared, carrying a short length of rope. And a long thick steel rod, probably a castoff from some engine room. After just a fleeting glance at Doc who was watching every move from the other end of the boat, he descended below, and deliberately gathered together pile after pile of bills, stuffing them back into the suitcase. It was not the neatest of packing jobs; but he got them all back in. The rope, which he then looped around the suitcase, made sure they stayed in. With not even a further glance at Doc, he moved back up the ladder with the case, and once again disappeared behind the tiny cabin at the rear. Promptly the boat changed direction. Its bow swung into the wind, hesitated, and then swung again.

"He's turned back!"

"John," replied Doc, tersely, "you stay put. I'm going to have a little talk with our friends."

With that he dropped into the hold, crossed it in just a few strides, and raced up the ladder. As he started to rise to his feet on the other side, just to the front and left of the wheelhouse, a strong hand grabbed him. And held him in his kneeling position.

It was the chief himself. Doc pushed. The man faltered. Now firmly on his feet, Doc went after him. The Turk lashed out with his steel rod. He missed Doc's forehead by millimeters.

Then Doc did a strange thing. He ran! And disappeared behind the other side of the wheelhouse. The captain was obviously not in a mood for hide and go seek. He charged after Doc. The American just stood there waiting, his back resting against the far rail of the boat—with a .32 Beretta in his right hand. With no apparent sense of urgency he shot the Turk in the right shoulder. The stunning effect of the bullet, and the lurching of the boat, sent him crashing to the deck, right at Doc's feet. One vicious kick to the head rendered him unconscious. A second made sure he remained that way for a while. The steel rod rolled out of his grasp. Doc picked it up, and flung it overboard.

The second Turk now emerged from the cabin. He also had taken precautions, this time in the form of a rusty iron pipe. But the sight of his boss lying on the deck, and a motion from the Beretta in Doc's hand, changed any thought he might have had of heroism. His first reaction sent him in the direction of the sea. But probably he remembered just in time that, in the good tradition of Turkish sailors, he could not swim. So he just stopped, sat down on the deck, and for some reason covered his head with his arms.

Then Gianfranco appeared. He looked scared.

"John," said Doc, in a perfectly steady voice, "do you know anything about boats?"

"Yes."

"Then turn the son-of-a-bitch around."

John did so with remarkable ease. Doc just stood beside him, watching in admiration, his gun hand loosely at his side.

"Any idea where Rhodes is?"

"It must be due west. Into the sun."

"Think you'll find it?"

"It's a big island, and we must be close. We'll make it."

"How come you know how to steer this thing?"

"I do a lot of sailing off Sicily. Don't worry about me. Worry about the two men out there."

"That's no problem. I can take care of those monkeys."

"I didn't mean that. It's what happens when we get to Rhodes."

"I'll also take care of that."

The prince fell silent, and his face remained expressionless, even when he spotted the rough outline of the mountains of Rhodes on the horizon, and then the contours of the huge breakwaters outside its main port. By the time they entered the harbor area, a large semi-circular body of protected water, it was 6 P.M. The prince pointed the boat at the docks which lay to their left, opposite the walled city. In fact, he headed straight between two ships which lay anchored there, both streamlined and gleaming white. Cruise ships. The docking itself was perfect. Doc managed the ropes, securing the boat to the pier both fore and aft with near professionalism. The Turks? The captain, now fully conscious, just sat on the deck, glumly holding his wounded shoulder. His mate huddled in his original catatonic position.

The dock area was deserted. Nobody!

"Strange," commented the prince, after he had shut off the engine.

"Probably the dockers here are like those everywhere else in the world. When the six o'clock whistle blows, they all go home."

"But what about the customs people?"

"Who knows. Maybe they sit in comfort at the gates, waiting for somebody to show up. Just as long as they stay there a little while longer."

"What do you intend to do?"

"Transfer."

"To where?"

"There."

There, as the huge letters indicated, was the *San Christofer*. Not fifty meters away.

"But . . ."

"But nothing. We just get our stuff and transfer. We're not going into Rhodes. That way we don't have to bother anybody in Rhodes. Right?"

"And the car?"

"Why ask for trouble? We'd need a crane to get it off. And that would mean a crane driver. And crane drivers can talk. So we leave it. Right where it is. And we tell those Turks to get their garbage scow out of here. Pronto. They'll cooperate. After all, they get one free Chevrolet."

"That's crazy. We might just as well have left the car in Turkey in the first place."

"You're right. But at the time you didn't think of it,

did you? Neither did I. Because I thought we'd need the car to get those damn suitcases past customs. But now there's not going to be any customs. So we get rid of the car."

"I don't know Doc, if . . ."

"No ifs. Just get moving. Over to the *San Christofer*. Find the purser, or whatever he's called. Give him a hundred dollars and tell him to send some of his boys over to pick up our luggage. Then give him another hundred and tell him we want no complications about the check-in formalities."

It worked. The Italians came. The Turks went. And nobody in Rhodes could have cared less. It was after six o'clock. Following a shower, a shave, and a much needed change of dress, the prince made his presence known on board. That evening they dined at the captain's table. He insisted that the after dinner drinks be compliments of Italian Lines. So they all stayed up until 3 A.M. before staggering off to bed. As a drunken afterthought, Doc left something he'd found on the floor after repacking the suitcases in his cabin earlier that evening. A tip. A wet 10,000 rial bill.

5

In Campione, across the lake from Lugano, it was just one in the morning, since Italy lies two time zones to the west of Asia Minor. They were lire, not rials, that the man in evening dress was recounting before passing them through the opening under the inch-thick glass to the two young men opposite him.

"How much did we make, Albert?"

"About twenty-four million."

"How much is that in dollars?"

"Around forty thousand."

"Jeez. That's more than last night."

"Yes, Marvin. It's working very nicely. But I think it is now time we went home."

So Albert and Marvin left the casino, walked across the boulevard through the gates where a tired-looking official just waved his hand. The waiting motor launch whisked them across the lake in fifteen minutes. By 2 A.M. both were sound asleep in Switzerland.

The next day, in fact the remainder of that week, Albert and Marvin were extremely busy: phone calls, meetings, negotiations during the daylight hours: then Campione by night. Until Saturday night, when they were politely, but firmly, refused further admission to the casino. As they again crossed the lake, for the fourteenth time in seven days, Albert told Marvin that it was just as well.

Five days later, two sun-tanned men strode into the Majestic Hotel in Lugano. The taller of them asked the clerk to connect him with Albert Fiore's room.

Mr. Fiore? He had checked out. When? Yesterday, together with the other American. Where had they gone to? No idea, signor. The bar? Yes it was open. Could he arrange that the doorman keep an eye on their car? But of course, and your generosity is appreciated, signor.

The bar was indeed open, but not busy. Drinking at noon is frowned on in Switzerland.

"Two Bloody Mary's, please. And bring them over to the table."

The bartender seemed to approve.

"Now why in the world would those two guys check out?" was Doc's puzzled question.

"Maybe we should have called them from the ship."

"It's not like Albert to do this," continued Doc. "Marvin, yes. But not Albert."

Somebody tapped him on the shoulder. Doc disliked any laying on of hands, and reacted angrily. Until he saw the huge grin on Marvin's face.

"Hi, Doc."

"Marvin, my boy. I thought we'd lost you. Where's Albert?"

"Busy."

"Where busy?"

"I promised not to tell you. It's a surprise."

"So it's time for games, is it. Not with me, Marvin. Now cut the crap. Where's Albert?"

Marvin just grinned.

"O.K., have your little fun. Sit down, Marvin, and tell us what you've been doing lately."

"Oh, we've been busy. And look, I don't think I should sit down. I promised Albert that if I found you, I'd bring you right up. So maybe we'd better go."

Doc looked like he was really going to blow his top, but then changed his mind.

"Come on, John. Let's humor Marvin."

So they left, with Marvin leading the way. Outside he climbed into a spanking new MG convertible.

"You guys got wheels?" he asked.

"Yes," was Doc's only reply, as his eyes shifted from the red MG to Marvin, and then back to the MG. He decided not to get drawn into another pointless debate with Marvin.

"Fine," continued Marvin, "just follow me." He started, and then gunned the engine a few times, testing Doc's nerves.

At the first intersection Marvin took a left. Almost immediately the road started to rise steeply. After ten minutes, they were well out of town, and negotiating one switchback after the other. After another ten minutes they passed through a medieval tower, and entered an ancient mountain village. The roadsign outside read: Garona—936 meters above sea level. Or so the prince said, since everything was in Italian. On the other side of the town, the MG suddenly swung off the road, and rocketed past a set of open gates, leading through the high stone wall on the left. Doc was caught unaware and overshot. Slowly he backed up, changed gears again, and inched his way through the gates. There, at a distance, stood Albert. Beside the swimming pool. Doc pulled up behind the MG, and both he and the prince got out.

A girl in a black dress and white apron emerged from the villa, and curtsied. Marvin made the introductions.

"Doc, this is Maria. Our maid. She'll take care of the baggage. She's a strong girl."

"Of course, Marvin," said Doc. "Now let's walk over to our swimming pool, past our house, and have a little talk with our Albert."

"Hi, Doc," were Albert's first words. "Hungry? We're planning on having lunch soon."

"Yes, Albert. That would be nice. Do you mind if I join you here for a couple of minutes first?"

"No. Pull up a chair. You too, John. Nice to see you again. Have a good trip?"

"Yes, thank you. It lasted a bit longer than we anticipated. But everything worked out."

Then Doc again. "Albert, I'd like to ask you a few simple questions."

"Sure."

"Well, for openers, what's with this place here?"

"We bought it."

"I see. And the MG?"

"We bought that too."

"Right. And of course the maid came with the house."

"How did you know, Doc?"

"Well, it's logical, isn't it. But let's push on to something else that's puzzling me."

"Sure, Doc. What is it?"

"Where did you get the money?" This time Doc yelled.

"Gee, Doc, don't get upset. We won it."

"Won it?"

"Yes. Marvin and I found out about this casino. It's in Italy, right across the lake from Lugano. You see, in Switzerland they have laws against gambling. But not in Italy. So everybody goes to the other side of the border. It's just like home, really. They have essentially no limits, because in some way—I'm not sure of the details—the Italian government is involved. So

I tried out something that I was working on, really just on an experimental basis. It seemed to work all right, so we decided to go all the way. As it turned out, the time was much too short for me to determine whether it really worked, or whether we just had a run of luck. Even at the University of Chicago, when we had access to an IBM 360, we determined that . . ."

"Albert, please excuse me for interrupting. Maybe we could come back to the University of Chicago later. But I feel there is another matter which I would like cleared up first."

"Of course, Doc."

"Good. Now my next question is: what did you use for money when you started?"

"Dollars. I got them from Marvin. Actually the whole thing was his idea in the first place."

"From Marvin. How much?"

"Fifty thousand dollars."

"From Marvin," Doc repeated.

"Excuse me," this from Marvin, who started to move toward the house.

"Oh no you don't, Marvin. You stay right here. Now Albert, in what form was this fifty thousand dollars?"

"Hundreds. Marvin gave me five hundred hundreds."

"New bills?"

"In fact they were. How did you guess, Doc?"

"Because I know our Marvin." Then Doc grabbed Marvin by the front of his shirt.

"O.K. Where did you get them, Marvin?"

"I brought them with me. Don't worry, Doc. They

were of extremely good quality. Hell, even in the States nobody would have spotted them. Those bills were the best I've ever done."

"You mean . . . ?" asked Albert, now frowning behind his glasses.

"Yes, Albert," replied Doc, "I mean."

"But Marvin," said Albert, "You should have told me!"

"Ah, come on you guys. It's over and done with. Let's forget about it."

"And if they find out? Did you have to identify yourself at that casino?"

"Sure," replied Marvin, "but only me. I did the playing and Albert just stood behind me and told me what to do. But don't worry."

"Why?"

"The passport I showed them was counterfeit too."

"Oh my God," whispered Doc. "All right. How much did you win?"

"We ended up with about four-hundred thousand dollars. But of course that includes our original fifty thousand."

The prince damn near fell off his chair. Doc merely shook his head—back and forth, for a full minute. Then he spoke again.

"So then you bought this house, and the car. Anything else?"

"Actually, yes. We took a lease on new banking premises. And we've arranged for the whole place to be done over. We've got the plans inside. You'll like it Doc. It's a great location. The office of American Express. They're moving into a new building, you see.

By chance we met the local manager at the bar of the hotel, and we got talking, and one thing led to the other."

"So how much have you already spent, or committed?"

"A quarter million. So we still have quite a bit left over, Doc."

Doc rose from his chair.

"I'm hungry. Let's have that lunch you were talking about."

Maria was waiting for them. The four men were no sooner seated in the elegant dining room than she appeared with a huge steaming platter of spaghetti. It soon disappeared, and a second followed. Maria turned a dark red when the Principe personally extended his congratulations on the excellence of her cuisine. It was, of course, him that she served first with coffee, and later with a yellowish liqueur.

"Gawd," exclaimed Doc, after the first gulp. "What the hell is that?"

"Grappa," replied the prince. "Here in Ticino they make some of the best, in any case the strongest grappa in the world. They say its alcoholic content can rise to as high as ninety percent."

"Where did she get it from?"

"Our wine cellar," replied Albert.

"Our wine cellar," repeated Doc, but after thinking it over, decided to let the subject pass without further comment.

"Albert," he said abruptly, "what do you know about silver?"

"Silver bullion?"

"Yes."

"It sells for $1.29 an ounce."

"Doesn't the price fluctuate?"

"During the past few years, no. The United States government has pegged the price at this level, and keeps it there by regulating the market."

"Why?"

"It's really a hangover from the days when silver, like gold, was part of the monetary system of the United States. It still is, in a way. After all, most of our coins are still made from silver. The U.S. government maintains an enormous inventory of the metal, not just for minting purposes, but also as a strategic raw material reserve. Silver is an important metal for our defense industry. That's why Uncle Sam controls the market and the price."

"But can you and I buy silver bullion?"

"Naturally."

"Where? From the government?"

"No. On the commodity exchanges—in New York, Chicago, or London."

"Anybody can do that?"

"Sure. Of course, you have to go through a broker, just like you do in the stock market. Actually, Doc, it's interesting you bring up silver. An increasing number of people feel a world-wide shortage is developing."

"I thought you said our government has piles of the stuff."

"They do, but every year this pile is diminishing, because they have to keep selling silver over the commodity exchanges in order to hold the price at $1.29

an ounce. But at some point, they'll have to stop, because, as I just told you Doc, the government is committed to keep a large stockpile as a strategic reserve."

"And then?"

"The price will zoom up."

"Albert, my boy, I'm going to let you in on a little secret. We have arranged to get 50% of the biggest silver mine on this earth."

"Where? In Canada?"

"No. In Iran."

"I've never heard of any silver mine in Iran."

"That's the point. Neither has anybody else. And nobody can. It's got to remain a secret."

"That's not going to be easy," said Albert immediately. "I mean you can hardly just hide a big operation like a silver mine."

"In Iran you can. John and I went over the whole setup. We're convinced it can be done, aren't we John?"

"Absolutely."

"All right, Doc, if you say so." Albert did not look convinced.

"Now Albert, there are still a few technical matters to be worked out. Maybe you can give us some ideas."

"I'll try."

"We'll have to set up a special account in the bank, and then make a loan of five million dollars to it. Think you could work that out?"

"Sure. That should be no great problem. But Doc, where are we going to get the five million from?"

"The rials. We've got four hundred million with us."

"But," interjected the prince, for the first time, "Agha said that he did not want his money to . . ."

"What Agha doesn't know at this point won't hurt him. After all, he wanted to deposit the money in the bank, and from now on it's up to the bank to decide what it does with its money."

"Yes, but . . ."

"Forget it. Now Albert, what do you know about rials?"

"Enough."

"How?"

"From our money dealer."

"Money dealer?"

"Yes, we hired one last Thursday. Also a securities dealer."

"On whose authority?"

"Doc, before you left you said we should try to improve things here. Well, we've tried."

"Where did you find these guys?"

"Also at American Express."

"I thought American Express was a travel office."

"In the States it is. Here it's also a bank."

"Why would these guys want to join a broken down bank like ours?"

"It's not so broken down any more. Wait until you see our new building, and how we're going to refurbish it. That's one reason why these fellows are coming. In addition, we're paying them a lot more."

"With what?"

"Doc, we've made out fine so far, and I'm sure things will get much better quickly."

"You're right, Albert. Either we move ahead, or

give up. And with that silver deal in our pocket, we're sure as hell not going to give up now. So what about my question: What's with rials?"

"There's a market for them in Geneva. Since nobody is supposed to have rials outside of Iran, it's a grey market. Still, the Geneva rate is only 2% below the official exchange rate, so it's a good deal. Our man said he can take care of everything the same day he gets the rials."

"Great, Albert. I hate to say this, but you and Marvin have done all right. Where is Marvin, by the way? He sneaked out of here without saying a word."

"Gee, I really don't know, Doc. Maybe it's because of Ringo."

At just this moment Marvin reappeared. With Ringo. Ringo took one quick look around the room, and headed straight for Doc. In fact, the front end of him ended sprawled across Doc's lap.

"Get him out of here!" Doc yelled.

"Ah, come on, Doc. He likes you," said Marvin.

Ringo's tail backed up Marvin's statement, as it wagged wildly in the air, brushing a coffee cup to the floor in the process. He even tried a few swipes of his tongue on Doc's face. Doc hesitated, wavered, and then gave the dog a few tentative pats on the head.

"You know, he really does. Marvin, you probably don't know this, but I have always had a great way with dogs." Ringo responded with a few more licks.

"That's enough boy," ordered Doc. "Sit!"

Ringo obeyed immediately, taking a position on his haunches, watching Doc's face eagerly for further instructions.

"Say, that's a really smart dog. Where did you get him, Marvin?"

"He came with the house."

"I never should have asked. Now listen, Marvin, this is not just some dumb dog. There can be no doubt that Ringo is a pure-bred Alsatian. They need lots of food, and the right food. What have you been feeding him?"

"Hamburger."

"That's not good enough. They need quality meat. And they need a walk every day. A long one."

"Sure, Doc. I'll take care of him. Can we keep him?"

"Of course. A fine dog like that. In fact, Marvin, I'll help you take care of him. After all, we need a watchdog around here."

"Doc, can I take him for a walk now?"

"Go ahead, my boy. But be careful of cars. Keep him on a leash."

The prince who had spoken very few words since returning to Swiss soil, now attempted to cut in.

"Doc," he said, "I have an idea."

"About what?"

"Well, it's like you said. Now we are going to definitely make something out of this bank. Is that not right?"

"Yes."

"And we will have this fine new building, new staff, everything new."

"Yes."

"Then we must seek to get recognition, publicity. So we get customers."

"Sure, but how?"

"I think I know how. We throw the biggest party Lugano has ever seen. I will invite all my friends. They will come, I'm sure. And they include some of the most famous names in Europe. Then we can invite local people. They will also come. The Swiss love aristocracy, because they have none of their own. In that, they are like Americans."

"Albert," asked Doc, "what do you think?"

"It's a great idea, Doc. In fact, terrific, if the prince can really pull it off like he says."

"Pull it off?" asked the prince, puzzled.

"That means produce. Like whether all those people would really show up."

"But of course they will. After all, we will pay their expenses."

That created a slight lull.

"So what," said Doc finally. "If it works it will be worth every dollar we put in. When?"

"The architects told me the renovation of our new bank building should be completed in June," said Albert.

"Then July 1?" suggested the prince.

"No," stated Doc, "July 4. It would be perfect. We could decorate the bank with lots of American—and, of course, Swiss—flags. Maybe even fireworks afterwards. In fact, prince, we must try to get the American ambassador to come. Then . . ."

6

In 1967, July 4th fell on a Friday. Normally, it went unnoticed in Lugano, as everywhere else in Europe. But not that year. For word had gotten out that some super-rich American bankers were putting on a real show. Typical. But still, not to be ignored. In fact, receiving an invitation to the big opening became a matter of local prestige. Rumor had it that half the aristocracy of Europe was coming. A very reliable source reported Princess Grazia of Monaco had definitely accepted. And this was followed up by a, perhaps, even more startling revelation: Elizabeth Taylor had insisted she be invited. To be sure, the authority in this instance was a well-known gossip. Swiss TV made a tentative probe, suggesting they might want to cover the affair. But a word from the chief executive of one of the large Swiss banks stopped that. Anyway, the prince would not have allowed it. He insisted that this remain an exclusive affair, not one to be peeped at by the masses. He also personally attended to every detail of the planning, except for the costs, which he left to the staff of the bank which had already increased to twenty-two by the time this memorable day arrived. A definite aura of success surrounded the Bank of Sicily and America in Switzerland.

At four o'clock the first limousine arrived in front of the bank. Uniformed doormen were there waiting.

The party of two, Prinz Johannes von und zu Hohen-
lohe and Prinzess Hildebrunn, noted for their punc-
tuality, were not in the slightest embarrassed to note
they were the first arrivals. They caught the reception
line in a state of slight disarray, but Annunzio soon
restored order. It was, of course, he who headed the
line. Beside him was, of all people, Joe Fiore, bursting
with pride and also almost bursting from the tuxedo
which, in spite of having cost over a thousand dollars,
still did not fit right. Next to him was Doc, and finally
Albert. Rather a meager lineup for an affair of this
size, but it was generally accepted as a display of
tasteful understatement.

The second arrival was La Marquesa d'Annecy.
The Marquis had been reunited with his forefathers
for at least twenty years. Her flaming red hair was
tied in an orange ribbon, and her immense bosom
heaved as the prince bowed gracefully to kiss her
hand. Joe Fiore, with a touch of real Las Vegas gal-
lantry, did the same, and even managed to utter a
close approximation of the going words. "Enchanté,
madam." Then came a bit of contrast: a short, fat
man who made his presence known through a succession of firm handshakes, clicks of heels, accompanied
each time by a sharp, guttural, "Bauer, Heinrich,
Hochtiefbau Duisburg, sehr angenehm." Nobody had
the faintest idea what the chap was saying until it was
later explained that he was Heinrich Bauer, formerly
of Hochtiefbau Construction of Duisburg, Germany,
now as Swiss as his tax advisors in Lugano. The next
pair of newcomers were Agha and Shireen Firdausi.
Shireen came in a low-cut dress of brilliant green. Her

eyes shone as they met Doc's, and her gloved hand stayed longer in his clasp than was required by protocol. Doc was so stunned by her appearance that he barely managed to bring out the necessary words. The mayor of Lugano and wife followed. Then the Ambassador of the United States and Mrs. Randolph. Since they represented the prize coup of the evening, the prince personally accompanied them down the reception line, and insisted on serving them their first drinks. By this time the new arrivals were already spilling over into the streets. At least a hundred spectators were out there, waiting for a glimpse of either Grace or Liz. But to no avail. The only movie star that finally came was Ursula Munding, famous in Switzerland for her 1938 portrayal of Heidi's father's sister, which made her Heidi's aunt, come to think of it.

By 5:30 the party inside the bank was developing into a resounding success. The caterers were being assisted by the bank staff who, with their natural Swiss multilingual talents, were able to make everyone more or less at home in his or her native tongue. Joe Fiore, finally released from the reception line, went straight to the improvised bar and asked for a shot of bourbon, neat. Then he got Albert aside.

"My boy, this is wonderful. Just wonderful. It must be costing us a packet, but it sure as hell is worth every nickel. Look, I want you to meet one of my friends whom I personally invited. He's over there, talking to Doc." So father and son moved.

"Tony," Joe said, "I want you to meet my boy, Albert. He was one of the men who has made all this possible. Albert, Tony Regazzoni, from New York."

While Joe stood beaming, Tony caught Albert in a huge embrace.

"Albert," he said, "I was just telling Doc. Your old man offered me and some of our mutual friends a piece of this bank, and like stupid bastards, we turned it down. But lemme tell you, I've changed my mind."

Then Joe Fiore spoke up. "I guessed as much, Tony, but so have I. I've decided that this is going to remain a family affair, my family."

"Now Joe, I know that you don't really mean that."

"Yes I do. And that's it. But look Tony, that doesn't mean we all can't work together. Everything I told you guys in Arizona still holds. We can manage your money, put it to work, and nobody can possibly find out. Isn't that right Doc?"

"That's right, Joe. In fact, I was just explaining our setup here to Tony. He's already promised to send over one million next week. And he said that from his organization in New York alone, he expects at least another ten million to follow. We've even worked out how the courier service will work."

"Is that right, Tony?"

"Look, Joe, I already told you I'm sold on this place. So I do something about it. Right? And I still want a piece of this action. But we'll talk about that later. You go and have a good time."

Then Marvin showed up. "Mr. Fiore, can I borrow Albert for a minute?"

"Who wants him?"

"Some guy from Amsterdam. He wants to know about silver."

"Silver! Albert don't know nothing about silver, do you Albert?"

"Yes, father, I do. I'll tell you about it later. O.K. Marvin, where is he?"

The guy's name was Richard von der Zuider. He knew Prince Gianfranco Annunzio di Siracusa from yachting. He'd heard silver was a good investment. Was that true? Yes it was. Was the U.S. government going to stop controlling the price? Albert felt that it was very likely very soon. And then? Then it could go to two dollars an ounce and beyond. Could the bank handle a rather sizeable investment in silver for him? Certainly. The best would be for Mr. von der Zuider to call at the bank on Monday. Would ten A.M. be too early? No. Good. He would bring his bank references from Amsterdam.

Doc, by this time, had joined the Firdausis. He was not the only one. Some nit who called himself the Duque de la Torrera had been trying to monopolize Shireen's attention ever since he had spotted her. And Heinrich Bauer was pumping Agha, trying to find out whether any quick money was to be made in Iran. His English was spotty, but he managed to convey, quite regularly, that he had twenty million marks, in cash, looking for a home. He expected at least ten percent return. But, as he explained after Doc had arrived, he would settle, temporarily, for five percent. Could his bank offer that? Doc suggested he come to the bank on Monday. Perhaps they could have lunch together? Heinrich did not hesitate. *Jawohl,* lunch would be perfect. He would bring along his bank references from Duisburg.

With some difficulty, Doc managed to get Agha into a private corner after that.

"Agha," he asked, "is everything going as planned?"

"Almost. We're a little behind schedule, but that's not your fault. The funds arrived in Kuwait much more quickly that I expected, and the letter of credit arrangements were completed just two days later. Then my Englishman, Howard, and I spent three weeks in Rhodesia. The problem was delivery. We now expect the equipment to arrive in Dubai in September. That means our first bullion will be ready for shipment probably in December."

"Did you hear the rumor about a possible change in the American government's policy on silver?"

"Yes, of course. That would make the whole venture all the better. Now tell me, has all the paper work been done here?"

"Yes. It will require some signatures."

"Excellent. You name the time and I'll be there. Of course, Shireen will also have to come. She has equal rights with me in this matter."

"Naturally. Perhaps we could best get together at a place we have outside of town. In fact, now that I think of it, you and Shireen must be our guests up there. For as long as you want."

"You are sure it will be no trouble?"

"Of course not."

"Then we accept. Doc, I suggest we continue our talks later. This is not exactly the place for us to go into any details."

"I agree. Anyway, it's time we move on."

At 6:30 the prince managed to subdue the din

sufficiently to announce in five languages that the limousines were waiting outside. It was quite a sight: somehow Annunzio had rounded up fifty luxury cars, ranging from Mercedes 600's, to Lincolns, to Bentleys to Citroens. They came from rental agencies as far away as Geneva, Zurich, Milano, and even Frankfurt. Lugano buzzed with the news that evening in almost every bar, restaurant and home. The convoy wound its way through Lugano, across the Swiss-Italian frontier, and then twenty-four kilometers along the narrow twisting road, through endless vineyards, to the shores of Lake Como. In Menaggio the lake steamer was waiting. The trip across took twenty minutes. And when they arrived at the dock of the Villa Serbelloni in Bellagio, thirty waiters, all dressed completely in white, including their gloves, were lined up on both sides of the stairway leading to the immense terrace of the hotel which, of itself, formed a small peninsula. They held trays of champagne, holding seven glasses each. The orchestra caught the spirit of the occasion and blasted out with "Quando, quando" in a manner which had nothing whatsoever to do with the style of Guy Lombardo, despite their common heritage.

Not since Jackie Kennedy's party in 1961, or was it 1962, had the Villa Serbelloni been given a carte blanche on expenses. Its management had not let such an opportunity pass. Hundreds of lanterns ringed the terrace, swaying gently in the warm breeze coming off Lago Como. The tables, set with seventy-year-old Sèvres dinner service, and fifty-year-old Baccarat crystal, loaded with gleaming Jetzler silverware, danced in the light of tall white candles which rose out of identical arrangements of pink and blue flowers. Beside each lady's placecard was a small orchid. The seating arrangements had required the full-time skills of the prince for two successive days. But as the guests took their places, and looked warily at their table partners, the looks of relieved satisfaction indicated that each felt he had been shown the respect due him. At the head table, the Ambassador's wife sat to the right of the prince. Across from them, Mr. Randolph had been paired with Shireen Firdausi, to his obvious pleasure. Joe Fiore and the mayor's wife, her husband and a duchess from Luxembourg, plus a scattered assortment of European aristocracy, none of the same nationality, had been given the remaining places of honor.

Almost immediately the food began to arrive. It is obligatory in Italy that one begins with prosciutto and melon, but tonight was an exception. Artichokes, stuffed with Strasbourg gooseliver mousse, sprinkled with white truffles, were chosen instead. The first wine to arrive: a 1957 Chablis Grand Cru. It was perfect for the dish that followed—grilled Italian scampi, delicately flavored by a mustard sauce which had been miraculously blended with cream from the Swiss Alps. Then came a surprise, one which even produced a subdued wave of applause: a lemon sorbet, but with the added touch of pink champagne which thirty waiters poured almost simultaneously over the icy crystals. The chef of the Villa Serbelloni, Giuseppi Ponti, had decided that this interlude of refreshment was not to be interrupted hurriedly. Only after thirty minutes did the main course arrive, a choice of Paillard di Vitello, with its piquant spices, or a Florentine steak. White Alsatian asparagus was the vegetable. The wine: 1949 Chateau Margaux. Dessert was Surprise Royale, a cassata covered with hot meringue, set aflame in marachine liqueur. At midnight exactly, coffee, cognac, and cigars were served.

Everyone agreed that the meal had been a masterpiece. In fact, it was with these words that the Honorable Charles Randolph began his speech. He went on to intone that he was proud to see the flag of the United States flying beside those of Italy and Switzerland on this Fourth of July. Actually there were no such flags in view, but he was working from a prepared text. He was proud to be part of this new world where Europe and America were living together in peace and harmony. And he was proud of his wife, Loraine, for insisting that they partake in this memorable occasion, in spite of the fact that as Ambassador to Switzerland, he had received many other invitations. He raised his glass to the success of this wonderful new bank.

All in all, it took one minute. The mayor of Lugano took ten, and would have taken a lot more had his wife not given him a dirty look. The prince ended the formalities by simply thanking his guests in six languages, the sixth being Parsee which he had picked up from Shireen over dinner. The dancing that followed was enormously popular. Joe Fiore had taken a real shine to the mayor's wife, and they did not miss a single waltz. Mr. Randolph latched on to a slightly tipsy countess from Brussels, and proved that age and drink was no deterrent to the cha-cha-cha. Doc and

Shireen danced almost uninterrupted until three.

Then, with a rather weak rendition of Arrivederci Roma, the orchestra signalled that the party was over. It was a happy and contented group that stepped onto the steamer waiting to take them back across the Lago Como to the fleet of limousines on the other side. By the morning of July 5, 1967, everyone knew that the International Bank of Sicily and America in Switzerland was a name to be reckoned with. As events later proved, this was a mixed blessing.

Part 2

(1968)

7

The sixteen members of the Board of Directors of the First National Bank of California met at two o'clock on the third Thursday of each month. The meetings usually lasted one hour, since the bank's Chairman, George Foreman, disliked gatherings of any type of more than sixty minutes duration. There was also the fact that he had a standing appointment for golf at 4:15, each Thursday afternoon at the Atherton Country Club. Likewise on Tuesdays and Fridays. The Club was a good forty-five minutes from downtown San Francisco.

Therefore at 2:59 on this Thursday, April 19, 1968, he announced that the meeting was adjourned. Most of the men thereupon left the vast Board room on the thirty-sixth floor, and returned to their menial chores as presidents of oil companies, chief executives of electronics conglomerates, senior partners of exclusive and ludicrously expensive law firms, and, in one case, to finish a drink at Harry's bar just off Montgomery Street. Although nepotism was definitely frowned on at the First National, the latter case was an exception, for in spite of his being the Chairman's brother, it was universally felt that Sam Foreman brought a much-needed touch of the common man to the decision-making process.

But not everybody left. Foreman—George, not Sam —had motioned to two men that he wished them to remain. They were Sid Chambers, his Vice Chairman, and Donald Luckman, a simple Vice President. Actually, Luckman did not belong at this meeting since he was hardly a member of the Board, nor even of the Senior Management. After all, the First National had forty-seven Vice Presidents. But the Chairman had asked him to sit—as an exception, it had been noted. So he had sat.

"I thought the meeting went well, didn't you?"

The you was obviously plural, so both Chambers and Luckman agreed. Fine meeting.

"I asked you to stay to follow up on that last item I had on the agenda: Our international program. Sid, as you know, we are simply not keeping up with the competition. Bank of America is all over the world. Wells Fargo has at least ten offices abroad. Even Security Pacific and U.C.B. down in Los Angeles are finally getting set up in both Europe and Asia. We haven't got a thing outside of this state. Now like I told the Board, that must change. And quickly. You saw the response. Even that stubborn sonofabitch from Analine Chemical agreed with me. That's the first time in living memory!"

A hearty laugh was enjoyed by all. Yes sir, you could say what you like about the old man, but he sure had a sense of humor.

"So," continued Foreman, "they gave me a carte blanche. Cost is not an issue. Speed is." Foreman glanced at his watch. Almost 3:15, only seventy-five minutes this side of tee-off. "I've decided to do this. We're going to have an international committee to implement this Board decision. Three men should be enough. If we have more, we'll never reach agreement without a lot of unnecessary talk."

Not a murmur of dissent thus far.

"I'll chair it. Sid, you'll be Vice Chairman. I'll call the meetings. Some of them will probably have to take place abroad. If we want to become bankers to the world, we must know the world."

The potential burden of having to spend springtime in Rome, summer in Norway, and fall in Hong Kong did not appear to press too hard on Sid's shoulders. He firmly concurred with the grass-roots philosophy of his chief.

"Fine. Now Luckman, you'll be the third. You're going to have the day-to-day responsibility for this project. I'm naming you head of the International Department and Senior Vice President. Your salary will be adjusted accordingly."

Donald Luckman was stunned. He was only forty-two years old. It was unheard of at the First National of California for anyone to be promoted to the giddy heights of Senior Vice President this side of fifty-five.

"Speak up, Luckman. You want the job or not?"

"But of course, sir. It just left me a bit speechless."

"Let's hope not for too long."

With that George Foreman rose abruptly. The two other men were only micro seconds behind. Before leaving, Foreman decided to make one more statement.

"Luckman, we're going to have to spend more time together. I want your views on how we should go about this. I'd also like you to hear mine. How about joining Mrs. Foreman and myself for dinner this evening? Seven-thirty at the Country Club in Atherton. Bring your wife."

Donald Luckman normally arrived home at 6:18. After one large martini at the station bar, he always caught the 5:16 Union Pacific which arrived in Palo Alto at 5:47. The run by Volkswagen from the parking lot to his $42,000 bungalow in Los Altos Hills averaged thirty-one minutes. By 6:20 he was into his second martini, since his wife invariably had a pitcher of the same waiting. Or half a pitcher, depending on how thirsty she had been before the dramatic arrival of her hubby.

But on this April afternoon in 1968, Don broke with tradition. First, no martini at the station. Then the 4:06. Finally the run by VW was cut to twenty-six minutes, a time achieved only once before in early 1966 when Debbie had gone to the doctor for a frog test. It had turned out to be gas, produced, it was conjectured, by bad olives in the martinis. So it was 5:03 when he crashed through the door of 2719 Sunrise Lane.

"Honey!" he yelled.

Silence.

"Debbie!"

Still nothing.

"Deborah!"

Then he heard it. The slosh of water from the bathroom. Deborah Luckman was involved in one of her more exciting pastimes: sitting in a bubble bath, dry martini glass beside her, the latest erotica in one hand, while the other was busy below the bubbles.

120

She had just hit a multiple orgasm, compliments of the Grove Press, when the satisfying peace was so rudely broken.

She was still a bit breathless, and peeved, when Don entered the steamy room. Until she realized what an opportunity this was for creative improvisation.

"Don. Take off your clothes and jump in. I feel horny."

"Debbie, don't be silly."

"What's so silly about that. I feel like it. And it's been . . ."

"Let's not get involved in one of those conversations again. Look, I've got some really great news."

"The bank burnt down."

"Stop it."

"You discovered your secretary is a lesbian."

Luckman knew this game, and he also knew he never won at it. He opted for an extended period of silence. So his wife simply ignored him as she stepped out of the bath and began to towel herself. For a thirty-eight-year-old woman, her body was in superb condition. The only possible way it might, perhaps, have been faulted was at bust level. She was over-endowed. She knew it, and was proud of it. Her final flourish with the pink towel was to carefully massage her right breast, then her left. Her nipples, also slightly larger than the American norm, as established by *Cosmopolitan,* responded immediately. Then she left, after dropping the towel at Don's feet.

"Damn," he exclaimed.

"Damn, damn, damn!"

Stepping over the towel, he picked up the half

empty martini glass from the side of the bathtub, and downed its contents in one go.

"Honey?" She was calling from the bedroom, where she lay sprawled across the bed on her stomach, head propped on both hands.

"Come on in here, Don." He obeyed.

Debbie's game plan had two parts. Phase I was to be oral-genital. In the Grove Press chapter she had just completed, despite over-success in the first stage, a sizable, in fact astonishing, erection had returned almost immediately to the visiting Congolese exchange student; it had subsequently been employed for fucking. Debbie was realistic enough not to plan on such. But at least a Phase I seemed feasible. It required essentially no active cooperation—just free access to a member of the opposite sex, one of which was less than a yard away along her current line of vision. So she reached. But before the reach became a grope, Don managed to back up.

After seventeen years of marriage, Don still did not go for that stuff. He was strictly a Saturday night, in the dark, missionary position fellow. Only about once a year, peculiarly enough around Christmas time, did he ever allow himself to be led into deviate activities. This was April.

"Debbie," he said firmly, "will you finally cut that stuff out and listen to me?"

There was no choice. She listened.

"I've been named Senior Vice President."

Disappointingly, the walls of the Eichler bungalow, though mere wood, did not tremble. Debbie, however, was moved.

"Don," she screamed, "we've made it!" She scrambled off the bed and caught Don, who stood his ground somewhat uncertainly, in a huge hug.

"Oh, Don, I'm so proud of you."

"I think you really mean that."

"I do," followed by another hug, this time slightly more intimate.

"There's more. A lot more. Want to hear it?"

She let him go.

"Guess who's asked us to dinner this evening? At the Atherton Country Club."

"Don!"

"Yes. Mr. and Mrs. George Foreman have requested the presence of Mr. and Mrs. Donald Luckman at 7:30. Dress will be informal."

For the briefest of moments she did not know what to say. Then she squinted.

"What's all this really about, Don?" Her face said there must be something somewhere. It just hadn't surfaced yet.

"Look, honey, don't start with those funny looks. Just shut up and listen for a minute."

The squint went.

"I've been put in charge of the international operations of the bank. That means Europe. Perhaps Asia. For months on end. Both of us."

"When?"

"Soon. We'll know exactly after this evening. This is Foreman's personal baby, and I'm going to be Foreman's personal boy."

"Don," said Deborah in a quiet, tense, voice, "this is not just another of your big dreams, is it? If you're kidding me, I swear, I'll kill you." The latter part of the sentence was not spoken nicely. Her husband did not even notice it. Seventeen years of marriage in California does that.

"Debbie, honey, I've never been more serious in my life. This is it. So start dressing. We are going to have the biggest evening in our lives!"

To prove it, he took her to bed. But there were no deviations.

Dining at the Atherton Country Club was not everyone's idea of a big night out. The average age of the members was sixty-five; their concept of exotic eating was to order a sirloin steak rare, instead of well done. The only thing anyone ever did to excess was drink: three large cocktails before dinner were accepted as standard. Often, in fact usually, the main subject of conversation during these sessions of alcoholic intake was the depravity of today's marijuana-addicted youth.

George Foreman drank nothing but Scotch—Chivas Regal, with two ice cubes and one inch of water. His wife, Marjory, drank gin. Straight. Gordon's. So when the Luckmans joined them in the lounge that evening, Donald ordered Scotch, Chivas Regal, with two ice cubes and one inch of water, while Deborah had Gordon's gin, straight. Mrs. Foreman commented on how remarkable it was that their tastes in drink were so similar. Then Mrs. Foreman said that Debbie should call her Marjory. Mr. Foreman said that Donald should call him George. Because they were going to be seeing a lot of each other in the future, and their difference in age was, after all, not that great. Was it? Of course not. When Marjory and Debbie and Donald and George finally moved on to dinner, Debbie had been fully briefed on the physical condition of Marjory: heart good, kidneys weak, hysterectomy successful. Debbie confided that she had discovered a distinct lump on her left breast last year, but it had turned out to be just fatty tissue, thank God. Thereafter they proceeded to eat.

"Now Donald," said Foreman, after coffee had arrived, "I think you and Debbie are going to be just perfect for this assignment. And Mama agrees. Don't you Mama?"

Mama did.

George Foreman then suggested that he and Donald should retire to the smoking room for coffee while the ladies continued their small talk in the lounge. George wanted to hear Donald's views on the project.

Actually all that Luckman ever got in during the following half hour was about six questions. Short questions. Because George had already thought things over, and he had come up with a tactical solution to their problem: Donald was to scout out an existing bank in Europe. When he found the right one, they'd buy it. What kind of a bank? One that was growing. One that was profitable. How big? Oh, say, with assets of around a hundred million dollars equivalent. That should cost about ten million, figuring a buck for every ten bucks in deposits more or less, which was what George had always figured when buying banks in the States, and he'd bought lots in his time. Until those left-wing radicals in the Justice Department had blown the antitrust whistle. Which made it all the more necessary for First National to expand abroad, outside the jurisdiction of the know-it-alls in Washington. Where in Europe? Maybe London. That's where everybody else went first. Perhaps Amsterdam. Or Zurich. It didn't matter that much.

A lot of people might think that's a hell of a way to approach spending ten million dollars, but then a lot of people don't run billion dollar banks. Like the man said, it's all relative.

The fact was that for George Foreman this was a rather small project. So having finished his monologue he ordered two small cognacs: Remy Martin, with water on the side.

The swirling and swallowing of the cognac was done in silence. Then Foreman had the last word, as he was used to having.

"Luckman, I want you to start moving the beginning of next week. Just get yourself a long airplane ticket. Two of them, come to think of it. You'll need your wife on this trip. She's got a lot of spunk."

Then Foreman leaned forward and in a soft voice said: "And remember, Luckman, not a word of this to anyone. If it leaks that we're in the market for a bank in Europe, everybody over there will be out to hold us up on price. This is secret and it must stay that way until we're ready to make a concrete move."

Fifteen minutes later the Luckmans' big night was over. Less than an hour later, both were sound asleep in Los Altos Hills, with the help of ten milligrams of

Valium each. Normally they only took five milligrams. But now Donald was a Senior Vice President.

When George Foreman got home—he lived only five minutes away—he neither took a Valium nor went to bed. After saying goodnight to his wife, he turned on the TV, and settled into his favorite chair in the den. Channel 4 flickered on. For years, Foreman had rarely managed more than five hours sleep a night. This meant that there was almost always a gap between the Country Club and bed. Thus Johnny Carson. He filled out time, and Foreman no longer liked to think about time. He was entering that period of the seventy-year itch . . . the craving for one last piece of really big action.

Johnny had already finished his standup, and was just welcoming Zsa Zsa Gabor to his show, for probably the 89th time. Foreman couldn't stand her. So he switched off.

The phone rang. Automatically, Foreman glanced at his watch. Two minutes short of midnight. Must be either a wrong number or a kook.

"Hello," he said cautiously.

"George Foreman?" The voice was hardly that of a kook.

"Yes," again carefully.

"Frank Cook. I hear you'd like to get in the banking business in Europe."

It had to be a hoax. Nobody ever talked to Frank Cook.

"Where are you calling from?"

"London."

"It must be the middle of the night there."

"It is."

"Mr. Cook, I hope you don't mind my being somewhat skeptical. We've never done business together. So I can hardly know whether you're authentic or not."

"I agree. You'll have to take my word for it."

"How could you possibly know we're interested in acquiring a bank in Europe?"

"Because it was the last item on the agenda of your Board meeting today. Should I recite the other items? Such as the five million dollar write off you're going to have to make on that bad loan to Nuclear Development Corporation? Or . . ."

"No."

"Fine. Shall I proceed with the real purpose of this call?"

"Please do."

"There's a bank in Lugano, Switzerland, called the International Bank of Sicily and America. It's what you're looking for. It can be gotten fairly cheap. And quickly. We'll help you get it. Provided you're prepared to move now."

"Why?"

"That later."

You don't argue with Frank Cook.

"We don't do things this way, Mr. Cook."

"Fine. Then just forget this call."

"Wait a minute!" Too hurriedly, but Foreman was more than just slightly off balance.

"I'm waiting."

"We'd like to do a bit of our own checking first."

"I understand that. Just as long as it's done right now."

"I've got a man leaving for Europe on Monday."

"What's his name?"

"Luckman. Donald Luckman."

"All right. I'll have one of my men contact him later next week."

"Where?"

"We'll keep in touch and decide that. Agreed?"

"Yes."

"Fine. Good night, Mr. Foreman. I'm looking forward to doing business with you."

Click.

Frank Cook!

George Foreman did something he hadn't done in ten years. He decided to have a drink at midnight—alone. This generation has seen only a handful of men in the class of Frank Cook: Gulbenkian, Ludwig, Hughes, Hunt, Getty, Englehardt. A race unto themselves. True billionaires. They had achieved heights that the likes of Onassis or his wife could only wishfully aspire to. Heights which a George Foreman could hardly dare dream of. Because theirs was the world of super-risk, the exact opposite of the world in which bankers are supposed to exist. But it was a world which held attraction for any mortal man. And George Foreman, in spite of what was said behind his back at the bank, was very mortal indeed. So he proceeded to do a second thing, which he hadn't done in at least twenty years. He picked up the phone after midnight. It rang ten minutes on the other end before somebody picked it up.

"Luckman?"

"Yes."

"George Foreman. I want you in my office at eight tomorrow morning. Sharp. Goodnight."

He almost slammed the phone down.

It felt good. The chase was on. And, finally, he was riding with the elite of this planet. Not bad for a sixty-eight year old. But one thought did linger.

Why did Frank Cook need him?

What was Frank Cook up to this time?

8

What was Frank Cook up to? Rigging the world's silver market, that's what.

The thought had occurred to him many times. But until July 14, 1967, it had not appeared feasible, for a quite simple reason. The United States government, due to its vast hoard of silver, controlled—completely controlled—that market. No one, not even Frank Cook, was megalomaniac enough to take on a situation like that.

But on July 14, 1967, Uncle Sam had given up. The reason? Up until that point the American government had been both willing and able to stabilize the price of silver at exactly $1.293 an ounce, by simply selling to all comers at that price. But gradually a shortage of silver developed. The photographic industry used vast, and ever increasing, amounts; the electronics industry, the nuclear industry, plus the old types of users in the silverware and jewelry industries —all were consuming the metal like crazy, at a rate far exceeding new mine output. Then on top of that, suddenly everybody started to hoard the stuff: in the form of Kennedy half dollars, Swiss five franc pieces, even plain silver bars. Because all over the world people began to feel that the value of their paper money was being eaten up by rising rates of inflation. There were only a few havens; but the surest of these were precious metals, especially silver. The U.S. government stopped the coinage of silver as a first step to conserve the metal. Dozens of other governments followed that example. Then they recalled silver coins, to melt them down, and replenish government inventories. But still the drain had continued. By law, the United States, through its agency the General Services Administration, had to maintain a minimum strategic reserve of silver, in case of war. So before that minimum was approached, the drain had to be halted. And the best way to halt it, was to let the price rise, rise to a point where the demand would level off to a reasonable level, to a level where it could be matched by new output from silver mines once more.

So the government turned silver loose.

And up the price went. Way up. By January, 1968 —just six months later—it stood at $2.40 an ounce. Double. There was no reason why it could not go to $5.00 an ounce, provided world demand held up, and the supply was held down. World demand no one individual, or group, can manipulate. But supply? That's something else. Harry Oppenheimer has proven that where diamonds are concerned. But no one had ever tried it on silver. Until Frank Cook.

Why Frank Cook? Because next to the United States government, he—or rather his companies—owned the largest silver inventory on earth. His group served as the middlemen in the silver business. When Kodak needed silver, it came to Frank Cook. So did General Nuclear. Also Metalgesellschaft in Germany, and Gaevert in Belgium, and the jewelry makers of Florence, and flatware producers in England. Of course, they did not come to Frank Cook directly. They went to International Precious Metals Inc. in New York, or Precious Metals Ltd. of London, or International Edelmetalle of Frankfurt, or Metaux Precieux Internationale of Paris. By feeding the customers sparingly, by making sure that no excess metal was ever allowed to float around in the international markets, Frank Cook was in a perfect position to make sure the price of silver went up. And up. And up. Which would mean that the value of Frank Cook's silver inventories would do the same. And thus his profits. But even Frank Cook's cash resources and credit lines were limited. He—that is, his computers—had first calculated whether they would suffice to corner the new silver market. The answer had been yes, but barely yes, provided no new source of silver emerged.

But that was exactly what happened in January of 1968. From nowhere. First, just a few hundred thousand ounces. Then a half million. Then a million. The speculators, who were unwittingly supporting Frank Cook's game plan in a beautiful fashion, suddenly got worried. There seemed to be more silver around than everyone had thought. The prices on the metal exchanges in London and New York hesitated, faltered, and then plunged. By February 23, the price was back to $2.00 an ounce. Frank Cook did not like that one bit.

So he—his people—started looking for the leak. In Hong Kong, in Panama, in Zurich, in Singapore. Where the hell was it coming from? In desperation, Frank Cook assigned his right hand man to the job, Nick Topping. He found it. In Dubai. And from there, the search quickly led to a man by the name of Firdausi. An Iranian. But it soon became obvious that the man did not have the financial resources to be able to swing a deal of this size. Again Topping went to work. And came up with the next answer: a bank in Lugano called the International Bank of Sicily and America. Firdausi had visited it three times during the past six months. An investigation of that bank had indicated, beyond any doubt, that there was something very fishy about the people involved there. Correctly employed, such information would mean that that bank could be had. Buy the bank, and you could probably buy Firdausi—and stop that silver. Provided, of course, they were partners in the silver thing. That would, in any case, have to be verified.

But Frank Cook could not risk buying that bank, or any bank. The last impression he wanted to create in the world's banking community was that he intended to join them—and become a competitor instead of a customer. If he did, every bank in Europe —maybe also in the States—would slash his credit lines to nothing. That was no solution. But he could, perhaps, set up the same play for somebody else— logically, another bank. And then play it by ear from there. But what bank?

Nothing developed for weeks. Then it was there, starting like many other business deals, with just a routine bit of intelligence. In this case it was a telex from the president of an electronics company on the West Coast, meant as a favor. He was on the Board of the First National Bank of California, and they had just decided to make a move into Europe. He thought Frank Cook might want to know—maybe they could start doing business together in Europe in the future. That was all—just a well-meant gesture.

The man in California almost fainted when Frank Cook called up to personally thank him—and to find out a few more things about the First National Bank of California. Then he moved immediately into action. Well, almost immediately. Before Frank Cook made any significant move he spent hours mulling it over— at home, alone, and at night. After the call had been completed, he sat there in the almost complete darkness of his library, pondering the next step.

"I'll keep Topping on this," he decided, "and get him to lend a helping hand to that fellow Foreman is sending over. Luckman." Frank Cook prided himself on his perfect memory where names were concerned.

"It's going to be like putting Muhammad Ali into the ring with Lillian Gish."

He smiled.

134

9

Donald Luckman would not have liked that Lillian Gish thing. Debbie might have. In any case, both were completely unaware of those dark thoughts of that dark man in the dark room. All Donald was trying to do was a simple scouting job: of a bank that his boss might want to buy. Foreman had told him to start easy. No immediate direct approaches. The best place to start would be Zurich, not Lugano. In Zurich they knew everything that was going on in banking circles in all of Switzerland. And in Zurich they knew how to keep their mouths shut. So that's where the Luckmans had gone.

Scouting out a bank in some countries is relatively easy. In Switzerland it is not. Because Swiss banks are quite complicated animals. They don't just take in savings, issue check books, and lend money. No, they also act as stockbrokers, they trade in Swiss francs, American dollars, Brazilian cruzeros, Iranian rials—sometimes through official channels, sometimes in grey or completely black markets. Their customers range from Swiss housewives to Cuban exiles to Americans trying to dodge unjust taxes at home. They own insurance companies, watch manufacturers, armament producers, shipping lines, and in one case, a big piece of a silver mine in Iran.

Normally when you acquire any corporation, banking or otherwise, the first step is to go through its

135

financial statement with a fine-tooth comb. This usually takes a team of auditors weeks, even months, due to the mass of information to be digested and analyzed. Not in Switzerland. About one hour by one man suffices. Corporate financial statements there provide about as much useful information to the general public as does the annual report of the CIA. Those issued by Swiss banks, substantially less.

Donald Luckman had discovered the futility of this approach almost immediately. He had acquired the barest skeleton of a balance sheet of the International Bank of Sicily and America, but it told him next to nothing. So he had moved on to step two: checking the bank out with the competition. In the States this is standard practice, and everyone is usually most happy to cooperate: to hint at any suspected bones in a competitor's back yard; to reveal how hard its president drinks; to discuss who the bank's major customers are; to put a definite limit on how much one would prudently lend that bank; and even to give a quite definite estimate on what the bank was worth, give or take a million or two.

But again—not in Switzerland, and especially not in Zurich, the heart of gnomeland, where even a request for the time of day is regarded with suspicion. This Luckman was also finding out the hard way. It was not that the right people weren't receiving him. With letters of introduction from George Foreman, Chairman of the Board of America's ninth largest bank, how could they refuse? But that didn't mean that they had to say anything useful. Luckman's last trump card was Walter Hofer, Chairman of the General Bank of Switzerland. But it turned out that Hofer was out of town—in Paris. So it was one of his top executives, Herr Dr. Kellermann, who had been more than happy to see him. Yes, Kellermann explained, they had received a letter of introduction from Mr. Foreman. In fact, it was only last year that he had had the pleasure of visiting Mr. Foreman in San Francisco. Such a lovely city. Their banks maintained correspondent accounts with each other, had for many years. The balances were, however, not big. They could be bigger, especially those in Zurich. Was that what Mr. Luckman wanted to talk about? No, not exactly. Aha. Well, perhaps over lunch one could hear more about what Mr. Luckman wanted. And over lunch it went like this:

"Now Mr. Kellermann," began Luckman, after the last piece of Wienerschnitzel had disappeared, "the real purpose of my visit is to inquire about another bank here in Switzerland."

"Oh?"

"Yes. It's in Lugano. The International Bank of Sicily and America."

"Ah, yes."

"Well, sir, I wondered what opinion your institution has of that bank."

"Yes, we know it."

"You do know it?"

"Yes, we do."

"Well, could you perhaps give me some idea of their net worth?"

"Net worth?"

"You know, the value of their capital and reserves,

after deduction of possible write offs for bad loans and the like."

"No, I'm afraid that's not possible."

"Not possible?"

"Yes."

"I see. Well, could you perhaps give me a feel for their credit standing? Like, what's the limit you people have put on any inter-bank loans to them."

"Ah, that we never discuss."

"I see. But you do do business with them."

"I would have to inquire further. That is not my department."

"I see. Would you say that their reputation is good, generally speaking?"

"I have heard nothing negative. Nor anything positive, as far as that goes. But of course . . ."

"That is not your department."

"Exactly."

"I notice from their latest statement, which is rather meager, that a rather substantial amount is listed on the asset side under 'Participations.' "

Luckman showed him the balance sheet. Kellermann put on his glasses and studied it carefully.

"Yes, I see that."

"Is that usual?"

"Is what usual?"

"To have such a large sum invested in that fashion."

"You mean under 'Participations'?"

"Yes."

"It is neither usual nor unusual. That item could include many things."

"Such as?"

"Well, it could merely be that the bank owns some shares of A.T.&T. Then again, it could mean that they own a factory of some type. That might be a bit more risky, I would think."

"Indeed. Now in this case . . ."

"I have no idea of what might be involved."

"There's one other item that struck me."

"Yes?"

"The footnote. The only footnote. It breaks down loans into foreign and domestic. It seems to me that an unusually large proportion of that bank's funds have gone outside of Switzerland."

Kellermann looked again.

"Yes. One could say that. But then again . . ."

Luckman put his piece of paper back into his briefcase.

"Just one more question, Herr Kellermann. Could you give me some idea of the ownership of that bank?"

"Ah, in Switzerland that is a most difficult question to answer. You see, the shares of most banks, in fact of most corporations of any type, are in bearer form. There is not, cannot be, any type of registration of ownership. Because the owner is that person, or company, which happens to be in possession of those shares at any particular moment in time. They may change hands often. Who knows?"

"But what about shareholders' meetings. The owners must come forward then?"

"A very good question. But you see, in Switzerland very few people ever attend shareholders' meetings. And almost all of them are lawyers; and behind the lawyers?"

"Who knows?"

"Precisely."

Luckman reached down and closed his briefcase.

"Mr. Kellermann," he said, "I guess that's about it. You have been most helpful."

"It was a great pleasure to have been of assistance to you, Mr. Luckman. I do hope you extend my compliments to Mr. Foreman upon your return."

Debbie was waiting for him back at the hotel. After one look at his face she said: "Struck out again, huh?"

"Yes."

"Now what?"

"I don't know."

"Well, I'm not just going to sit around this dump alone, while you spend your days getting fat on Swiss lunches."

"God," thought Luckman, "this was to be the dream of her life. Europe! Switzerland! And after three days she's already at it again."

"Honey," he said, "I'd hardly call this a dump. It's costing sixty dollars a day."

"Sure. And the shower doesn't work. There's no air conditioning. The bartender throws daggers at me every time I walk in alone. Thinks I'm a hooker, probably. Say, maybe he's got something there. Might keep my mind occupied."

Don just looked at her. Air conditioning in April in Switzerland?

"Now, seriously, Don, tell me something."

"What?"

"I thought this bank you want to buy is in Lugano."

"It is."

"Then what in God's name are we doing in Zurich?"

"Look, Debbie, one has to approach such matters subtly. I prefer asking questions here, rather than in Lugano. This is a big banking center. They're used to Americans. Lugano is a small town; they'd be bound to hear about me, and start asking questions of their own."

"So what?"

"Don't act so damn stupid."

"I think you're the one that's being stupid. You can hardly buy a bank without the bank knowing about it sooner or later. It's like trying to screw a girl over the telephone."

"I don't think your analogy is either funny or apt."

"You wouldn't."

"All right. What do you suggest?"

"That we pack right now and go to Lugano."

"Debbie, we're staying here, and that's final."

He started taking off his jacket.

"What are you doing?"

"I'm going to take a nap. Alone."

"What am I supposed to do?"

"Read a book. Go shopping. I really don't care."

So she went down to the lobby, bought a *Time* magazine, a *Herald Tribune, Playboy,* and a German illustrated called the *Stern.* By the time she got back up to the room, Donald was snoring. In fact he was still snoring three hours later when the phone rang. It woke him up, but Debbie got to the phone first.

"It's for you," she said, "San Francisco."

Donald managed a few "Yes sir's." Then he wrote a number down on the pad beside the phone, added a few more "yes sir's" and hung up.

"Who was that?" asked Debbie. "Your mother?"

"Debbie, sometimes . . ."

"All right. Who?"

"Mr. Foreman."

"Oh?"

"Yes."

"And?"

"We're leaving. Tomorrow."

"No. He can't do that to us! We've barely gotten here. What does he expect you to do. Perform miracles?"

"Shut up, Debbie. We're leaving, but not for home. For Lugano."

To his credit, he actually grinned when he said it. And to Debbie's credit, she only said, "I told you so" half a dozen times before the evening was over.

They took the Trans-European Express which left Zurich at 7:30 and arrived in Lugano at 11:58. They went directly to the Hotel Villa Castagnola where Donald had booked a suite. He immediately called the number given to him by Foreman the prior day. A meeting was fixed for 5 P.M. in Luckman's suite. Debbie disappeared into the bedroom at five to five, leaving the door just slightly open.

The man who stepped through the door at five on the dot was tall, darkly tanned, and dressed in sports clothes. The hand he extended to Luckman was big, and leathery.

"I'm Nick Topping. Mind if I take off my jacket?"

"No. Go right ahead. I'll get a hanger from . . ."

"Don't bother. I'll just plunk it."

"Would you like something to drink?"

"No. Not right now. Maybe later. But I will sit down."

Luckman kept his jacket on. All bankers do.

"You know why I'm here?"

"No, not exactly. I received a call from our head office yesterday asking me to come down here to talk to you. That was all."

"Good. Well, let's start by me telling you who I am. I'm in charge of public relations for International Minerals Consultants of Panama."

"I see."

"Fine. Now we're both interested in the same object here in Lugano."

"We are?"

"Yes. The Bank of Sicily and America."

"That I was not told."

"I know. That's why I'm telling you now."

"Why are you interested?"

"Because of something that bank owns. Or may own. Or may own part of. It's something you wouldn't want to keep, if you buy that bank."

"What is it?"

"We'll come to that later."

"Is it listed in that bank's statement under 'Participations'?"

"Sonny, you're brighter than you look."

"Do all those foreign loans tie in with the same thing?"

"They probably do."

"That could add up to $25 million—a quarter of the bank's assets."

"Right again. But like I said, it's something you wouldn't like to keep. Too risky."

"What about the rest of the bank?"

"In good shape. You'll be happy with it."

"Provided it's for sale."

"It will be. We'll take care of that end of it for you. Provided a few things check out first. We'll start checking tomorrow."

"How?"

"By taking a little trip together."

"Where to?"

"Kuwait."

"Kuwait?"

"Right. I'll make all the arrangements. You'll just need to have your passport and suitcase ready to go."

"Look, I'm not sure what kind of game you're playing, but you can be very sure that I'm not going along with it. I came over here to look at a bank situation in Lugano. I have no intention whatsoever of going with you to Kuwait or any other place."

"You will. In fact," continued Topping, "I think you'd better get on the phone to your boss in San Francisco right now." He glanced at his watch. "You might just catch him before he goes beddy-bye."

He got up.

"I'll call you tonight with the flight time."

Luckman just watched him in amazement, as Topping went blithely on: "There is one thing you could do. After you've checked back with your home office, of course."

"That is?"

"Make an appointment with the General Manager of the Bank of London and the Near East in Kuwait —for tomorrow afternoon. Don't mention me under any circumstances. If they get curious, just make it sound like a courtesy call. I understand you bankers make the rounds regularly."

"Anything else?" Luckman was getting a bit peeved.

"No, that should do it." Nick Topping picked up his jacket and once again extended his huge hand.

"See you tomorrow. Maybe we can have that drink then."

And he left.

Two seconds after the door had closed, Debbie came flying out of the bedroom.

"Donald! What was all that about?"

"You were listening, I suppose."

"Could hardly help not listening. That man's voice would carry across the lake. Is he as big as he sounds?"

"Bigger."

"This whole thing is starting to sound a bit screwy to me."

"You're not the only one."

"Are you sure everything's on the level?"

"Now look, Debbie. Do you think Mr. Foreman would ever get involved in anything that was not on the level?"

"No. I guess not. Well, all right. Off we go to Kuwait."

"Off *I* go to Kuwait. Provided head office says so. You stay here."

"Oh no you don't, Donald. You promised that we were going to do all these things together. I'm not going to sit around this place all alone, just like I had to in Zurich."

"I'm afraid you are, Debbie. Look, we can fix something up. Maybe a tour of northern Italy. Or the Alps. The bank will pay under these circumstances. So . . ."

"Look, buster. Nobody's going to package tour me. If I go, I go the way I want to. And I'll make the arrangements."

"All right Debbie," with a silent "Jeezus" to go with it.

The call to San Francisco went through quickly. George Foreman came on the line almost immediately. And his instructions were curt and exact. Luckman should work together with Topping in all matters, no questions asked at this stage. If Topping wanted him to go to the Persian Gulf, he should go. Report back when he got back.

"Yes sir, Mr. Foreman." The George and Donald bit was obviously not on over telephones.

Debbie didn't even turn around to ask after he had hung up. In fact, her lack of interest could hardly have been more pronounced when he announced later in the day that he would be leaving very early the next morning for Kuwait. What was she going to do during his absence? Not to worry. She'd think of something. Just leave some traveler's checks—endorsed!

The following day when he crept out of bed shortly

after dawn, he wondered whether he should wake her or not. He decided not. He left a note, saying he would call her—provided he could get through—from somewhere letting her know when he would be arriving back. He could not help but whisper a tender goodbye when he took a last peek into the bedroom before leaving. Just as he stepped into the corridor, there seemed to be a faint response, like:

"Fuck off, baby."

But maybe it was just his imagination.

10

Kuwait is certainly the least interesting Arab city on earth. Because it has been built by the glass-curtain-on-steel-frame school of architects provided courtesy of the cultural department of Standard Oil of New Jersey. There are almost as many air-conditioning units per square mile as on Manhattan; certainly as many Cadillac limousines, and definitely as much money. Which accounts for the fact that, like in Manhattan, there are also many banks.

When Donald Luckman walked into the Bank of London and the Near East's branch there, he was nervous. Because his was a mission of intrigue, one that required subtlety, cunning and coolness. Or so Nick Topping had said during the briefing session at the hotel. Actually, all he had to do was inveigle the local manager into spilling the beans about the bank's relationship with a man called Agha Firdausi.

Who was Agha Firdausi? An Iranian. What did he have to do with the bank in Lugano? All in due time, was the cryptic response of Nick Topping. Just get in there and feel your way around.

The local manager turned out to be walrus-moustached, red in the face, and loud-voiced. More or less par for the course for Englishmen east of Suez. When referring to Americans, he consistently used the term "you chaps," and was just as consistent in referring to the local residents of the Gulf as "wogs." He left the distinct impression that he considered both to have advanced to rather similar levels in the process of evolution. He was brimming with advice for young American bankers visiting Kuwait. It was summed up in the full-voiced statement:

"Too many of you chaps here already, you know."

At this point, Luckman cut in to inform him that the First National Bank of California had no intention of setting themselves up in Kuwait. This met with condescending approval. But, Luckman went on, he would appreciate getting a reading on a party that had recently approached them for a sizeable credit. Chap called Firdausi. Luckman wasn't sure whether Iranians fell into the wog or chap category, so he gambled and won.

"Fine chap, Firdausi. Good man. Lives just up the line in Iran. No problem there. Good for five million on his own. In dollars, not sterling. Heard that he's got a charming sister. A real looker. Never met her though. He's also got Swiss money behind him. Lots of it.

Keeps coming in. Big in silver, Firdausi. Biggest on the Gulf, they tell me. Don't quite know where he gets the stuff. None of my business, of course."

"Perhaps you might give me the name of that Swiss bank. We'd probably like to check with them too."

"Small bank. In Lugano. Never heard of it before. Something to do with Sicilians, I think. Can't be too many of those. But if you want me to get the file . . ."

"No, no. As you say, there can hardly be many of those in Lugano." Luckman got up.

"I would appreciate your keeping my inquiry confidential," he said as he shook the Englishman's hand.

"But of course. No trouble there, dear fellow. We British bankers know how to keep our mouths shut."

Back in the hotel—the Kuwait Hilton—Nick Topping was waiting for him.

"Well?"

"So it's silver," triumphantly.

"Maybe, maybe not. Just give me the facts. Then we can move on to the speculative bit."

So Luckman related what had transpired at the bank. Topping did not interrupt once.

But when Luckman was done, Topping smiled.

"Good boy. This gives us the definite confirmation of a tie-in between Firdausi and that bank."

"But where does the silver fit in?"

"Since months the word's been out on the Gulf that Firdausi has become Mr. Big in silver, all of a sudden. It is also said that it's coming out of Iran, from a new mine that's been developed recently."

"But surely that's very easy to confirm, without all this roundabout rigamarole."

"Like how?"

"Checking out Firdausi's properties in Iran. I assume that's where this mine must be situated."

"We tried. The place is guarded like the Shah's palace. One of our people got killed."

"What about the equipment? You can hardly start up a major mining venture without bringing in tons of it. All you'd have to do is check it out with the customs people in Iran."

"Sonny, don't be naïve. Nobody pays customs duties in this part of the world."

"You mean you believe that somebody could smuggle in all that stuff without anybody knowing?"

"I don't just believe. I know."

"O.K. I'll take your word for it. I also can hardly help but deduce that you're after that silver mine. Fine. So why don't you just approach this Firdausi and try to acquire it?"

"Because maybe he doesn't own it all. Maybe he doesn't even control it. Maybe that bank in Lugano does. Right? Remember that big item termed 'Participations'?"

"Right," said Luckman. "Right."

"Look," said Topping, "if I were you I'd try not to get too far ahead of this thing. You're slightly out of your depth. For the moment, why don't you just follow the leader and not ask too many more questions O.K.? I'm the leader, if you need reminding."

"Agreed. What next."

"Dubai."

"Why?"

"The silver, goddammit."

"I thought this mine was supposed to be in Iran?"

"It is."

"Then why Dubai?"

"Because that's where the silver from the mine in Iran will end up. At least temporarily."

"I see. And we're going to arrange to hi-jack it. Then you won't need the mine."

Luckman was getting a bit frisky. Twelve hours away from Debbie was working wonders.

"Donald," said Topping, "they must really miss you around the bank these days. No, we're not going to hi-jack anything. At least not on this trip. We are going to merely try to determine if it's there. The silver."

"I thought you now knew?"

"If I *knew,* then we wouldn't still be here sweating our ass off in this godforsaken desert, would we? We've *heard* something, that's all. First, the rumors around the Gulf. Now something a bit more reliable, from your banker friend here in Kuwait. But we still don't *know*. If we luck out in Dubai, then we will know."

"O.K.," replied Luckman, "lead on. When do we leave?"

"Tomorrow. We're expected at the Dubai airport at eleven."

And so they were. By a dark little man whose appearance did not betray any sign of either prosperity or honesty. Apparently the only way he communicated with his fellow man was through hissed whispers. And in this case, the hissing was exclusively for the ears of Nick Topping: his left ear, to be more precise. Before they reached the hotel, the car stopped and the grubby Arab slunk out and disappeared into the equally grubby crowd in what appeared to be the main square of Dubai.

"So what was that all about," asked Luckman. "You trying to buy a used camel or something?"

"Donald, you have just had the pleasure of associating with one of the most unsavory characters on the entire Gulf. He and his pals consider simple theft as demeaning."

"I also detected that he must consider taking baths equally so."

"He does leave a rather pungent odor behind, doesn't he? No matter. He may solve all of our problems for us. We shall see. Hopefully this evening."

"See what?"

"Let me put it this way. Our smelly friend has promised to produce the body."

"Body!"

"Only figuratively speaking. Like in *corpus delicti*."

"Whose body?"

"Wait and see."

After they had checked into their hotel, and had lunch, Nick Topping announced that he was going to take a nap. Donald Luckman thought he'd have a look around Dubai, but after ten minutes in the blistering heat, gave that up. Then, suddenly, he remembered Debbie. It took almost two hours to get through to Lugano. Once she was on the other end, Luckman gave her a play-by-play account of the last twenty-four hours, expecting her to share his excitement. But all he got in response was an occasional "Uh huh." And at the end. "Well, have fun with your little Arab friends." Then she hung up, leaving Luckman with an empty feeling in the pit of his stomach. Why, he thought, must she always put a damper on everything? A cool shower helped. But when he lay down on the bed, sleep did not come, although, God knows, he was fatigued. He was still lying on the bed, mind shifting from Debbie, to Dubai, and back to Debbie when the phone rang. It was Topping. He would meet him in the lobby at nine.

It was dark when the two men left the De Luxe Ambassador Hotel by foot. They were immediately swallowed up in the masses of people moving to and from the city's teeming bazaars. People of many nations: mostly Arabs, of course, but also Chinese, Indians, Iranians, black Africans. White faces were rare. Nick Topping barely took notice of the exotic surroundings as he pushed his way through the narrow streets. Suddenly they emerged from the stifling heat and odors of the old city into the port area. The stench was perhaps even more penetrating, but at least there was a breeze coming off the Persian Gulf. The port was jammed. Huge sea-going modern yachts, hundreds of djerbas, oil tankers—all seemed to be competing for parking places in the water.

On land donkeys mingled with seamen, crates of cackling chicken competed with wailing beggars. Suddenly a man reached from the crowd to touch Nick Topping's shoulder. He reacted like a wounded tiger, spinning and going into a crouch. Then, just as suddenly, he relaxed, as he recognized the man beyond the hand.

"Don't ever do that again or I'll cut it off."

The dark little Arab who had met them at the airport did not react. He just looked Topping boldly in the face, and said:

"Come with me. We will have to wait."

After the three men entered the dingy Indian café, the Arab went immediately to a table in the rear.

"In one hour," he said to Topping. "We shall have tea. Yes?"

Green tea in battered cups it was. The Arab put four heaping spoons of sugar in his. The Americans drank theirs straight. The Arab apparently felt no need for conversation, nor did Nick Topping. But Luckman did.

"What's all this about, Nick?"

"You'll see."

And that was that. It was not exactly an ideal place to spend an hour. The restaurant reeked of curry, and was infested with flies. One overhead circular fan revolved slowly in a totally futile attempt to move the heavy air. Luckman must have consulted his watch ten times before, finally, another man entered the deserted café. He just nodded to his compatriot at their table, who said: "It's here." The signal to go.

As they left, the darkness outside was total. The crowds had thinned, but there were still a lot of people milling about. The smell of fish now filled the air, replacing the curry. The temperature had sunk considerably. Luckman had trouble keeping up with the other three men, as they hurried along the waterfront, past boats of every size and description.

"This one," said their Arab, as they halted before the smallest and dirtiest of the djerbas. Luckman followed the others, clambering aboard with difficulty, since there was practically no light to guide him.

Within minutes a small engine was started, and they moved slowly out into the harbor. But not very far. No more than 200 yards from the waterfront, still busy with the loading and unloading of small vessels, the engine was cut. The boat hovered there in complete darkness. The dim lights from the main pier did not penetrate that far. Luckman sat alone on a crude bench alongside the starboard railing. The other three men had somehow disappeared. Then two of them, their Arab and Nick Topping, reappeared.

"That one," said the Arab, as his arm pointed to a rather large fishing vessel which had apparently just docked.

Then both men raised large binoculars to their eyes. Night glasses. The djerba was obviously well equipped.

"There he comes!" said the Arab.

Luckman strained his eyes toward the pier, but saw nothing or no one that seemed out of place.

"The man in white?" asked Topping, after he had swung the glasses about ten degrees to the right.

"Yes."

"Is he alone?"

"Yes."

The two men stood almost motionless for at least fifteen minutes, watching the pier.

"I think that first truck is fully loaded and ready to

go," said Topping finally. "You'd better signal your man."

The Arab immediately lowered the binoculars from his eyes, and moved toward the stern of the djerba. From a box he extracted a new instrument—a signalling lamp. He used it for no more than ten seconds. Luckman observed all this with nothing less than astonishment. Maybe everything was on the up and up, but it sure as hell didn't look that way.

After stowing the signalling lamp, the Arab returned to Nick Topping's side, and reassumed his vigil with the night glasses.

"There goes the truck," said Topping, after another ten minutes. "Let's hope your man has his timing right."

Now, for the first time, there was excitement in his voice. Another three minutes passed in silence. Then:

"He's got him!" This time it was the Arab. Now both binoculars were trained on the waterfront itself. "And I think he managed to tip it over."

"O.K.," said Topping. "Let's get out of here."

Within seconds the engine was started, and still without showing any lights whatsoever, they returned to their original berth in the port of Dubai. Almost the moment the djerba came alongside shore, Topping and his friend jumped out, leaving the second Arab to complete the docking procedures. Luckman was far behind when he too left the boat and hurried to catch up with the two other men.

After no more than 100 meters, all stopped. Once again they were almost directly in front of the Indian café. Another 50 meters away, a large crowd had gathered. Apparently two trucks had collided in the middle of the broad concrete strip which ran along the entire waterfront. One of the trucks had tipped over, and part of its cargo—wooden crates about a yard long and two feet high—had been spilled out. At least a half dozen men, in the middle of the crowd, were hurriedly trying to load them into a third truck. A man in a tropical white suit was giving the orders. The whole operation was completed in no more than twenty minutes. The third truck then pulled off, leaving the crowd of curious Arabs surrounding the two wrecks, both empty. Apparently no one had been hurt. It was just one of those accidents which happen almost daily in the chaos of a port on the Persian Gulf.

"I think we should have another tea," was the only comment of the dark, dirty consultant of Nick Topping. So back to the rear of the Indian café they went. By now it was almost eleven o'clock. Another Arab— yet a new one—was at the table waiting. For three minutes he spoke rapidly, and uninterrupted, in Arabic. Then he answered three questions; rose abruptly, and left.

"All right," said Topping. "Let's have it."

"Everything is confirmed," said the Arab, his words coming out in a staccato fashion. "The crates contained silver bars. One split open. Two of my men saw the silver. There can be absolutely no doubt."

"Where are they taking it?"

"Undoubtedly to the warehouse of Mr. Nebbu, the Indian. He is a partner of the Iranian. It is heavily guarded, and it is impossible to get any information from the people working there. Nebbu pays very well, and his employees are all Indians. They are very loyal to him."

"Can you be sure the silver is going there?"

"Yes. Another of my men is watching the warehouse. He will identify every truck that makes any deliveries tonight, or in the process of the next few days. This will allow us to also determine rather exactly the amount of silver Firdausi is landing."

"Are you still watching Firdausi?"

"Yes. He arrived around six o'clock this evening at the airport, and we have watched him ever since. He is, by the way, also staying at the De Luxe Ambassador. His sister is with him."

"Well, Ali, you and your people have, as usual, done a superb job. Would you like your money now?"

"Yes. In cash, as arranged. But I'm afraid that it will cost slightly more than I originally estimated."

"Why?"

"I'm afraid the truck will now be a total loss."

"I understand." With that, Topping reached into the inside pocket of his jacket and removed both an envelope and his wallet. After extracting some bills from his wallet, he laid them on top of the envelope and pushed the neat little pile across the table. They disappeared into Ali's clothes almost in the same motion.

"It is a pleasure to do business with you, Mr. Topping. You shall hear further from me." He rose, glided through the restaurant, and out the door into the darkness beyond.

Now Donald Luckman rose, but was told to sit down again by Topping.

"We don't want to be seen with that lot any more than is necessary."

"I'm not sure I want to be seen with you any more either," replied Luckman, and this time there was not the slightest touch of humor in his voice.

"What's wrong with you?"

"Wrong with me! Look, you and your pals here engineered that whole thing, didn't you?"

"Of course."

"What if somebody had been killed in that crash!"

"Nobody was."

"What kind of business is this, anyway?"

No answer. Then two minutes later:

"O.K. Let's go back to the hotel. We'll walk."

They walked in complete silence. Twenty minutes later they entered the De Luxe Ambassador.

The man in white was at the desk asking for his key. Beside him was a beautiful young girl.

Luckman, seeing them, said, "Look, Nick, that's . . ."

"Shut up." Topping grabbed Luckman under the elbow, and almost lifted him into the waiting elevator. He then pressed the button immediately for the fifth floor.

"Come on to my room for a minute, Luckman. I see I'll have to explain a few things to you."

In the room, Topping produced a large bottle of whiskey, and poured two glasses. He didn't bother to ask about ice, since none was available. Luckman didn't care in the least. In fact, he had downed half of the glass before he even sat down.

"Now I'll make it quick," said Topping. "That man

downstairs is Agha Firdausi. And the girl with him is his sister. That was his djerba that brought in the load of silver. It's the second load that's come in so far to-night. My friend Ali, and his pals, alerted us they were coming. But they didn't convince me. Now I'm convinced. Firdausi and that bank in Lugano have struck on a major source of silver in Iran. And they've obviously set everything up in Switzerland very cleverly. Lately they've started dumping it in London or New York. They are warehousing the silver here in Dubai."

"What you say makes sense. But why you have been willing to go to such lengths to establish all this, does not. Hiring a bunch of thugs. Staging what might have been a fatal accident. Sneaking around like thieves. You already said that a man got killed trying to break into the property of Firdausi. At the time I thought you were putting me on. But no longer. I don't want anything more to do with this."

"Luckman, you were instructed to look at a bank in Lugano, with the objective of possibly acquiring it. My instructions were to find out where all that silver was coming from via Dubai. And if it was coming from a mine in Iran, to acquire said mine. Your bank obviously owns part of my mine. Your bank also appears to have Firdausi in its hip pocket. Because he's borrowed from them up to the hilt to finance this whole project. Now listen carefully. We will get that bank for you. All we want in return is that you let us have that mine. We will pay very handsomely for it. In fact, the odds are that, when all is said and done, you are going to get that bank for *nothing*. Now wouldn't that make you a big hero back in San Francisco?"

"Not if it turns out that we're dealing with a bunch of crooks."

"Easy, easy. What's crooked?"

Luckman's eyes narrowed.

"Well?"

"Nothing much. Except for that accident, that attempted break-in in Iran, and probably a dozen other things I don't know about. And there's bound to be more."

"Why?"

"Because there's no way you could get the owners of that bank to part with it. No way—legally. Because, together with Firdausi they've got one great big money machine going. Why in the world should they sell out to us?"

"Leave that to me. Believe me, it will all be done legally. We always work that way."

"Sure you do. Which brings me to another point. Who exactly is 'we'?"

"People who are interested in silver."

"That tells me one hell of a lot."

"Look, would your boss back in California tell you to work with me if he didn't know who we are?"

Again Luckman had to think.

"Hardly, no."

"Does your boss want you to buy that bank?"

"Yes, apparently."

"Do you know how to swing it?"

"No. Like I said, there simply can be no way, legally. Except at an enormous price."

"O.K. Now let's go back to square one. I know how to acquire that bank. I'll need a little help from you, but not a great deal. And I guarantee—guarantee—that we can close the deal within sixty days. Maybe a lot less. Now we're going to stay in Dubai for at least two more days. I've got to know exactly how much silver Firdausi is bringing in, and it will take my friends that long to find out. You just take a little rest. Except for one thing. You get on the blower to your boss. Tell him exactly what I just told you. And then ask him whether you are to proceed. Then let me know. I'll be in and out of the hotel."

Luckman did just that only one hour later.

He was given Foreman's personal authority to proceed, as rapidly as possible.

That night he slept easily. He was covered.

11

The green *Michelin* says of Gandria: "a little village right on the shore of the Lake of Lugano, much frequented by artists. Its flowery terrace, its pergolas, leafy arbours and arcaded houses make a charming picture." The red *Michelin* lists but one restaurant, the Antico. It not only does not have three stars, it has not even one. But the concierge of the Hotel Villa Castagnola insisted that this was pure and simple French prejudice. Because Italians did not smear thick red wine sauces over their food, the inspectors from

162

that tire company obviously regarded all their restaurants as primitive. Anyway, he said, what does a tire company know about food? His logic was unassailable. So Debbie Luckman asked him to book a table for just one. When? Eightish. She also booked a limousine. If the bank was paying, it might as well live up to its reputation as a multi-billion dollar institution.

The village itself clung to the edge of the rocky mountain which descended directly into the waters of the lake itself. Its narrow stairs were hardly suitable for even Fiat 500's, much less Daimler limousines. So Debbie had to walk the last two hundred yards from the parking lot above. She kept looking for the "pergolas" in the fading light, but not knowing exactly what they were, failed to detect any. The many leafy arbors made up for it. The Antico itself was unexpectedly interesting. It seemed to have been built in a large cavern in the rocks, facing the lake below. The terrace was closed. All tables were reserved, but nobody was there except for a sole gentleman in the tiny bar at the rear.

"So what," thought Debbie. Damned if she'd stay in that hotel alone for one more night. And damned if she wasn't going to have a drink at the bar.

The barman eyed her with interest, especially the area between the neck and waist. He even licked his lips slightly before saying "Buona sera, signora." He knew full well that she was American, but he also knew full well that Americans loved to be mistaken for something slightly more sophisticated. So he kept up the game.

"Quanto chiede all'ora?"

Debbie looked bewildered. Then the sole other occupant of the premises intervened.

"Excuse me, madame. I'm afraid our friend behind the bar is trying to be amusing. May I, perhaps, be of assistance to you?"

It was now Debbie's turn to do some eyeing. She liked what she saw.

"Well," she said, "that is most kind of you."

The tall slender man rose from his bar stool, and extended his hand.

"May I introduce myself? Gianfranco Pietro Annunzio di Siracusa."

"Oh," replied Debbie. "I'm Deborah Luckman."

"Deborah. That is a lovely name. Now the drinks. What may I order for you?"

"A daiquiri, please."

A few sharp words sent the barman scurrying. The grin on his face had totally disappeared. The prince was drinking champagne. He raised his glass to Debbie after her daiquiri had arrived.

"To a most charming surprise. You have brightened my evening considerably."

Debbie actually shivered. Not with cold, but with the thrill of it all. *This* was Europe, the one she had been searching for ever since landing in that dreary Zurich. God, she thought, I hope he doesn't go away. Better talk to him.

"Are you from here?" Not exactly clever, but it kept the options open.

"No, no. I'm from Sicily. From Syracuse."

"You are here on business?"

"I suppose so. Although I am not really a businessman. And you?"

"I'm with my, eh, husband. He's in banking."

"In Lugano?"

"No. In San Francisco. But he is trying to buy a bank in Lugano."

"Ha," exclaimed the prince. "Well, tell him to be careful."

"Why do you say that?"

"Because, my dear, I have had some slight experience in that regard." Then he looked at his watch.

Debbie's eagerness suddenly subsided.

"I'm so sorry. I must be keeping you."

"Not at all. Quite the contrary. I have been expecting a friend, but he seems to have been delayed. May I suggest something?"

He did not wait for an answer.

"Why don't we dine together. Unless, of course, you are expecting someone. Your husband, perhaps?"

"No, no," she replied. "He's in the Near East somewhere." She hesitated then. "I would be most happy to dine with you. But I must confess something. I did not get your name. Everyone seems to speak so quickly in Italian."

"Just call me John. All my American friends do. And now I suggest we move to a table. It will be more comfortable."

Almost as soon as they had changed places, the restaurant started to fill up: with people, laughter, noise, confusion. For Debbie, the next three hours passed completely unnoticed. She had decided to switch to champagne, they were already on their third bottle, deep in conversation, when a man touched the prince on the shoulder.

"I'm sorry to be so late."

"Doc! I hardly expected you any more."

"Nor did you miss me, it would seem," said Doc, as his eyes shifted across the table.

This brought the prince to his feet.

"Excuse me," he said, "I must introduce you."

"Mathew, this is Deborah Luckman. She is from San Francisco."

Doc extended his hand, and Debbie took it delicately. This one, she thought, is even better. Gawd, what an evening it is turning out to be!

"Delighted to meet you," said the deep mellifluous voice, "I do hope I may join you." With that he drew up a chair from an adjoining table, and waved at the waiter.

"Just bring another glass," he said, "and another bottle of champagne."

Now it was Debbie who looked at her watch.

"But . . ."

"No buts," said Doc. "If you have been kind enough to make up my unforgivable lateness to the prince, the least I can do is offer you a nightcap."

"The prince?"

"Ah, he didn't tell you?"

"No," she said, now looking at John with awe.

Annunzio stammered something about it not being very important.

"Doc," he continued, searching for a diversion of interest, "her husband is in banking. And he is trying to buy a bank here in Lugano."

"Oh, any particular bank?"

Debbie replied, "Yes. One that has something to do with Sicily and America."

"How very interesting. What bank is your husband with in America?"

"The First National of California."

"Yes, I've heard of it. Very big, I think."

"Yes it is. Are you also in banking?"

"We . . ." started the prince, but he was immediately cut off.

"We," said Doc, "are in the investment business. But we hardly want to start talking about business at this hour of the evening, do we?" The glance he shot at the prince was deadly. Debbie didn't notice a thing. In fact, after so much alcohol she was starting to have trouble keeping anything in focus. The conversation shifted abruptly to the delights which the Italian part of Switzerland offered to visitors and residents alike. It was agreed that Debbie should be shown some of the sights. Doc volunteered to serve as her guide. He would phone her hotel.

All three were on somewhat unsteady legs as they left the restaurant fully two hours later. Debbie insisted on pecking both men on the cheek as they said their farewells in the parking area above the village. The one she gave Doc was, however, a bit too extended to qualify as a simple peck. And the pat he gave her behind was too lingering to be accidental. All the way back to the hotel she hummed a tune over and over again. The driver was tempted to turn on the radio to drown her out. But simple greed held him back. The fifty franc note she pressed on him as a tip, mistaking it for a ten, proved his Italian instinct correct.

The International Bank of Sicily and America opened its doors at nine. Within minutes, it was bustling with tourists exchanging money, local businessmen arranging transfers, housewives depositing savings. Around ten o'clock the more important type of clients began arriving. They were discreetly ushered into an elevator, and met on one of the upper levels by a bank executive. The issues they discussed were the state of the American economy, the weakness of the dollar, the strength of the German mark, the boom in cocoa prices. The decisions they reached often led to shifts of millions of dollars from one market to the other, from one currency to the other. The commissions generated as a result of these switches, the fees charged for advice given—the interest charged if margin was involved—all added up rapidly. Less than a year after the takeover the Bank of Sicily and America had become an enormously profitable institution. The reason: the bank seemed to possess an almost uncanny knack for being in the right thing at the right time. The word had spread. The money poured in.

Every morning at ten the executive committee of the bank met in the Board room. Often these sessions lasted no longer than five minutes, and usually consisted of everybody listening carefully to Albert Fiore as he meticulously outlined the day-to-day adjustments in the bank's strategy and tactics. At first, fresh recruits—Swiss bankers provided by executive headhunters through periodic raids of other banks—were highly skeptical of what Albert told them to do. He was much too young to know anything, he was American, and he looked and acted more like a budding professor than a smart money manager. But such doubts were of short duration. Because, his ideas worked.

This particular morning the meeting started late. The reason was that Doc had insisted that Albert hear about the happenings the prior evening in Gandria. They talked softly in the corridor—rather Doc talked softly. Albert just listened, nodding his head occasionally. Finally, when Doc had completed his narrative, he stated his conclusions:

"Doc, this could be either good or bad. In any case, it's all too flimsy to act on at the moment. Let's wait until you get something in greater depth. Then we can figure out our response. Now let's get that meeting going."

The prince was waiting patiently at the head of the table as they entered. The moment everyone spotted Doc and Albert, the murmuring ceased. As usual, the prince, as Chairman, officially greeted everyone, and then turned the proceedings over to Albert.

"Gentlemen," he started, "this morning we are going to discuss commodities. I suspect that some of you are not too familiar with the workings of commodities markets, so I will explain the essentials. They are really quite simple. It will not be necessary to take notes. If anyone has questions or problems later, you must simply come to me."

Albert always said almost exactly the same words when explaining a new area of finance. It was simple.

169

"You have to really understand only three basic concepts. These are: long, short, futures. Three words."

In spite of his suggestion to the contrary, everyone at the table, including the prince and Doc, wrote down the three words.

"Let's start with 'long.' When you go long in the commodities market, it simply means that you are the buyer. You are entering into a contract to buy a commodity from another party for delivery at some time in the future. Like: 'I agree to buy 10,000 ounces of silver from you, at $1.50 an ounce, for delivery three months from now.' Any problems with that?"

He looked around the room. No problems. Going long meant you were a buyer.

"Good. Now 'short.' Going short means that you are a seller. You agree to sell those 10,000 ounces of silver, at $1.60 an ounce, to the other party of the contract. And you agree to deliver that silver three months from now. Got it?"

They got it.

"Futures are simply the name given to these types of contracts, where the commodity involved, though contracted for now, will be physically transferred at some time in the future. In our example, those 10,000 ounces of silver will first have to be delivered three months from now from the seller, who went short, to the buyer, who went long. Got it?"

More or less.

"Now we come to the heart of the matter. Normally, the fellow who is selling in the commodity futures market does not own any of that commodity.

170

And the fellow who buys, usually never intends to ever really use that commodity. O.K.?"

No. That one definitely did not get across.

"How," said one of their account executives, "can you sell something you have not got?"

"Because the actual contract is done through a commodity broker who guarantees that you will be able to get it, when the time comes to deliver."

"Why should he do that?"

"Because you give him a guarantee to do so. A cash down payment. They call it margin in the commodity business. But don't let that confuse you. It's just a cash guarantee."

Now the youngest member of the group spoke up. He had a beard, but this did little to conceal the fact that he was only twenty-three.

"Why should anybody sell anything he has not got?"

"To make money," was Albert's prompt response.

"How?"

"Let's go back to silver. Say I went short and you went long on that futures contract. You agreed to buy 10,000 ounces of silver from me three months from now, and I agreed to deliver it to you then. We also agreed that you would pay me $1.60 an ounce. Right?"

"Right." One had to give the kid credit. He was not afraid to ask "stupid" questions.

"O.K. During the next three months, the price of silver falls. Say to $1.30 an ounce. The day I have to deliver that silver to you—the silver I never had—I go out and really buy it. Then a minute later I hand it over to you. And you pay me. But you have to pay me $1.60 an ounce. I only had to buy it, a minute beforehand, for $1.30 an ounce. Voilà. I've made thirty cents an ounce. On 10,000 ounces that's $3,000 dollars."

"What about me?" asked the young man.

Now Doc broke in. "You have been screwed!"

The laughter broke the ice. Now other men, the older ones, started to ask questions.

"Could you explain what would have happened if the silver price would have gone up, instead of down?"

"Sure. Then I, who went short, would have had to actually buy the silver when the contract became due, at a higher price. Say $1.90 an ounce. But I would have had to hand it over to our friend here a minute later for $1.60 an ounce. Then he would have been the one who made $3,000."

"What determines which way the price goes in something like silver?" asked another man.

"Supply and demand like in any other market. But in commodities it is more complicated. There the determining factor is what people *expect* the supply/demand picture will be in the future, since almost all commodity trading is done for future deliveries. Let's say there's shortage of silver now. Some people may think that this shortage will get even more acute in the future, driving the price up. So they'll go long. Others may feel that a new flood of silver may be about to hit the market, driving the price down three, or six months from now. They'll go short. So it's future expectations that are the key here."

The group seemed satisfied. But then another man spoke up.

"Albert, explain that margin business again."

"I will, since it's highly important. It's what makes commodities so interesting, and so dangerous. Key to all commodities futures trading is that, normally, you only put up margin, in other words a cash guarantee, of 10% of the actual value of the commodities you are buying or selling. Now in our case of silver, the actual value of the 10,000 ounces at $1.60 an ounce of silver would be $16,000. Right?"

Albert paused.

"But you only would have had to put up 10%. Or $1,600 in cash. Get it?"

"Yes," somebody volunteered.

"That means that I would have made $3,000 profit on just $1,600 in three months. That's almost impossible to do in any other market."

"Exactly. You can double, triple, or quadruple your money in a very short time in commodities."

"Or get wiped out!" said the young man with the beard.

Albert now looked at his watch.

"Gentlemen," he continued, "the reason I've brought this up is the following. We shall be recommending to our clients that they buy, or go long, on silver. For delivery in three months. Because the price of silver is going to go up. Now let me show you exactly where it appears to be headed."

Albert unrolled a huge chart, and with the help of the prince tacked it on the wall.

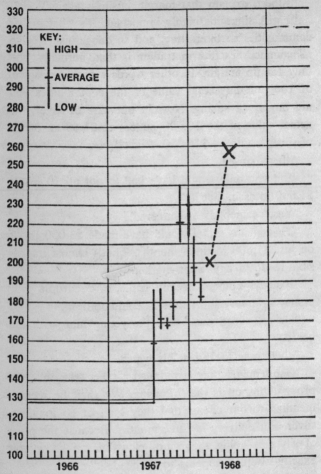

CENTS PER TROY OUNCE

KEY:

HIGH

AVERAGE

LOW

1966   1967   1968

"This shows what has happened to silver during the past six months. It came from $1.29 in July, moved all the way up to over $2.40 at year end, then retreated almost all the way back to $2.00. Now it's starting to climb again. It's a buy for two reasons. First, a silver craze has developed among the small investors in the United States. Hundreds of thousands of people are trying to get a piece of the action before it's too late. Last summer, speculators held future contracts amounting to well below 200 million ounces. Today, it's a half billion ounces. Times two bucks. That means they have over a billion dollars on the line. And it's rising every day, as more and more suckers pour in. I use the word suckers advisedly, because those that are long are going to make a lot of money. At least for a while. Because in addition to the little guys, there seems to be some big guys, or big guy, that is rigging this market. On the upside. When both the little guys and the big guys are pushing in the same direction, that's the time to join them. Which is what I propose we do.

"Now look at this chart once again. The little 'x' is where we are now. The big 'X' is where I think the silver price is heading. If I'm right, $10,000 invested today, on margin, should triple by summer."

He paused.

"I think our clients might like that."

The faces of everyone in the room shone. Albert was out to do it again. The clients would not like it—they'd love it!

"How should we go about this technically?" asked

175

their most senior account executive, one that they had gotten from the Union Bank of Switzerland by offering him twice his former salary.

"Just give the orders to my office," said Albert. "I'll keep an eye on them after that."

Within five minutes the switchboard of the Bank of Sicily and America lit up like a Christmas tree. With outgoing calls to selected clients in dozens of countries. Silver futures were hot!

The only man in the bank with any lingering doubts was Doc. He stayed behind in the Board room with Albert after everybody else had left.

"Albert, one thing puzzles me. Our mine down in Iran is starting to pump out silver like crazy. Won't that start affecting the price?"

"Probably. But not until late summer. That's when Firdausi plans to achieve full output. Then we'll look at the whole thing again."

Doc shrugged. He knew it never paid to ask Albert a question.

"In the meantime," Albert continued, "by getting speculators to buy we push the price up, don't we? So we make it both ways. We sell our physical silver from Iran at better and better prices, and we make profits for our customers in the futures market. It's what the Europeans call one hand washing the other."

That answer fully satisfied Doc. And it pleased him to see that little Albert had more than a little larceny in his soul.

As the Europeans also say: the apple never falls far from the tree. Joe Fiore could be proud of his boy.

12

Debbie was in her bath at the Hotel Villa Castagnola. But she was involved in purely ablutionary activities. Why indulge in childish practices, she had told herself firmly, when the real thing was close at hand. At least it had better be!

Funny about Debbie. She was by no means promiscuous. Aside from Donald, she had only slept with two other men in her life; boys, really, since it had happened in college, almost twenty years ago, long before she'd even met Donald. But somehow, somewhere along the line, something seemed to have snapped inside her. It was hard to say exactly when, but certainly no more than a year ago. What gave way was her determination to stay faithful to Donald no matter what. Up to that point, she had been resigned to getting along quite nicely for the rest of her life on a low-key limited diet of sex. But suddenly it had dawned on her that within a few years, after forty, she would probably have no choice in the matter. Who wanted to screw old women these days? The trouble was that in Los Altos Hills nobody seemed terribly interested in screwing relatively young ones either! Not that she'd exactly put herself on the market. But she'd given a few broad hints at more than one cocktail party. The most brazen had occurred in Roger Wright's kitchen, while she was helping him with the drinks. His only reaction was to drop ice cubes all over the floor, and flee to the safety of numbers in the living room. Maybe he's a latent fairy, she thought. Those good looking ones often are, it seems. If that turned out to be the case with Mathew!

But no. That couldn't be. He'd picked her up after lunch and they'd spent all afternoon driving around Ticino. To be sure, he'd kept everything on the up and up the entire time. Until he'd dropped her back at the hotel.

"Why don't we dine together this evening?" he'd said. Where? A little restaurant in the village where Mathew lived. Maybe she'd like to see his villa after dinner. For a nightcap. All right?

She'd left no doubt whatsoever that it would be all right. So it had been agreed. Doc would pick her up at eight. That was in half an hour; she'd better get moving.

Doc was just stepping into his car in Garona; actually it was Marvin's MG. It seemed like a more appropriate vehicle for the occasion. Which was to be the not-so-subtle seduction of Deborah Luckman.

"Well," he thought as he wheeled through the gates, "at least she has a nice face and big knockers."

But he knew he was kidding himself. Because he'd have to bring her back to the villa for the crucial stages of the operation. And that would mean eventually, in fact inevitably, his bedroom. Which was the place where he'd discovered that Shireen Firdausi was the girl he wanted—not just for one night stands, but for real. Christ, here he was forty-four years old, and acting like some seventeen-year-old nit! But goddammit, he thought, she's everything I want. She can mean happiness. That was a word he'd almost forgotten. But since Shireen had shared his life for those eight glorious days in summer, it was a word that could no longer be forgotten. In fact, even now when he thought of her he felt a gut ache. They actually exchanged letters every day! And he phoned her twice a week. Yet neither of them really ever had anything to either write or say. But he could hardly wait until the mail arrived each morning, or until Wednesdays and Saturdays when he could hear her voice again. And to top everything off, this was bloody Saturday! He had picked up the phone probably ten times, but somehow, knowing what was scheduled for this evening, he could not bring himself to place the call. Shit!

At eight on the dot he pulled up in front of the Villa Castagnola. Debbie was waiting for him in the lobby. She made a smashing impact. The fact that her little black dress was buttoned up to the neck only emphasized her superb body. She had that healthy, suntanned, California-girl look, in spite of her maturity. The Italians in the lobby were almost going off their nut as they imagined themselves sinking into that magnificent body of delicious female flesh. For all their charm, Italians are not terribly imaginative when it comes to sex. They like it quick, hot, and ample: like spaghetti and meat balls at lunchtime. The disappointment was universal when Doc arrived to snatch the prize from their eager clutches. But since generations, Italians have learned to live with defeat; and at least half a dozen mamas enjoyed unexpectedly vigorous matings later that evening as a result of the visions which Debbie had given rise to in the lobby at eight.

Even Doc was put slightly off his stride when he saw her. By gawd, he thought, this is one of the nicest pieces of ass I've met up with in many a year. Both were suddenly tense when they greeted each other, in spite of the fact that they had spent the entire afternoon together.

This tenseness remained with them all the way up to Garona, and even through the meal at the local restaurant. It was as if both knew what was going to happen, but neither dared bring it out into the open. Until Doc had paid the check.

"You still interested in that nightcap?" he asked.

She looked straight into his eyes without saying a word, and then just pushed back her chair. Doc was immediately on his feet, and when he touched her elbow to guide her toward the exit, both his hand and her arm were moist.

They took the car, even though they only had to go 100 meters. The courtyard was lit, as was the swimming pool, when they entered the grounds. But the house lay in darkness. It remained that way except for a small table lamp in the living room, and the glow of the fireplace, which some invisible hand seemed to have lit not long before their arrival. Debbie noticed this, but said nothing. She settled into the deep settee facing it. There had been a chill in the air outside, especially in the open MG. Here in the villa, everything was warm and cozy. There was a smell of burning wood in the air, which soon mingled with the bouquet of cognac.

"Mm," whispered Debbie, as Doc sat down at her side, "this is what it's all about, isn't it?"

Doc surprised himself by agreeing, and not just with words. The only flaw was that Debbie happened to be the wrong person to share this moment. But there was no denying the fact that she was a tremendously attractive girl. This was felt beyond any doubt in Doc's loins, so much so that he lost control of the situation. This was to be the time for carefully filling in the story of exactly what Debbie's husband was up to. But instead he found his hands unbuttoning the little black dress, while Debbie's hands were busy at his belt. They were both on the rug in front of the fireplace within seconds, and when Doc entered her he could feel her trembling, pushing, enveloping him all at the same time in one tremendous moment, a moment which lasted but a short time before he ejaculated into her with a loud groan which was shared, and repeated, by Debbie, as her body clung to keep him within her as long as possible. Her convulsions finally began to ebb, and with a sigh, she relaxed in Doc's arms.

"Thank you, Mathew," she said, in the softest of voices, as her hand wandered ever so gently to his cheek.

Doc wanted to feel ashamed, but he couldn't. Because he could not help but feel a deep liking for this strange woman. Not love, no. But a warmness, a recognition that, in many ways, they were two of a kind. People who had kept their emotions under control for so long that they were almost afraid to let them leak out into the open ever again. Yet both had done so, and both were happy that it had been with each other.

They did not finish their cognac. Instead Doc took her by the hand, and without a word, led her up the staircase to his bedroom. Under the covers, they were almost immediately together again. But this time it lasted for a long time. The violence of their first meeting was replaced by a mutual desire to extend, to hold on to, the total physical pleasure they had discovered they were able to provide.

By four in the morning, Debbie felt fucked to a degree that was wildly beyond anything she thought possible. Then she fell into a deep sleep. So did Doc.

It was 9:30 the next morning when both woke. The first words came from Debbie:

"Mathew?"

"Yes."

"Any regrets?"

"Don't be silly. And you?"

She leaned on top of him, took his head between both hands and bestowed a single kiss. Then, in a sudden whirl of action she was out of bed.

"I'm happy," she said, "and I'm hungry. So let's both take a bath—together—and then have breakfast."

They splashed around like little kids for at least half an hour. When they descended the stairs afterwards, the aroma of bacon and eggs was there to greet them. So was Maria. She kept her eyes averted as she served them in the breakfast room; it would be more difficult for her to day dream about Doc after this.

"Mathew," said Debbie, suddenly. "You do know that I'm married, don't you?"

"Of course. But you hardly think that I'm so indiscreet as . . ."

"I didn't mean that. It's just that, somehow, I want to tell you more about Donald."

"Look, Debbie, I don't really want . . ."

Again she interrupted. "But I do. Because I don't want you to think that I'm the unfaithful type. This is the only time I've deceived Donald in seventeen years."

"Debbie, I believe you. It doesn't matter."

"But what I want to tell you is why. It's been building up for a long time. Then, out of the blue, we were sent to Europe. I was sure everything would get better as a result. But Donald, instead of making this our second honeymoon like we planned, he just treated me like excess baggage. Dammit, Mathew, I refuse to be treated that way any longer!"

Doc just nodded.

"The last straw was on Thursday. He had the bloody nerve to go to the Near East, to Kuwait, *with another man!* Leaving me here to twiddle my thumbs. And just because of a crazy scheme involving some bank here and a silver mine in Iran."

Doc had planned to use Debbie for all it was worth. But now? After last night? Not so easy. Still he had a job to do.

"Tell me more."

"I don't know any more. But why are you now so interested in my husband?"

"I've got reasons. But, take my suggestion for what it's worth: it is that you forget about this whole thing. Just blank it out of your mind. You are not going to help yourself, your husband, or me by getting involved."

Doc got up, and moved behind Debbie. He touched her shoulder, and then began to slowly caress her hair.

Maria came back into the breakfast room with fresh coffee. But when she saw the two of them, she stopped and fled back into the kitchen. What was that woman trying to do!

Ten minutes later Debbie and Doc were on their way down the twisting mountain road leading back to Lugano. He apologized for not being able to have lunch with her. It didn't matter, she pointed out. Her husband would probably be back in the hotel before noon anyway. What more was there to say? He left her standing in a daze outside the Villa Castagnola. And then sped back into the center of town.

13

Albert, the prince, and Marvin were somber as Doc filled them in.

When Doc was done Albert spoke:

"It doesn't make sense."

"What do you mean," answered Doc violently,

"we're sitting on top of a mint and they are going to try to take it away. They'll blow the whistle on us unless we deal. Remember, Albert, your old man and his pals are not exactly elders of the Mormon church."

"But that's what doesn't make sense. Big American banks don't think or do things that way. There's got to be something else. Somebody else. Didn't you say that that woman mentioned that her husband was down on the Gulf with another man?"

"Yes."

"Did she further identify him?"

"No. But I had the feeling he was not from that bank."

"How could they possibly know about that mine?" This from the prince.

"Maybe Firdausi's double-crossing us." That from Doc. Who then glared at the prince. "Are you guys up to some new fancy tricks?"

The prince just sat there dumbfounded.

Albert interrupted. "No, that's not possible."

"Why not?"

"We've got Firdausi 100% in our hands. Don't you remember the terms of those loan agreements, where we provided Firdausi with working capital? We've put $20 million of the bank's money into that venture down there—on top of the original investment. Firdausi has personally co-signed every note. They are all callable within thirty days. And if he can't pay up, we have the right to take over his half of the venture, and he knows it."

"Maybe," said Doc reluctantly, "but maybe he's trying to use these California guys to take over the bank in order to get off the hook. Then he'd have that mine all to himself."

"No, Doc," said Albert, "because if somebody else takes over, they will still hold those same notes, with the same conditions. No, you're looking in the wrong direction."

"So what's the right direction, dammit?"

"Frankly," said Albert, "I simply do not know. But it has to be somebody who desperately wants that silver. The bank can only be of secondary interest. When you come right down to it, banks are a dime a dozen in Switzerland. It's got to be the silver."

At that point a secretary walked in with a note in her hand. She hesitated, and then handed it to Doc.

"Well I'll be goddammed," he exclaimed. "Look at that!"

He handed the note to Albert.

"Read it," Doc said.

So Albert did. "A Mr. Nicholas Topping is waiting outside in the reception room. He would like to talk to someone in the bank about possible mutual interests in Iran."

The dumbfounded look returned to the prince's face. Even Albert was nonplussed. Only Marvin, as usual, showed no emotion.

"Well?" asked Doc, his eyes shifting around the conference table.

"No use speculating any further," said Albert. "He's the man. And he thinks he's got everything lined up. So let's hear it."

"Bring him in," Doc told the secretary. "And don't let anybody else in here until I say so."

Then to the prince. "You play Chairman of the Board. I want to just sit back and watch this guy for a while."

"Marvin," he continued, "get out of here and make sure this guy is photographed front, back and sideways before he gets out of the building. Then you personally tail him after he leaves. I want to know where he's staying."

Marvin had barely closed the door, when it was opened again by the same secretary. Nick Topping was right behind her. No sports clothes this time. Blue serge, white shirt, highly polished shoes. Even a thin leather briefcase. He stopped just beyond the threshold, waiting for the other side to make the first move.

The prince made it. "Mr. Topping?"

"Yes." Loud, clear, and tough.

"My name is Gianfranco Pietro Annunzio di Siracusa. I am Chairman of this bank. I have asked two of my colleagues to join me."

He just waved his hand lazily at the other men sitting around the table, indicating no intention of introducing them personally. Nor did either Doc or Albert rise to do so themselves.

Topping blithely ignored this.

"Why don't you take a seat, Mr. Topping. Perhaps down there." He pointed at the far end of the table. Topping did as requested. When seated, the sun from the windows on the opposite side of the conference room shone directly in his eyes. The prince then took his seat, at the other end of the long oak table. Doc and Albert faced each other mid-way down. Topping looked carefully at each man in turn, glanced into the sun, reached into his breast pocket, and put on his sunglasses.

No one said a word. The prince broke the ice.

"I believe you have suggested we may have some mutuality of interest, Mr. Topping?"

Completely ignoring both the question, and the prince, Topping turned toward Doc.

"How do you find Lugano, Mr. Smythe, after so many years in Las Vegas? Excuse me. It's *Doctor* Smythe I'm told."

Doc just stared at him. So Topping turned toward Albert on the other side of the table.

"Mr. Fiore, I believe. I do hope next time you speak to your father, you give him my best regards. We once ran into each other a few years ago. In Miami. We had mutual friends. From Cuba. I'm not sure our interests were necessarily mutual on that occasion. I sincerely hope they are now."

"O.K., Topping," said Doc finally, "cut out the fucking around. What do you want?"

"First, I'd appreciate if you could pull those goddammed curtains and get the sun out of my eyes."

Doc motioned to the prince. The curtains were pulled. Topping took off his sunglasses.

"That's better. Now who's in charge here?"

The prince started to say something. Until Doc interrupted: "I am, Topping."

"And who's that monkey?" Topping's head nodded slightly toward the other end of the table—at the prince, who turned darkly red.

"He's nothing," replied Doc.

"Right. Where's Marvin?" continued Topping.

"He went out to arrange for somebody to take your picture," replied Doc. "But I don't think that's going to be necessary."

"No. And he won't have to follow me home either. I'm staying at the Metropole, Room 612."

"How was your flight from Dubai?"

"Comfortable."

"Where's your little pal?"

Topping just raised his eyebrows.

"Come on, Topping. You're cute, but not that cute. Why didn't you bring Luckman along?"

Topping smiled.

"Doc, you're all that they told me you were. I think you and I are going to get along."

"Don't plan on it," replied Doc. Then, "Are you sure your boss knows what he's taking on?"

"Cut it out, Doc. Fishing with that kind of lousy bait will get you nowhere. You should be ashamed of yourself."

Doc grinned.

"O.K., Topping. Lay it on the table."

"Be happy to. Doc, I am acting for principals that desire to make you a very fine offer for this bank. I think, indeed I hope, that you will find it irresistible. Now don't get me wrong. Nobody is out to screw you. My principals will pay a fair price. Provided this matter can be settled quickly, cleanly, and quietly."

"Otherwise?"

"Doc, let's not get our relationship off to a bad start."

"Spell it out, Topping. Otherwise I'll kick your ass out of here in ten seconds flat."

"All right Doc. Otherwise we let the poor, unsuspecting, innocent Swiss know that the Mafia have invaded their holy of holies of banking. We've got a file probably ten feet thick on Joe Fiore, you, and all your pals. If that lands in the lap of the Bank Commission in Berne, you'll be out of business in less than a week. Is that clear enough?"

"Boy, one thing I've got to say about you, Topping. You don't lack nerve. What's to prevent us from letting you walk through that window, and mess up the sidewalks of Lugano?"

"Come on, Doc. Let's keep this on a gentlemanly level."

Again Doc grinned. He was enjoying himself, apparently happy to be back in his element.

"Sure, Topping. Say, is it all right if I call you Nick?"

"But of course. I want you to think of us as buddies."

"O.K. Nick, now why don't you cut that crap about you being an agent for principals interested in this bank?"

"But it's true, Doc."

"So what was that stuff about Iran that you were telling the secretary outside?"

"Doc, I'm happy you brought that subject up. It might have slipped my mind." Now it was Topping that grinned.

"When we heard of your interest in Iran," continued Doc, "our only conclusion was that you were a rug merchant. Topping is an Armenian name, isn't it?"

Topping laughed aloud.

"Are you big in rugs, Doc?"

"I can get fairly big on them," was the reply. Which was quite enough for Albert.

"Mr. Topping," he said, "I'd appreciate your showing us your credentials."

Topping's grin slowly disappeared. He looked at Doc, shrugged, and opened his briefcase. From it, he withdrew two small visiting cards, one for Albert, one for Doc. None for the prince.

"Nick," said Doc in a disgusted voice, after just one glance, "what kind of Mickey Mouse stuff is that? International Mineral Consultants of Panama City, and Monrovia, Liberia. You should be ashamed of yourself."

Topping dipped into the thin leather case again. This time a letter appeared. He hesitated slightly, then gave it to Doc. Doc read it, then read it again, and finally gave it to Albert.

"It looks authentic," Albert said just seconds later.

"It is," replied Topping. "So return it." Albert did.

"Why should the Chairman of the Board of a big American Bank like the First National of California appoint your crummy little company as its agent?" asked Doc.

"Probably because Mr. Foreman knows my world-wide reputation for honesty and forthrightness."

Doc liked that.

"Do you have an offer prepared?" interjected Albert.

"Yes. But it will have to be oral for the moment."

"All right," replied Albert, "make it."

"Fifty million dollars. Cash."

"For a crummy little bank like this?" was Doc's incredulous response.

"Provided one small thing," said Topping.

"You foreclose on your loans to Firdausi, and take over 100% of the equity of that property in Iran—prior to your getting that fifty million."

"Firdausi?" asked Doc. "What's that?"

"That's an Iranian with a good-looking sister, who owes you guys a mint. Something to do with silver, they tell me in Dubai."

"It's not enough," said Albert, quietly.

"What would be?" asked Topping.

"Sixty-five million," was Albert's reply.

"How about fifty-five?"

"Maybe we could split the difference."

"Perhaps."

"Hold on!" bellowed Doc. "Albert! Are you out of your fucking pinhead mind? That silver mine alone is worth a couple hundred million!"

"I know," replied Albert. "But if the Swiss banking authorities ever get involved, we could well end up with neither the bank, nor that mine. They would probably put in a receiver, or liquidator, who could eventually sell off all the bank's assets—the good ones to the Swiss, cheap, and the rest to some Americans, or Germans, or whoever, expensive. I suspect that the mining property would end up Swiss."

"Whose side you on, anyway, Albert?" asked Doc, pleadingly.

"I am a realist, Doc." For a minute Albert Fiore sounded exactly like his father. And his eyes behind the glasses had the same icy blue tint. In spite of this, Doc could not contain himself. His fist rose, and came down on the table with a resounding crash.

"I'm not," he said, "not going to let the likes of this jerk and his big banking pals in California get away with this. I swear it, Topping. I'd rather kill you first."

For the first time, Topping looked a bit nervous. His eyes went to Albert.

"Doc," began Albert patiently, "there's no sense in . . ."

"Now you shut up a minute, Albert. We have built this bank from nothing into something. Something to be very proud of.

"We did it 100% straight. You and me and even Marvin. We did it and we did it together. Haven't you got any goddammed pride? Or guts?"

Albert just sat there.

"And what about the Firdausis? You just going to sell them down the river after all they've done for us? In my opinion that would stink! What kind of a kid are you? A goddammed walking computer, that's all. And one that can't even figure too well."

Albert asked a question.

"Mr. Topping, where would the funds come from?"

"My company, acting on behalf of our principal, the First National Bank of California would place them in escrow, preferably in a bank in London. Provided my conditions on the foreclosure of that Iranian property are met. The funds would be released to whomever your owners appoint, upon delivery of

100% of the outstanding shares of this bank. The shares are in bearer form, I believe?"

"They are."

"The key is the foreclosure on that property. Are you in a position to do it?"

"We are."

"How quickly?"

"Theoretically within thirty days."

"And practically?"

"The same period of time, provided Firdausi does not entangle us in some legal battle."

"Is that possible?"

"Anything's possible where that amount of money is involved."

"Is it probable?"

"That depends."

"On what?"

"On how this is presented to Firdausi. Obviously, we can't just try to walk away with the whole thing. He must get some sort of reasonable compensation. On the other hand, the logic of our position must be explained to him. If we don't foreclose on friendly terms, the Swiss will—on much less friendly terms, as you have so kindly pointed out."

"Who would explain all this to Firdausi?"

"Probably the prince. He knows him best."

"You mentioned reasonable compensation," said Topping. "What do you have in mind?"

"He's got a rather large inventory of silver in Dubai, as you no doubt know. Mine output was up to 3 million ounces a month last month. Much of it's been warehoused. I would suggest we leave what's in Dubai to Firdausi."

"That we hadn't planned on," said Topping.

Now it was Albert that shrugged. "Well, as I said, the alternative could well be a legal battle. A long one."

"That will add to our cost," continued Topping, frowning.

Again Albert just shrugged.

"How do you know mine output is up to three million ounces?" inquired Topping.

"That's what the latest warehouse receipts from Dubai indicate," replied Albert.

"Albert, you I like," said Topping. "You're honest. We checked everything out in Dubai. Our estimates agree with your figure. What's output projected at for the rest of the year?"

"By mid-summer, it should be up to five million ounces a month. That will be peak."

"For how long?"

"That is impossible to determine, according to Firdausi's engineers. But probably for quite a while."

"That would mean around 60 million ounces a year."

"Boy, are you ever smart," said Doc, "smarter than Albert, in any case. Do you know how much that is worth a year, Albert?"

"At current prices, well over $100 million," came the calm reply.

"So," yelled Doc, "why don't you tell this jackass to get the fuck out of here!" Then more quietly: "Albert, don't let this guy psych you out. He's bluffing.

Believe me. Let's stop this whole conversation right here. O.K.?"

Again no response from Albert.

So Doc turned to Topping.

"In any case, Topping, you're wasting your time. No one in this room, including little Albert, has any authority whatsoever to talk about selling this bank. And I, for one, am going to make damn sure that no one does. You want this bank? Fine. If the owner says so, it's fine with me. But if I know the owner, you are going to end up wishing you'd never walked into this place."

With that Doc got up and left the conference room, slamming the door almost off its hinges in the process.

"I see that Doc is easily excited," commented Topping.

"Topping," replied Albert, "maybe you'd better leave too. There's such a thing as going too far. With the resulting consequences."

Topping got the point. Before he left, he put just one further question.

"Shall I call you, or . . . ?"

"I will be calling you. I'd suggest you stay away from here in the meantime."

The prince sat there, apparently deep in thoughts.

"A great pity," he said, as finally both he and Albert got up to leave.

Topping went directly from the bank to the Hotel Villa Castagnola. Luckman was waiting for him in the lobby. They went to Luckman's suite on the fifth floor.

"Well?" asked Luckman, after the door had closed.

"They'll deal."

"How much?"

"Sixty million."

"How much is that in dollars?"

"I'm talking dollars, sonny."

"You are out of your mind!"

"You, as I've said once or twice before, are out of your depth, Luckman."

"We'd never pay a price like that."

"Who said you're going to have to?"

"Sixty million dollars!" exclaimed Luckman, in an awed voice. Then, "Look, I think I've made it quite clear that our bank would never enter into a deal of that size for a little bank in Switzerland. It's just plain stupid to even discuss the matter further. When I report this back to Mr. Foreman, that's going to be the last we'll ever see of each other. That I can guarantee."

Topping said nothing. He just opened his thin leather briefcase.

"Here's a letter that was waiting for me at the hotel when I arrived this morning. I think you should read it."

Luckman read it. Then read it again.

"It's not possible. Foreman appointed *you* as our agent? No."

"But yes. And before you make a fool of yourself by calling Foreman, I would suggest you cool off, maybe have a nice little drinkie, and then I will sit down with you and map this whole thing out. Like I told you, I'm going to make a big hero out of you,

Luckman. Now give me that letter back." Luckman obeyed.

Topping glanced at his watch.

"I've got a few things to do. Hell, I'm not even unpacked yet. Why don't we reconvene around five. I'll come here. I like this hotel. It's kind of rundown. Let's meet in the bar."

The bar at the Villa Castagnola has wicker furniture. It also serves one of the worst dry martinis in Europe—which means that they are sincerely vile. Luckman winced as he tried to get rid of the stuff in a second gulp. Topping approached his table at exactly this moment.

"Luckman, do I affect you that badly?"

"Worse."

"What's that you're drinking?" as he took a chair.

"A really great martini. You must try one."

"Not on your life." Topping ordered a Campari and soda.

"Shall we get down to business?"

"Why not? It shouldn't take long."

"Donald, you don't trust me."

"Topping, why don't you get on with it."

"O.K. It's really very simple. Step one: the bank here in Lugano is going to foreclose on the mining property in Iran by calling in the loans Firdausi has co-signed. That will give it 100% ownership. Step two: your bank in California transfers $60 million to an escrow account at Winthrop's Bank in London, to be released against delivery of all of the outstanding shares of the International Bank of Sicily and America. Originally, there were fifty thousand shares. But since then, the new owners have put in a lot more capital, to keep up with the growth in deposits in the bank. Right now there are 250,000 shares outstanding. They will have to deliver every one of them, in good negotiable form, to collect their money."

"The bank's only worth ten million dollars at most. But be that as it may for the moment. What happens next in your scenario?"

"After taking over the Swiss bank, you transfer title of that Iranian property to a second escrow account at Winthrop's. Against that we pay in $85 million."

"Who is we?"

"A company in Liechtenstein. It's called Friendship International."

"It would be. But hold on a minute, Topping. Why $85 million?"

"Because your Swiss bank carries that Iranian property, with loans, at around $25 million book value on its balance sheet. Which they will have to write off if the property is sold. Right? Christ, Luckman, I thought you were a banker!"

"And then?" Luckman was struggling a bit.

"That's it. We get our mine. You get your bank. For nothing! And you said yourself, the bank's worth $10 million. You see what I meant, Luckman. I'm going to make a big hero out of you."

"So simple."

"Yes, except for one small additional detail."

"Now it comes."

"What do you mean?"

"Nothing. Only that I knew there just had to be a little detail somewhere."

"It's something quite harmless."

"What?"

"You're going to have to make a full report on the Lugano bank, as a basis for the takeover, aren't you?"

"Of course."

"That means a type of audit. Right?"

"Yes. You don't think the people back at head office are going to shell out that kind of money on the basis of a phone call, do you?"

"Exactly. Now that report will ultimately go to the full Board of Directors of your bank. Right?"

"Naturally, again assuming that we would enter into a deal like this, which I'm sure we won't. Every acquisition involving more than $5 million *must,* eventually, receive full Board approval. In practice, such approval is normally given after the fact. Especially in our bank, where Mr. Foreman has been personally responsible for its growing from nothing to one of the largest banks in the United States during the past thirty years."

"That's not the point. My point is that eventually everybody on that Board gets into the act."

"I'd hardly call it an act."

"Well I would. Because you've got a lot of blabber-mouths on the Board of that bank. Your boardroom is like a sieve."

"Come off it, Topping. But even if what you say is true, so what?"

"This. We don't want people, especially in the United States, blabbering about that Iranian mine. So

200

we want any mention of it deleted from your audit report on the Lugano bank."

"Impossible. It can't be done. That would leave $25 million in assets unaccounted for."

"Not necessarily. One would just have to create some alternate documentation related to those assets."

"Like what?"

"That is where creativity enters in. What would you suggest, Donald?"

"Maybe a string of Iranian whorehouses?"

"But why should a bank want to sell a solid investment like that? Luckman, you disappoint me."

"Now look, Topping, you cannot be serious?"

"But I am. Deadly serious."

"Don't you realize that would be a flagrant violation of the law?"

"Whose law? Not the Swiss. You won't be altering any records in Switzerland. It's just a report you are making to an American bank. It has nothing to do with the Swiss."

"And America?"

"No problem. We've looked into that. The Federal Reserve has essentially no reporting rules whatsoever related to the acquisition of a foreign bank by a domestic U.S. bank. You can't break laws when none exist."

That stopped Luckman for the moment. He was on unsure grounds, especially because Topping's words had the ring of truth. After all, it could be checked out very easily.

"So what do we say instead?"

"When you think of Iran, what first comes into your head?" asked Topping.

"Oil."

"Good boy. Now is that Firdausi property anywhere near the Iranian oil fields?"

"How should I know."

"Well it is. Right on the edge."

"So?"

"So a quite logical project would be the financing of a storage facility. You know, big tanks full of crude oil, waiting to be shipped out as demand requires. They arise beside major oil fields all over the world. And banks love to get involved. What better collateral can a bank have than huge tanks full of crude oil?"

"I remember a few years back where American Express thought that huge tanks full of salad oil were pretty safe. Until they checked the tanks in Illinois and Texas, and found out they were empty."

"Luckman, what's that got to do with it?"

"Nothing. Except that the fellow who funnied up the documentation is sitting in jail for God knows how long."

"Luckman, you're going off in the wrong direction. That was a big swindle. People lost huge amounts of money. This is quite different. Nobody's going to lose anything here. When nobody loses money, nobody cares. That is Nick Topping's first principle regarding human behavior."

"O.K. Topping. I'll try to remember that. For a few minutes, in any case. And just to keep this lunatic conversation going a bit longer, might I ask who is going to produce all the phoney documentation proving the existence of your oil tanks full of oil?"

"That's easy. There's a fellow named Marvin Skinner working in that bank here in Lugano. He's one of the best counterfeiters on earth."

"Working with the bank?" Luckman's composure finally disintegrated.

"Sure. But don't tell anyone. He could produce storage receipts for crude oil in Iranian tanks of a quality that would make Exxon blush."

"Do the current owners of that bank know about this man Skinner?"

"Luckman, don't make a big thing of it. Skinner will no longer be with that bank after you take it over, will he? I mean, you can hardly expect the top executives of that place to stay on after you take it over. Anyway, you probably wouldn't want him to stay."

"I should think not. But now you've really blown it. How can we tell that he hasn't phonied up all the records of the bank, including the rest of the balance sheet?"

"Because he hasn't. Anyway, your big job will be to go into that bank and make sure. Right?"

"We'll never get to that point. In fact, I'm sure we'll never get beyond this conversation. Mr. Foreman would never touch a deal like this."

"I'd suggest you leave that decision to him," stated Topping dryly. "In fact, it's one he's going to have to make rather soon. We're in a hurry to close this deal. So Foreman's going to have to decide whether he wants this bank presented to him on a platter, or not.

And it's up to you to determine that. Now. So let's go over the entire thing again. This time take notes."

Luckman did as he was told. When they were done, Topping left, leaving behind a suggestion that Luckman call Foreman. Right away.

14

During the next hour, three key phone conversations took place. They were responsible for irrevocably setting into motion a series of events that were going to rock the Swiss banking community, cause total havoc in the world silver markets, cost naive speculators literally billions of dollars, and make a fortune for a few not so naive investors. What a much nicer world this would be if Alexander Graham Bell had been a botanist.

The first call went from Donald Luckman in the Hotel Villa Castagnola in Lugano to George Foreman in his office at the First National Bank of California in San Francisco. It went like this:

"Mr. Foreman? Donald Luckman in Switzerland."

"One moment." Someone was requested to leave Foreman's office and to come back in about fifteen minutes. "All right, Luckman, go ahead."

"I understand that you appointed Mr. Nicholas Topping as the bank's agent in regard to the possible acquisition of the Bank of Sicily and America here in Lugano." Luckman tried to not sound peeved, and did not succeed.

"Your understanding is correct, Luckman."

"I am going to merely report on what Topping has done so far, without endorsing any part of it."

"Report, Luckman. And spare me the running commentary."

"Topping claims the bank is available. He also claims that it will be available with 100% ownership of that Iranian mining property. I already explained about the mine, and Topping's interest in it, when I called you from Dubai."

"You did. How much will it cost us?"

"It's not basically a matter of cost. It's one of risk. Topping is talking big numbers. Very big. And unless Topping is representing an absolutely impeccable party, we could . . ."

George Foreman interrupted: "He is. In fact, Topping represents an organization that has a net worth at least four or five times our own. Furthermore, it is owned and run by one man—Frank Cook. I assume even you must have heard of him, Luckman."

Luckman had, and murmured such into the phone.

"Cook and I have been in constant communication with each other—which, I assure you, is not all that convenient since he's in London and I'm out here on the West Coast. The point of all this is the following: I'm not at all interested in your endorsement or non-endorsement of what Topping has done. He does what Frank Cook tells him to do, just as I expect you to do exactly what I tell you to do. If this deal is done, Cook and I will do it. And you and Topping will take care of the details. I gather you understand this, and will act accordingly from now on, Luckman."

"Of course, sir, but I didn't realize that . . ."

"Now you do."

"Yes, sir."

"So go on with your report. I asked you a very simple question, if you recall. I'll repeat it: How much will that Swiss bank cost us?"

"Nothing."

"What's it worth?"

"I don't know."

"Guess."

"Ten million."

"What would be the mechanics?"

"Complicated," replied Luckman, who then hurried to continue. "It would involve us purchasing all of the outstanding shares of the Swiss bank through an escrow arrangement at a London bank for $60 million. Then we would take the Iranian property out of the Swiss bank, and put it into a second escrow account. Frank Cook's group, using a Liechtenstein company, would buy it for $85 million. $25 million of that would go to the Swiss bank to reimburse them for the sale of the Iranian property; the rest would go back to California. So like I said, our net cost would be zero."

"I don't see anything complicated about that," said Foreman.

"So far, not. But the buyer of the Iranian property further requires that all references to the silver mine be deleted from any audit report we—I—might make on that Swiss bank."

"So?"

"Well, Mr. Foreman, with all due respect, in my opinion . . ."

"Luckman, remember you're in Switzerland now. Not California. The mores of the banking and business community over there are quite different from our own. Just look at the Italians and the French! They don't even pay taxes. If we want to operate successfully in that part of the world, we must adapt. Now's the time to start."

"But . . ."

"So I want you to proceed along the lines Topping has suggested."

Luckman swallowed.

"Yes, sir."

"I want you to go into that bank as soon as possible. Make an audit report. If everything's all right, send it to me with your recommendation that we acquire the bank."

"Yes, sir."

"Where will those escrow arrangements be set up in London?"

"At Winthrop's. They're on Lombard Street."

"Fine. You should include a request for the proper funds in your report to me. I'll make sure they get there. Provided, of course, everything proves out in your audit."

"Yes, sir."

"Good work, Luckman. We've been given a marvelous opportunity here, and you are following through beautifully. I plan to come over there as soon as possible following the closing. Marjory will come along.

We're both looking forward to picking up where we left off at the Country Club the other week. Marjory thinks the world of your wife, you know. Please give her our best regards."

"Yes, sir."

There were two clicks signalling the termination of Luckman's call: one when Foreman hung up five thousand miles away in California; the other, when Luckman's wife, ten yards away in the adjoining bedroom, replaced the receiver on the extension.

The second phone conversation took place between Nick Topping in the Hotel Metropole, in Lugano and Frank Cook in his residence just outside Marlowe on the Thames, in Buckinghamshire, England. It was rather short.

"Mr. Cook, Topping here."

"Yes, Nick."

"Looks like we can get it for eighty-five million."

"What's it worth?"

"They're producing at three million ounces a month now, and expect it to go to five by mid-year. That would put peak annual output at around sixty million ounces. At current price, over $100 million. Who knows how much is still below the ground. Probably triple that amount. So my guess is that the property is worth at least a quarter of a billion."

"And it will be worth a lot more to us if we can keep that stuff in the ground for a while."

"Exactly, Mr. Cook. We'll make it twice over, just like you said. Now in the future market. Later by selling spot bullion after we've jacked the price up."

"How's that fellow Luckman working out?"

"As expected. But he'll come around, provided you've taken care of the San Francisco end."

"I have."

"Good."

"How long until you can wrap this up, Topping?"

"Oh, probably in a couple of weeks."

"That means we'll have to have around eighty-five million cash ready to go at that time."

"Right. Any problem there?"

"No. How will it work technically?"

"Back-to-back escrow arrangements. The Fiore group puts the shares of the bank, and 100% equity of that mine in escrow. The California bank pays out $60 million to the Fiore group."

"Then?"

"The California bank puts the mining property into a second escrow. Against that, we deliver $85 million. They keep $60 million and put the extra $25 million into the Swiss bank to replace the mining assets they sell us. Everything's clean after that."

"Will the Fiore group cause trouble?"

"I doubt it. Young Albert was quite reasonable. That Doc Smythe is a pain in the ass, though. Still, I think he'll cool off."

"Good. And that Iranian fellow?"

"He'll play, as soon as he understands that one way or the other, he's going to get squeezed out. But we'll probably have to leave him a little. Like the silver warehoused already in Dubai."

"Good work, Nick. When it's so far, come on back

to London. I want you here when those escrow arrangements are set up."

"Will do."

The third call was a conference call—at least on the Swiss end. Involved were Doc and Albert in the Bank of Sicily and America in Lugano, and Joe Fiore in Las Vegas. Doc spoke first, once they had gotten through.

"Joe, it's me, Doc. Albert's on another phone."

"Something wrong?"

"Hello, Dad," this from Albert.

"Something wrong, Albert?"

"That depends."

"Oh no it doesn't," Doc cut in, "there's definitely something wrong here, Joe. It's something we can take care of. But we may need a little help."

"Well what is it, for Christ's sake!"

"Somebody's trying to take over the bank."

"They can't do that!" screamed Joe.

"Exactly what I said," agreed Doc.

"Who?"

"Some wise guy by the name of Nick Topping. Says he knows you."

"Topping?"

"Yeah. A big guy. Probably forty-five. Mumbled something about Miami and some Cubans."

"*That* Topping." Then silence.

"Bad news, Joe?"

"Not good."

"Who's he working for?"

"One of the real heavies. Man named Frank Cook."

"Is he out of Miami?"

"No you dumb bastard. He's one of the richest guys alive."

"What's Topping's job?"

"Hatchet man. For Cook. He used to be with the Treasury Department. Narcotics. Then he went to work for I.T.T. in Latin America. Moved on to some Belgian company, and worked for them in the Congo. Real dangerous sonofabitch."

"Ever heard of a bank called the First National of California?"

"Vaguely."

"They're big. Topping says he's acting as their agent."

"Bullshit. Topping works for Frank Cook. Period."

"Sure, Joe. I see that. But for some reason they must have talked that California bank into fronting for them."

"Why?"

"I'm not completely sure. But I do know this: Topping couldn't care less about this bank. He's only after that silver mine."

"That figures. Frank Cook's the biggest in silver."

"How come you know so much about Frank Cook, Joe?"

"For a while he was in the hotel business out here. Before Hughes. Then he pulled out, all of a sudden."

"Topping seems to know all about us."

"That's his angle?"

"Yeah."

"Has he made an offer?"

"Fifty million. Albert countered with sixty-five. Probably would end up around sixty."

"I've only put in ten so far," said Fiore.

"Joe! You're not going to let some guy like Topping push you around, are you?"

"Topping, no. Frank Cook, maybe."

"Is this guy Cook superman or something?"

"Almost."

"Look, Joe, we've been together a long time now. Right?"

"Yeah."

"I've never asked any favors, or anything. I've done my job, and done it fine. Right?"

"Yeah."

"Now I'm going to ask for a favor."

A pause.

"Yeah?"

"Don't give in to these guys. At least not yet. I'll find an angle. Joe, I *always* find an angle."

"Doc, you're out of your league this time."

Then, for the first time, Albert broke in.

"Dad, it's not just us that's involved."

"What do you mean?"

"The Firdausis. Our partners in that Iranian project. You met them last summer."

"What's their problem?"

"The key provision of the takeover bid is that we foreclose on the entire property in Iran."

"Can we?"

"Yes."

"So what's the problem?"

212

"It must be done quickly. And he may give us trouble."

"Albert," stated his father, "maybe you're a bit young to take on something like that."

"I agree," interjected Doc.

"Doc, you keep out of this," answered Joe Fiore. "Albert, what did you have in mind?"

"That the prince and I go down to Iran and talk the whole situation over with the Firdausis."

"It's stupid," said Doc.

"Doc," Fiore warned. "Shut up. Now Albert, why that prince?"

"Because he knows Firdausi best. They're even related."

"Now wait a minute," Doc again, "there's no need for that.

"I tell you, Joe, I'll find a way out of this. Come on, give me a chance."

There was a long pause on the Las Vegas end of the line.

"O.K.," replied Joe Fiore finally. "You try whatever you want, Doc. Just don't blow this deal. Albert, you go down there with that prince and talk to Firdausi. In the meantime *both* of you make as if we're playing ball with Frank Cook and his boy Topping. You understand that, Doc?"

"How long do I have?"

"Albert," asked his father, "how long?"

"I would say a week, ten days at most. Topping made it quite clear that they're in a hurry."

"All right. One week. Then I want both of you to come back to me. And Doc, I warn you just one more time. Don't blow this deal unless you come up with a perfect solution. Frank Cook has us by the short hairs. He does not like losing. He'd rather see the whole bank go down the drain, silver mine and all, than get beaten by us. Unless we develop an even better lock on him. That won't be easy. In fact, my guess is that it will be impossible. But you've got one week to try."

"Fair enough, Joe." Doc's voice was steady, but barely.

"And Albert," Joe said, "you be very careful down there in that Iran. You hear?"

"Yes, Dad."

"Just one more thing, Joe," said Doc.

"Yeah?"

"Am I still in charge here?"

"You are. As long as you follow orders."

15

Doc also intended to stay in charge. Because he was convinced that he had finally achieved something that he wanted to keep—permanently. He did not kid himself in the slightest as to what that something was. Respect.

Respect. The respect of society. The respect of colleagues. Respect of himself by himself. Which was, when he thought of it—and he had thought of it quite a bit lately—an almost impossible achievement. He never had known a father. His mother was, when all the illusions were dismissed, really nothing more than a whore. And a cheap one at that. His real name? Synkiewicz. Even in Milwaukee they had laughed at that. His education? The streets. The exercise yards of prisons. His occupation? Organized crime. Taking other people's money. If necessary, hurting other people to get their money. Not out of malice. Out of necessity.

But now, such necessity did not exist. Nor need it ever again. He, Doc Smythe, was finally a person like everyone else; he lived a life like everyone else; not just as an act, for some devious purpose, but as a result of what he, and Albert, and Marvin, and the prince had put together. Honestly. He earned what he now had, dammit.

But he would not be allowed to keep it unless he figured this whole new thing right. Doc was hardly naive, but that evening, following his talk with Joe Fiore, he was puzzled, disappointed, angered. The world to which he had aspired was not what it should be. Bankers were supposed to be gentlemen. Corporate executives were supposed to live by rule books, which quite definitely set down what was right and wrong for the upper middle class man to do, both in the office and at home. Strongarm tactics, Nick Toppings, blackmail were supposed to be part of his old world, not this new one.

But they were part of both worlds. Perhaps equally. The only difference was that of terminology. The Joe Fiores weren't bosses, they were Chairmen of Boards. His counterpart would be classified as a security consultant. Marvin's alter ego in the good world would

215

be known, and admired, as a creative accountant. Albert? No doubt a computer—a machine that was just as completely without ethics as its white collared masters. And the prince. That was easy. The PR man who could arrange for the seduction of everything from the press, to politicians, to ambitious girls.

It was well past eleven o'clock, and the evening was warm, though not warm enough to sit outside. But Doc had wanted to be in the fresh air, alone. So he had been walking, first up the mountain road which extended eventually into a cul de sac above Garona, and now back to the villa that had become a home for Doc like nowhere else had ever been.

"But," he thought, as the lights of the house came into sight, "do they kill? Is that where the real difference lies? The ultimate borderline? Obviously they destroy, by tossing, pushing, forcing people into the rubbish heap. By removing a man from his job, or his money, or his reputation. But do they actually kill?"

The question was hardly academic, because Doc had already reached a conclusion. It might be necessary to kill Frank Cook. Certainly he would have to get to Cook, try to make a deal, lean on him hard. And if none of that worked, kill him.

That would stop everything cold. Just as would happen if somebody finally got to Joe Fiore. In the fight for succession, only confusion would exist—nobody would dare move lest they risk offending the next man who would assume that type of absolute power which can only exist in big business or big crime.

And then he could go back to what should be the

rule book. Because Doc was still convinced that it was there, and lived up to by the vast majority of the good people of this earth. The Frank Cooks, the Nick Toppings, even that California bank—they *had* to be aberrations, exceptions, which always pop up, even in the best of classes.

Albert was sitting in the living room reading, as usual, when Doc finally entered their villa.

"Well?" he asked. "Figure a way out?"

"No," was Doc's curt reply.

"So what happens next?"

"We get together with Topping and his pal from that California bank tomorrow, and get the paperwork moving. Then you might just as well take off for Iran, provided the prince can set things up down there immediately."

"And what are you going to be doing, Doc?"

"Just keep thinking, Albert. Until I come up with an angle. Maybe you can help me a bit."

"Sure. How?"

"What's this guy Frank Cook up to?"

"He obviously wants to get that mine out of production immediately."

"Why?"

"To make silver even scarcer than it is right now. The price has gone from $1.29 to almost $2.45 an ounce. If supply gets even tighter, it could go to three dollars and beyond."

"And that's what Cooks wants?"

"Obviously."

"Is this fellow Cook big enough to swing something like that all alone?"

"Provided he keeps the speculators in line."

"Explain that."

"Well, as long as people all over the world think that silver is going to get scarcer and scarcer, they'll keep buying the stuff on the commodity exchanges. But if they think that all of a sudden a lot of new silver could start coming out of the woodwork, wrecking the price, they'll all run for cover. Leaving Mr. Cook holding a great big bag full of silver which will maybe be worth $1.29 an ounce again before long."

"So if people learn about our little mine, that would be bad news for Mr. Cook."

"Obviously. That's why he wants all mention of it deleted from our books."

"Thanks, Albert. You're a smart kid."

"So what are you going to do, Doc?"

"Like I said before. Think."

But while thinking, Doc had to play it straight. Already at 8:30 the next morning he was on the phone to Nick Topping. At eleven he, Albert, and Marvin were back in the Board room of the bank, waiting for the other side to arrive. The prince was busy in his office, trying to get a phone connection with Iran.

Topping and Luckman arrived fifteen minutes late. That was Topping's idea. Luckman, whose apprehension had kept him awake most of the night, felt better almost the minute he entered the Bank of Sicily and America in Switzerland. For he was once again in an atmosphere he felt comfortable with: lines of people in front of tellers' windows, adding machines crackling in the background, marble floors, indirect lighting, hushed voices, dark blue suits.

The man that interested him most after they had arrived at the Board room was Marvin. And when they had been introduced, some of the earlier apprehension returned. No blue suit on Marvin! Plaid jacket, yellow open shirt, green trousers, and white moccasins, topped off by a wide grin.

Topping could not resist taking advantage of a situation like this.

"Marvin," he said, "made any good Swiss money lately?"

Doc liked that.

"Marvin, why don't you show him some samples," he said. "No, don't bother. I've got a few on me." He reached into his pocket for his billfold, extracted a one hundred Swiss franc note, and handed it to Topping. Topping held it up, smelled it, then rubbed it.

"At least it's dry," he commented, "and it sure looks a lot better than some of the dollars Marvin used to turn out."

He turned the bill over. "It's even got a naked gal on the back, big tits and all. And pretty flowers! I can see why you came over here, Marvin. Making Swiss notes must be a lot more fun than drawing pictures of Benjamin Franklin for those hundred dollar bills." Then to Doc: "May I keep it?"

"Sure," replied Doc, "provided you buy me lunch."

"A deal."

"Mr. Luckman," interjected Albert, "I suggest you ignore the horseplay. I understand that you will be responsible for reviewing the books of our bank on behalf of the First National Bank of California."

"That is correct."

"Do you have identification?"

"I do." And he showed it.

"Where would you like to start?"

"I assume that you have regular reports on the bank's status from your Swiss auditors?"

"Yes."

"In what language?"

"Italian. But we have had English translations made —and certified."

"The last audit was when?"

"It was completed about a month ago."

"That should make things easier. I think I'd like to start with them, and then proceed to make spot checks of the important positions."

"I anticipated that. I've arranged for you to have an office on this floor, and our chief accountant will be available to you, for as long as you require, to explain everything."

"I'll need a secretary, who understands English."

"That's also been done. I think it would probably help if I arrange for a circular to be sent to every officer of the bank, stating that you are to have full access to all records. I'm afraid that most of us will be out of town the rest of this week. So we want to be sure that everything you need is done today. Of course, Marvin will be here."

"You mean Mr. Skinner?"

"Yes. In fact, if you agree Mr. Skinner can take you to your office, and get things going for you. O.K., Marvin?"

Mr. Skinner was only too happy to be of service.

Then the phone rang. Doc picked it up, listened for a minute, and hung up.

"That was John. Firdausi's not at home. He's in Teheran. You can get a plane there tomorrow morning. The prince's fixing it up right now. So you'd better get to work on the papers Firdausi's going to have to sign."

Albert departed, leaving Doc and Nick Topping by themselves.

"Nick," said Doc, "too early for that lunch you're going to buy me?"

"Too early to eat, but never too early to drink."

"Do you know the Donatis?"

"No. But I'll trust you, Doc. At least where food's concerned."

It was only five blocks from the bank, so they walked. They took a corner table, a bottle of Frascati, and Doc asked the waiter to put together some antipasto—but there was no hurry. He even managed to do so in Italian.

"You're quite the gracious host, Doc," remarked Topping. "Who taught you the lingo, anyway?"

"The prince."

"He's some character. Where did you find him?"

"I didn't. Joe Fiore did."

"I guess Joe's getting old. But apparently Joe got to you after our little chat yesterday."

"He did."

"So where do we stand?"

"We play ball with you, provided you play ball with us. Simple. And when I say 'you' I don't mean errand boys like yourself, Topping."

"Aha. You know something that you're not telling me, Doc."

"That's right. I know all about who's calling your signals."

"So so. Don't keep me in suspense."

"And one of the new rules of the game is that I deal directly with him."

"Can't be done."

"I would suggest you ask Frank Cook first."

"You're wasting my time, Doc. Mr. Cook has bigger things on his mind than you."

"Albert told me that."

"What did Albert tell you?"

"That your Mr. Cook is trying to cook the silver market."

"And?"

"Maybe he needs to be sure that nobody turns off the gas."

"Like who?"

"Me."

"How?"

"A few phone calls to a few people. About the mysteries of Persia."

"You wouldn't do that, Doc. Joe Fiore would kill you."

"Joe's in Vegas."

"What do you want from Mr. Cook?"

"Maybe a little love and understanding. Plus a contribution to my pension fund."

"You don't need Mr. Cook for that, Doc. Good old Nick here can see if a little charity might not be in place and fix things up."

"I told you before. I don't deal with messenger boys. Where's this Cook hang out, anyway?"

"In England."

"Why?"

"He likes his privacy. That one can get in England, like nowhere else. Doc, tell me something. What are you going to do after this bank thing's over?"

"I haven't given it much thought."

"I take it you're pretty pissed off with the Fiore crowd."

"You take it correctly."

"Maybe we do have something to talk about."

"We including Frank Cook?"

"Yes. I'll find out. In the meantime, Doc, don't do something stupid. I hardly think you want both Joe Fiore and Frank Cook mad at you at the same time. Right?"

"When?"

"Tonight soon enough?"

"It is. A little more wine, Nick?"

"Don't mind if I do, Doc."

That evening Topping did as promised. But Cook only agreed to meet with Doc after it had been confirmed that Firdausi had fallen into line. So it was tentatively agreed that Topping should bring Doc over to England on Thursday. They could meet at Cook's place the following morning—again, provided that the whole deal was on.

Topping telephoned all this to Doc at the villa in Garona. Doc didn't like the delay, but agreed nevertheless. Which gave Frank Cook a few extra days to live.

16

Pan Am has a lot of flights from Europe to Teheran. It's not that there's that many people who want to go there; it's just that Teheran is an ideal fueling stop on the longhaul flights to India, Thailand, Hong Kong, or Singapore, where they load up again before moving on to Japan or Australia.

It's about a four hour trip from Milan, about the same time it takes from New York to Los Angeles. But it's more fun, since the cabin is usually full of rather exotic types: Indian girls in the saris, Japanese in their business suits which never seem to quite fit, Australians with their big mouths, and, in 1968, a smattering of Europeans and Americans off to Southeast Asia to get their fair share of that huge flow of dollars that Uncle Sam was pouring into the area in order to restore clean living among the natives.

The prince and Albert had something less than clean living on their minds as they sat out the hours up front in the 707.

"Albert," asked the prince, for the third time, "are you sure it's going to work?"

"Provided you make sure that Firdausi understands the position we are in."

"But I never told him exactly who you people are. He thinks you are very famous American bankers."

"Now you are going to have to be more exact, John."

"I don't know," replied the prince, slowly shaking his head. "You must understand that the Firdausi family is one of the oldest and most respected in Iran."

"All the more reason for them to cooperate," said Albert. "I hardly think they will want to become involved in a major international scandal which would link them with my father and his friends in Las Vegas." He said this without any sign of regret or bitterness.

"You are right, Albert. At least I hope so." They lapsed into a long period of silence, as the plane hummed its way east. Then:

"Albert, what do you make of Doc?"

"I like him."

"I do too. Very much. But what will he try to do?"

"I frankly do not know."

"Could it be something very bad?"

"I hope not. But with Doc, you can never tell."

"But he is such a kind man, really. At first, I was very afraid of him. But now I am afraid for him." The prince sighed. "Albert, I also talked briefly to the sister."

"The sister?"

"Shireen."

"And?"

"She asked about Doc. Whether or not he would be coming."

"She likes him very much?"

"I'm afraid so. But she has no idea of what type of a man he was."

"People change, you know," said Albert. "You

don't have to tell her everything. What does she expect of Doc?"

"I think she'd like to marry him."

"But that's crazy. Why?"

"She wants to get out of Iran. Women there are still treated like servants. Or worse yet, like they did not even exist. In some parts of the Arab world until a few years ago, a father had a perfect right to kill a new-born baby if it was female."

"That's disgusting."

"They don't do that in Iran. But still—it is no place for a woman like Shireen. She was educated in England, you know. And she wants, desperately, to go back to Europe."

"Then she should go—and leave Doc alone," said Albert. "Have you ever talked to Doc about her?"

"Only once."

"What did he say?"

"Oh, you know Doc. He just told me to mind my own business."

Again a long pause.

"Albert?" It was the prince once more.

"Albert, what do you think I should do after this is over?"

"Can't you find something in Italy?"

"Yes, probably. But it will not be easy for me."

"Why not? With your family background?"

"But that is the trouble. We are regarded as laughable. As ridiculous remnants of the past. As amusing degenerates. I cannot stand that any longer. Do you think maybe Doc could do something?"

"Ask him."

"Albert, I'm afraid to. Would you?"

"Yes, John. But first let's wait and see what happens in Teheran."

Agha Firdausi was waiting for them at the gate. The greetings were perfunctory. There was too much in the air for them to be otherwise.

A Mercedes with driver awaited them outside. He quickly drove them along the broad boulevard named after a local golfing champion: Khiaban-I Eisenhower. In the center of town they swung north along the Khiaban-I Pahlavi. Teheran does not quite measure up to what one expects to find in the mysterious Orient. Squat, uninteresting buildings, skinny trees, the world's most chaotic traffic conditions—Tokyo, of course, excepted. Twenty minutes later they were already on the outskirts of the city. Signs indicated the imminent presence of the inevitable Hilton. But they passed it, as the road gradually began to rise into the foothills of the mountains faintly visible in the night sky. Their destination was the Darband Hotel. Even at night it was dazzling. If Agha Firdausi was out to impress, he was succeeding. The prince and Albert had been given a two-bedroom suite. There were flowers and a huge basket of fruit in each bedroom— compliments of the manager. Firdausi suggested that they meet in the restaurant a bit later. He wanted to get down to business immediately. As yet they had not exchanged one word about silver.

"I don't like the feel of this," Albert stated, once he and the prince were alone upstairs.

"Nor I. It's not like him to be this way," said John.

"I wonder where his sister is?"

"I don't know. And I thought it best not to ask."

"John, would you mind taking the lead with Firdausi?"

"No, Albert. As long as you take over when we get to technical matters."

"Should I bring my briefcase along?"

"I should think so. Either we settle things tonight, or I'm afraid we never shall."

Twenty minutes later they entered the restaurant. Agha Firdausi was awaiting them at a corner table—alone.

He rose to greet them.

"I assumed you must have eaten quite a bit already on the airplane," he said, "so I have taken the liberty of just ordering something light."

The something was caviar, with vodka, and champagne. The glasses had been filled. Firdausi used his vodka glass for a toast: "To our continuing success and friendship!"

The three glasses met. And then embarrassing silence.

"You have problems, Gianfranco?" asked Firdausi.

"Yes we do," replied the prince.

"Serious ones?"

"Yes."

"Then tell me. Now."

The prince did, starting with Joe Fiore, and ending with the prospect that the Swiss banking authorities would close the bank, foreclose on all outstanding debts, including those cosigned by Firdausi himself.

"That would mean," Agha finally said, "that I lose the silver mine."

"Unless you can come up with $20 million within thirty days to pay off those notes," said Albert, speaking up for the first time.

"Where would I get $20 million?" was Firdausi's response. "But," he continued, "there is something I find difficult to understand. Do you mean, Gianfranco, that the bank is owned by a Mafia boss?"

"Yes."

"And Doc is one of them?"

"Yes."

"And Albert here?"

"Yes."

"Why didn't you tell me this in the beginning?"

The prince just shrugged. Albert said nothing. Firdausi slowly shook his head.

"I have been warned many times," Firdausi said, "about doing business with Americans. They smile, they joke, they come with stacks of documents, with lawyers—all very thorough and efficient, yet easygoing. They talk of fairness, of wanting to learn from their foreign partners. They want to be friends, forever. Until everything is signed. Then the surprises start to happen. The lies. The double-crosses."

He turned to the prince. "That you are willing to be part of such, Gianfranco. You should be ashamed of yourself." The last words were spoken bitterly. "Now I shall lose everything. Just like your father did in Sicily. Then I too shall have to become a prostitute like yourself, Gianfranco. And what is to happen to Shireen?"

"One minute, Mr. Firdausi," interrupted Albert. "You do not understand."

Firdausi's voice rose for the first time. "Who are you to tell me I don't understand? You are worse than my cousin. You make a profession of stealing—of taking advantage of the weak. In Iran we shoot people like you."

"Please," interjected the prince, "let him talk, Agha. It is bad, but not nearly as bad as you think."

"Not as bad as I think?" Now Firdausi was shouting. "I lose the property that has been in our family for centuries. I lose a business that was making millions upon millions of dollars. I even lose all the savings which I was stupid enough to entrust to you, Gianfranco, and that Mafia bank of yours."

"Mr. Firdausi," interrupted Albert again. "You are wrong, I would suggest you hear me out."

Firdausi slumped back into his chair. The vodka glasses had been refilled. He emptied his. The prince followed his example.

"Go ahead," he said, quietly this time.

"First, your savings. You deposited five million dollars with us last year."

"Yes."

Albert opened his briefcase.

"I have a check here for five million, five-hundred thousand dollars. It includes full interest. It is a cashier's check issued by the Chase Manhattan Bank in New York—in your name."

Albert showed it to Firdausi, but did not let it leave his hands.

"That is at least something," said Firdausi, grudgingly.

"There is more," replied Albert.

"Go on."

"How much silver is warehoused in Dubai?"

"You know that. I send the warehouse receipts every week."

"Our records indicate 4.1 million ounces."

"That's about right, yes."

"Actually, that silver is our joint property."

"Naturally."

"We propose to turn the entire amount over to you."

"When?"

"Now, if everything else can be adjusted. I have the necessary documents here." Albert pointed to his briefcase.

Firdausi's face brightened for the first time.

"May I see that document?"

"But of course."

Actually, it was nothing but a simple assignment. The warehouse receipts had been attached. The proper signatures, from the Swiss side, were already there.

"That silver is worth about $10 million, at today's prices," said Firdausi.

"Yes."

"That still leaves me five million short of the twenty million I need to pay off those notes. But," Firdausi continued, now flushed, "I can probably borrow that in Kuwait. In fact, I'm sure I can, against the warehouse receipts of the silver in Dubai. Now I see what you meant, Mr. Fiore. I apologize for some of my earlier remarks. All it will mean is that our partnership will be dissolved. My property will once again belong to our family. Completely."

"No," said Albert.

"What did you say?"

"I said no. The property will not belong to your family."

Again Firdausi's voice rose, "I'm afraid, young man, that what I do with my money is my affair."

"It is. But, Mr. Firdausi, you will not have any money, or any silver bullion, unless we give it to you."

"Give! Give! How can you give me my own money?" Again he was shouting.

"Quite simply. We have it. You don't."

So there it was. Right on the table. And Firdausi knew it. He nervously wiped his mouth, then his forehead, with a table napkin.

"What do you want of me?"

"The mine. Which means your entire property in Khuzistan."

"You want me to sell you something that's worth a fortune for $15 million of my own money?"

"The silver's not yours."

"Half of it is. Remember, we're supposed to be partners."

"All right. Have it your way. The situation is still the same. We want full title to that property, in return for $5.5 million cash, and 4.1 million ounces of silver bullion. As we say at home: take it or leave it."

"And if I leave it? Then you will send Doc after me? Isn't that the way you people work?"

Albert picked up his briefcase, and put both the

232

check and the agreement of assignment on the silver bullion back into it. He snapped it closed, and leaned over to put it back down on the floor beside his chair.

From the far side of the room, an orchestra suddenly began playing and at the same moment, the prince leaped to his feet. Albert was startled by all the action. His glasses had slid down his nose, and he wildly tried to push them back up with one hand, seeking to regain his balance with the other, while still protecting his briefcase. Was this to be an Iranian hit?

Hardly. It was Shireen Firdausi. Agha Firdausi was almost as shocked to see her as Albert was relieved. Before anyone could say a word, even the prince, he again shouted:

"Shireen, I thought I told you to stay in your room!"

His sister ignored him completely, as she embraced her cousin.

"Gianfranco. Oh, Gianfranco." And she burst into tears.

The roomful of Iranian big spenders, plus a sprinkling of British expatriates, were getting their money's worth that evening. Women who broke into tears in the middle of dining rooms are appreciated world-wide, especially if they are good looking. And Shireen Firdausi definitely was. But Gianfranco Annunzio di Siracusa was up to any occasion. With a great flourish, he put one arm around Shireen, and with his other waved to the headwaiter, who almost dashed to his side.

"Flowers," he commanded. And somehow, within

seconds, a bouquet appeared, apparently snatched from a free table. The prince seized them from the waiter's hands, and presented them to Shireen with a tremendous bow.

And the tears were replaced by a choking smile.

"You are," she said, "a great big—what do you call it—a great big clown, Gianfranco." And she kissed him.

The audience beamed. Albert gaped. And Agha Firdausi hissed:

"Sit down! Both of you. This is ridiculous!"

"Agha," said the prince, "don't act so damned Iranian. Come, Shireen, we both need a bit of champagne."

Again he put the headwaiter to work. He wanted a bottle of Dom Perignon—not the other whatever it was they had been drinking. And he wanted it now—not in ten minutes.

He also wanted a place set for Shireen—instantaneously—and some more caviar for all. Black, not red. Then he proceeded to chat up Shireen—in French.

Albert's computerized mind had difficulty following all this. At twenty-seven, females were still a total mystery to him, a mystery he was not terribly interested in solving, since, he had long ago concluded, their emotions were simply not reducible to anything even faintly resembling predictable logic. So ignoring all the preceding events, he returned to the business at hand.

"Mr. Firdausi," he said, "I assume you have decided to leave it."

"I have decided to cease discussing it," was the harsh answer.

"Which is exactly the same."

"It is not. I must reflect."

"We do not have that much time."

"How much time do you have?"

"Until the end of the week. No longer."

"You shall have my reply before then. Now if you will excuse my sister and myself." Firdausi rose abruptly, so abruptly his chair fell over.

"Come," he said to his sister.

Her face turned from the prince to his.

"Please, Agha," she said, "don't. What has gotten into you?"

He roughly grabbed her hand and pulled her to her feet.

"We go," he said.

Again the prince intervened: "If you want to go, Agha, go. But I intend to dance with Shireen."

What ensued was a brief tug-of-war, with Shireen in the middle, until Agha, redfaced with embarrassment and slightly puffing from exertion, let go. And when the pair moved off, he just glared after them, immobile.

"Mr. Firdausi," said Albert. "Please sit down again. Gianfranco means well."

Now Albert got the glare. But it is difficult to hate Albert for very long, especially when his glasses are perched precariously near the tip of his nose, as they were once again.

So Firdausi picked up his chair and sat on it. Stiffly.

"It's disgusting."

"What is?"

"The habits you people have brought to our country. Just look at the display those women are making of themselves!"

To be sure, a number of mini-skirts were flouncing rather high as the orchestra beat out the Persian version of "Strangers in the Night." The prince and Shireen, both tall, with equally black hair, dominated the scene on the dance floor with their grace of movement, and striking good looks.

"At least Gianfranco is a gentleman of the old school," admitted Firdausi.

"You are closely related?" asked Albert, trying to calm the waters.

"It is none of your business, actually," replied Firdausi. "But the answer is no. It goes a long way back, and is very complicated. You would not understand these things."

The music continued, and so did Shireen and Gianfranco.

"Another vodka?" suggested Agha, grudgingly. Albert could hardly stand the stuff, but he agreed.

"At least," Firdausi said, "she will finally get that Doc off her mind now."

Albert decided to let that one pass.

"Mr. Fiore," began Firdausi anew. "Is all that you have been telling me true?"

"Please call me Albert. And the answer is yes. It is true."

"Who is behind all this?"

"An extremely powerful group. So powerful that

236

even we can do nothing about it. That is not my conclusion. It is the conclusion of my father."

"Who are they?"

"I am not in a position to say. I'm sorry. But that's the way it is."

"They are in the silver business?"

"Yes."

"They are criminals?"

"In a sense, yes."

"If I agree to your proposal, what happens then?"

"We want mine output stopped immediately."

"Stopped?" said Firdausi, "but that is crazy!"

"Perhaps," replied Albert. "But that is what they want. It would mean that you would have to go down there right away and make the necessary arrangements. With the prince."

"So. To make sure I don't double-cross you, I assume."

"Yes."

"And Gianfranco has agreed to this? To do this to me and Shireen?"

"Yes. He also has no choice. But he agrees with me that it is the best, in fact the only, way out for you. And Shireen."

"Do you realize this means that we must move out of our home, put many many people out of work—men whose families have been faithful to us for generations?"

"They will have work again when the mine is reopened."

"And when will that be?"

Albert just shrugged.

Agha took yet another glass of vodka. Iranians, like Russians, thrive on the stuff.

"What else would I have to sign?"

"Sign?"

"If I agree to your proposal."

Albert reached down once again to his briefcase, and extracted a new document.

"Just this," he said, and handed it to Firdausi. It was thick.

Firdausi flipped a few pages, and put it back on the table.

"What is it?"

"A release."

"A what?"

"It says, in about a hundred different ways, that you will never sue us. In Switzerland, Iran, or anywhere else on this globe. Ever."

"I see. You thought I would?"

Again Albert just shrugged.

"Show me those other papers."

"You mean the assignment of the silver?"

"Yes. And the check."

Albert showed them, and this time let Firdausi pick up the $5.5 million check.

Firdausi read the check, once, then again, and yet again. His hand then wiped across his face. It was damp. Then yet another vodka—straight down.

He reached inside his jacket. For a pen.

"Where do I sign?" he asked.

"Here," said Albert, "and here."

Firdausi signed. And just as he had attached the second signature, the music, finally, stopped. The sweat glistened on his forehead. Shireen and the prince both stared at him when they reached the table after leaving the dance floor.

"Agha," exclaimed his sister, "what is wrong?"

"Nothing, my dear. Nothing. It is over."

"What are you talking about?"

"I have sold everything. We are—we are now gypsies, like Gianfranco."

"Agha, are you sick?" Not only was her brother bathed in sweat, he was now white as a sheet.

"No, my dear. Let me be. I will explain everything later. While you pack."

"Pack? Whatever for?"

"Because we are leaving for Abadan in the morning."

Her face clouded.

"And Gianfranco is coming with us," Firdausi continued. "Come. Sit down both of you. We still have much champagne and caviar. And there is still time to dance. Let us speak of other things." They did. At least he did, explaining that he loved poetry. Especially that of Omar Khayyám. And with the help of a few more vodkas, he began to recite, first in the original, then in English. Albert listened carefully, as Albert always did.

The next morning all four went to the airport. Albert boarded a nonstop BOAC flight to London. The prince, Agha, and Shireen took Iranian Flight Number 7: Teheran—Abadan—Kuwait—Dubai.

None of them got off the plane in Abadan.

17

When Albert arrived in London, he went directly from the airport to the hotel. He then made two short phone calls. The first was to his father in Las Vegas, who did little more than grunt as Albert explained what had happened. All that was now required, Albert explained, was that someone bring the shares of the Bank of Sicily and America—every one of them—to London. Against delivery—now that the bank owned 100% of the silver mine—Albert could collect $60 million. The shares would be sent immediately. By hand, his father said. From where, and by whom, he did not say. Joe Fiore disliked telephones. Anything new from Doc? No. Better talk to him, his father advised. And tell him that if he fucked things up now, he was in big trouble. "Got that Albert?"

"Yes, father."

"And when you get that money, keep it in England. You hear? Maybe you can find a way to use it."

"Yes, father."

"You're a good boy, Albert."

"Yes, father."

Then Albert called Doc. Was everything going on schedule in Switzerland? It was, more or less. That twit Luckman was taking everything a bit seriously, but it appeared as if his audit report would be done by the weekend.

"What happened in Iran, Albert?"

"Firdausi agreed. I have all the signed documents with me."

"That's great. That means that we now own that silver mine, lock, stock and barrel?"

"For the moment, yes. I just talked to my father, Doc."

"And?"

"He's sending the shares over. And he asked me to tell you not to interfere."

"He said that I would have ten days."

"I know."

"Well, they're not up yet."

"Doc, my father sounded quite firm."

"I don't give a goddam how he sounded."

Albert said nothing.

"Albert, where are you talking from?"

"The Carlton Tower."

"Where's that?"

"The West End. On Cadogan Square."

"Fix me up a room starting Thursday night."

"Just for you?"

"Yes. Luckman can make his own arrangements. So can Topping."

"What about Marvin?"

"He's staying here. To close up the house in Garona."

"What about the dog?"

"The what?"

"Ringo."

"How the fuck should I know. It's you and your father who seem to have everything figured out."

Again Albert kept silent.

"One more thing, Albert. Is the prince doing what he's supposed to do?"

"Yes. He went down to Khuzistan this morning."

"You're sure those agreements you've got from Firdausi are airtight?"

"Yes."

"O.K. Albert. I'll see you at the end of the week."

At six the next evening, the hall porter telephoned Albert in his room. Someone had left a large package for him. Should he have it brought up? Yes.

It was a large cardboard box. Inside were hundreds of engraved certificates. Each certificate was in lieu of 100 shares of the Bank of Sicily and America. They were, it was printed, the property of the bearer. Their value? Provided everything went well, 60 million dollars.

Albert pushed the box into the closet. Then he went down to the Rib Room. They serve the best roast beef in London there. And Albert liked roast beef.

It was Thursday, May 12, 1968, when Doc boarded the Alitalia flight for London. The airlines had not yet gotten around to installing their fancy detection devices, so Doc was not at all concerned about the fact that he had a .32 pistol strapped inside his jacket. He was concerned that Donald Luckman had brought his wife with him. He had sat beside her in the back seat of the limo all the way to the airport. They had exchanged but a few polite words. But it was impossible to avoid constant physical contact as the car wove its way down the Autostrada from Lugano, to the Milan airport. Donald Luckman had said even less. He'd just nervously clutched his briefcase in his lap. It held the audit report which would recommend that the First National Bank of California buy a small bank in Lugano for sixty million dollars. The man who had made it possible, Nick Topping, had occupied the front seat, and had further occupied himself with a running commentary on Italian drivers. He was the only one that seemed happy.

He was still happy in the airplane, as it proceeded across the Alps toward England.

"Say," he said to Doc who sat beside him, "that Debbie Luckman is something else."

"I hadn't noticed," replied Doc.

"But her husband!" continued Topping. "I think he's going to have a heart attack before this is all over. Did you read his report?"

"Partially."

"Actually, you guys put together a pretty good bank there. But the best reading was about that phoney stuff Marvin put together. Christ, he's really good. And I like his grin. We could probably use somebody like him."

"Yeah," said Doc, "couldn't we all."

"What's your problem, anyway, Doc? You said that Albert had wrapped everything up down in Iran. You haven't got a worry in the world now."

"Oh no?"

"Look, forget about that bank. And the Fiores. I've set up that meeting with Mr. Cook. He's going to like you."

"For when?"

243

"Tomorrow morning. At ten."

"Where?"

"His place."

"Where's that?"

"In the country."

"How'll I get there?"

"I'll take you. Where are you staying?"

"The Carlton Tower."

"I'll pick you up at nine. O.K.?"

"Yeah. If something happens, where can I reach you."

"At Mr. Cook's place."

"Got his telephone number?"

"Sure. You have to call long distance from London. Place called Marlowe. In Buckinghamshire. Number's 86083. Got that?"

Doc got it, and wrote it down on the back of his airplane ticket.

Then he got up to stretch his legs. Donald Luckman immediately joined him in the aisle.

"Are you sure those shares will be in London?" he asked.

"I told you so, didn't I?" was the surly response.

"Well, they'd better be. Mr. Foreman is coming tomorrow from San Francisco, and he expects to close this deal in the afternoon."

"How come you're so eager, all of a sudden?"

"I'm not eager. I just want to make sure. Now, we expect you to be at Winthrop's Bank with the shares, and with proof of 100% ownership of that, uh, property in Iran. At three."

"Otherwise Mr. Foreman is going to spank you, right?"

"He wants everything reconfirmed tomorrow. You should call me at my hotel at two."

"Yes, sir. Anything else?"

After which Doc returned to his seat. He didn't even bother to say goodbye to anyone after passing through customs. He called Albert when he arrived at the hotel. They drank one Scotch at the bar.

Doc told Albert what the schedule was. Three at Winthrop's Bank. On Lombard Street. He should bring the shares, which he assumed Albert had. Albert had.

"I'll meet you in the lobby here at 2:30," said Doc, after he had paid the bar bill.

"Why don't we have breakfast or at least lunch together?"

"Because I'm going to be busy."

"Oh?"

"And Albert, if something comes up, you can give me a call at this number." He handed him the ripped off corner of an airplane ticket.

"Doc, you're not . . ."

"Albert, go to bed. It's a big day tomorrow."

Albert did so, but had great trouble falling asleep. Not Doc.

Long ago he had learned that a good night's rest was indispensable before a job.

To get to Buckinghamshire from Knightsbridge is easy. Cross Hyde Park past the Serpentine, then circle the Royal Lancaster Hotel and proceed a few blocks north to Western Avenue. Then a left, direction Oxford, down the A 40. First it's a row of factories, but slowly it thins out, and suddenly you are in the middle of the green and pleasant countryside which is uniquely English.

"How long a drive is it?" asked Doc.

"An hour. Not even, at this time of day," was Topping's reply.

"How come Cook lives way out there?"

"He likes his privacy."

By 9:30 they had reached Gerrards Cross, and a few miles later approached Beaconsfield. Then a left took them toward the Thames valley.

"Hey, Topping. How come they call this Buckinghamshire?"

"Damned if I know."

"Say, you drive pretty good on the wrong side of the road."

"Practice, my friend. You'll catch on a lot quicker than you think."

"What makes you think I plan on staying that long?"

"You'll stay." They sped on.

"Nick," continued Doc, after a long pause, "where's the airport from here?"

"What do you want to know that for?"

"Maybe I'll want to settle down here after all."

"You could pick worse spots. Actually, Heathrow is very near. If you head back toward London you just have to take a right at the traffic signal in Gerrards Cross. Down Windsor Road."

"And then?"

"Just stay on it until you get to Slough. There you

pick up the M4, and you're at the airport in ten minutes."

Closer than I figured, thought Doc. The only problem is when, and where to after that. I'll have to get out of Europe, that's for sure. And stay away from the States for a while too, until Joe cools off.

"Frank Cook must have a lot of people in that house of his?"

"What makes you think that?" countered Topping.

"He runs a big show, right?"

"Sure. But not from his home. He's just got an old bag of a secretary. Ugly. Talks like she's got marbles in her mouth. And a chauffeur, who's also the gardener."

"That's all?"

"I told you. Frank Cook likes his privacy. He comes into the offices in London about twice a month. For maybe two or three hours. He likes to use the telephone. Well, we're almost here."

"I thought you said it was on the river?"

"It is. Just hold your horses a minute, Doc. What are you so nervous about all of a sudden?"

I've got my reasons, thought Doc.

The car was already in the outskirts of Marlowe, when it swung left down a narrow, hedged lane. At the end of the lane were huge gates, and on either side of the gates, high brick walls. Topping left the car running, and repeatedly pushed a button mounted below a loudspeaker, imbedded in the wall to the left. A loud bell sounded three times. A few minutes later a stocky man in gardener's clothing appeared.

"Mr. Topping, sir," he said. "Is the Gov'nor expecting you?"

"He is, Henry."

"I'll let him know you're here." He picked up a phone from a wooden box mounted on the other side of the gate, said a few words, hung up, and without any further conversation unlocked the gates and swung them open.

"Thanks, Henry," yelled Topping, as they passed through. Almost immediately the gates began to close.

Not quite as easy as Topping pretended, thought Doc, as he observed every move. But still—easy enough.

Topping pulled up the Ford Cortina beside a grey Daimler in the large area at the side of the house, adjacent to the stables. The smell of freshly mown grass filled the air as the two men stepped out. It was quiet. No dogs, Doc noted.

"You want to see the river, right?"

"Why not," replied Doc, "as long as it's there."

It was there, he found out, separated from the back of the mansion by a vast expanse of lawn and gardens. The Thames at this point more resembled the Avon than the huge dirty river one is used to from London. It was Friday, so for many English the weekend had already started. Having picked up their rented motor launches at Maidenhead, or perhaps Bourne End, they were wending their way up toward Oxford, navigating lock after lock with some difficulty, but trying to give the impression that every Englishman is a born sailor.

"Nice," commented Doc.

"Yeah," said Topping.

Which took care of the tourist end of things. It was a very bright day, so Doc put on his sun glasses. This proved to be a mistake. Because when he followed Topping through the curtained French doors which led into the house from the terrace at the rear, he could not see a thing. Not only was it dark, but cold as well. He shivered.

Topping looked at his watch.

"We're two minutes early. Take a seat."

Sun glasses off, and with eyes rapidly adjusting, Doc quickly scanned the room. It was vast, heavily carpeted, lined with objects of art varying from vases on pedestals to massively framed oil paintings. The only lighting in the place came from a large glassed-in cabinet in one corner. Doc decided not to sit down, but to walk over and investigate.

"Gawd," was his comment. "Is it all real?"

"The jade? Sure. Mr. Cook has one of the best collections in the world. Bought most of it from Farouk after they kicked him out of Egypt. He says he paid less than a million dollars for it then. Who knows what it's worth today."

The door at the far end of the room opened. A very thin middle-aged woman emerged.

"Mister Cook will see you now," she articulated. Topping was right, thought Doc. She sounds like she's got a mouthful of crumpets.

Topping led the way. The first impression Doc had was of books. Thousands and thousands of them lining the wall. Then the fireplace. Not the usual coal-burning affair, but one which contained a roaring wood fire. It provided the only light in the room. There were obviously windows, but they had been heavily curtained. In front of the curtains was a massive oak desk, with not a paper on it. Behind the desk sat Frank Cook.

He was thin. His hair was white, and combed straight back. He wore a blue jacket, with silver buttons down the front and on each sleeve. But all this seemed to merely provide a setting for the dominant feature: his eyes. They actually glinted. No doubt it was only the mirror effect, produced by the darting flames from the fireplace. But they were eyes which one never forgot. Nor the eyebrows. Heavy, like those of Ben-Gurion. Completely white. The eyelids were half-closed. And they stayed that way. For a full minute Frank Cook's gaze held Doc, unblinkingly. And Doc stood there as if mesmerized.

"Be seated. No. Here." Frank Cook's hand motioned toward two chairs directly opposite his desk. The voice was flat. Not English. Not American. But also not showing any traces of continental origin. As Doc took the chair which had been assigned to him, he noticed two further things. Cook's right hand remained out of sight. And when seated, his head was a good foot higher than the level of his visitors.

"Mr. Smythe. You wanted to see me. What about?"

"The silver mine at Choga Zambil."

"Yes?"

"We now own it. One hundred percent."

"And?"

"I propose we deal directly."

"Spell it out."

"Call off the First National Bank of California."

"Then?"

"Then we continue with our banking business in Switzerland as before. And we give you half of that mine. For nothing. You can run it. We'll just stay on as silent partners."

"So. You are offering me something for nothing. Is that it?"

"Yes."

"But you are also taking away something for nothing. The other half of the mine which you want to retain."

"Incorrect. You will have to pay almost one hundred million dollars for ownership of that mine. My way, you will not have to invest one nickel."

"What's that mine worth?"

"Probably a quarter of a billion."

"Half of a quarter of a billion is one eighth of a billion. That's what you expect me to give you."

"Yes, if you put it that way. As I said, you are going to have to pay out almost a hundred million as it is. The difference between one-eighth billion and one hundred million is small. And we, as your partners, take half the risk off your hands. You must admit, there is risk in any mining venture. Even this one."

"Smythe, you're good. Very good. But the answer is no. Not because what you say doesn't make sense. It does. But it conflicts with the one basic rule I have always followed in business. Always. Do you want to know what it is?"

Doc did not reply.

"I will tell you," continued Cook. The whole time the only movement from behind the desk was provided by his lips. His head, his hand, his body—all remained completely immobile. And his eyes kept boring in, unrelenting. "No partners. Ever. Including now. And including you. That's final."

Doc hesitated for no more than two seconds. "As I understand it then—you'd rather be dead than have me as a partner."

"Mr. Smythe," replied Cook, "if you have nothing further to add, you probably should leave."

Nick Topping sat about four feet to the right of Doc, sunk well down into his chair. Frank Cook was about ten feet away, almost dead ahead. The secretary had disappeared. The room, with its unbroken line of book cases on both sides, the heavily curtained windows at the end, would be as soundproof as one could wish for. And the gardener was hardly standing right outside.

The phone rang. Frank Cook let it ring, not taking his eyes off of Doc for one second. Doc stared right back. Topping, puzzled by what was going on, finally couldn't take it any longer.

"The phone," he said. For the first time, Frank Cook looked at Topping.

"Take it." As Topping rose, Cook's eyes went back to Doc. A very light smile crossed his face.

Topping barely had the phone in his hands when he swung around, with an utterly surprised look on his face.

"Doc, it's for you. Albert."

As Doc got up to take the receiver, Frank Cook's right arm moved slightly. But the hand remained out of sight. Doc's senses were at a screaming pitch. Unless he kept control of himself, he'd blow everything. Because somehow Frank Cook seemed to know.

He put the receiver to his ear and listened. For three minutes—one hundred and eighty long seconds—without saying a word. Then:

"Yes, Albert, I heard. I understand." With that, he carefully hung up. And as he sunk back into his chair, his features seemed to shrink. His face was ashen. His hands shook.

"Bad news, Mr. Smythe?" Cook's eyes had not missed a thing.

"Yes. I'm afraid I have been wasting your time."

"Your partners double-crossed you?"

"You could say that, yes."

"So you see what I meant just a few minutes ago. Never, never have partners."

Now his right hand appeared on top of the desk. It held a Smith and Wesson .45. A small cannon.

"Anyway," continued Cook, "what you had in mind would never have worked. But I admire you for considering it."

The hand reached to the right and opened a drawer. It deposited the .45 and closed the drawer silently.

"Smythe, I want to talk to you when this is over," said Cook. "You're all that Topping said you were. And a lot more. I think we could work together. Though not as partners." Frank Cook stood up suddenly, and extended his hand.

Doc also rose, seemed to think it over, and then grasped it, firmly.

"Mr. Cook," he said, "you win. I guess you're used to winning. But sometime, somebody's bound to get you. In the meantime, I'll think over your offer."

Then to Topping "Let's get the fuck out of here."

Topping looked to Frank Cook, and got the nod.

The sunlight almost blinded Doc when they emerged from the house. Neither Topping nor he spoke a word to each other until they were halfway back to London. Finally Topping broke the silence.

"Doc, are you really carrying a shooter?"

"Yes."

"You crazy son-of-a-bitch."

"So crazy I'm not, especially with you around. But if that phone hadn't rung, I would have been back there."

"You sure are a crazy son-of-a-bitch. But Mr. Cook likes you, just like I told you he would."

Topping dropped Doc at the Carlton Tower. Doc went straight to the bar and had a drink. Then another. At 2:30 he met Albert in the lobby. Albert had a large cardboard box in his arms. At three they entered the venerable old London merchant bank, Winthrop's.

Sir Robert Winthrop himself was there to greet them. The others had already arrived. They were waiting upstairs. George Foreman, Chairman of the First National Bank of California did not bother to rise when they entered the room. So neither did Donald Luckman. In fact, Foreman chose to ignore the presence of both Doc and Albert completely. Without even glancing at them he asked Sir Robert whether everyone was present. Winthrop was used to eccentric behavior, having been a merchant banker for almost forty years, he just let his eyes move from one person to the next, deliberately, and announced that yes, it would seem so.

Then he solemnly intoned his thanks that both parties had chosen his bank to act as the escrow agent in this transaction. Winthrop's, in its 329-year history, had provided a helping hand to many a deal which had, later, been looked back upon as financial milestones. It was especially a pleasure to be acting on behalf of two such venerable banks as the First National of California, and the Bank of Sicily and America. The fact that the latter was as unvenerable as banks come didn't seem to bother him in the least.

The next act lasted less than five minutes. First, Albert opened his cardboard box and stacked certificates, each worth 100 shares of the Bank of Sicily and America, on the table. Luckman came over to that side of the table, examined a few of the certificates, gave a look of satisfaction to his boss, and again took his place.

"Satisfied?" asked Sir Robert.

"Yes," answered George Foreman.

Then Foreman extracted a simple cashier's check in the amount of $60,000,000 and no cents from the briefcase which Donald Luckman helped him open.

"As I understand it," said Sir Robert after the check had been handed to him, "the sixty million is to be deposited to a joint sight account in the names of

Mr. Joseph L. Fiore and Mr. Albert P. Fiore. Is that correct, gentlemen?"

Albert said "Yes."

"And both parties agree," continued Sir Robert, "on the condition of the object which is herewith changing hands." He waved a copy of Donald Luckman's audit report on the Swiss bank which had been lying on the table in front of him since the start of the proceedings.

Both Foreman and Fiore said yes at the same time.

Sir Robert beamed. "Now I will call in two of my assistants who have the documentation prepared for signature. I assume both parties are now prepared to execute them?"

Both parties were. And did.

After Sir Robert had mumbled his final benediction, Doc and Albert rose to shake hands all around the conference table. But as they approached George Foreman, he abruptly turned his back. So Donald Luckman did the same, leaving Doc and Albert with nothing more to do but leave.

Thus it was that at 3:35 on Friday, May 13, the banking careers of Doc Smythe and Albert Fiore came to a rather ignominious end.

"Bastards," said Doc, as they climbed into a taxi in Lombard Street. But he had the widest of possible grins on his face when he said it.

A half hour later, after the obligatory sherry with Sir Robert, George Foreman and Donald Luckman also left the bank. Their spirits were high as their opulent Bentley took them back toward the not so opulent London Hilton.

Next stop was Foreman's suite on the top floor of the hotel, but Luckman got off first on the 12th floor. He wanted to pick up his wife and a dossier. He found the dossier, but not the wife. Because, as he found out a few minutes later, she was up in the Foremans' suite. And everybody was once again back on the Debbie and Marjory, George and Donald basis. George was playing bartender.

"My boy," he said, "you have done a truly remarkable job. That audit report was a masterpiece."

Donald blushed, and muttered something appropriate. Then he handed Foreman the dossier he had just picked up. "I thought you should have this right away. It will provide the basis for the closing with Frank Cook on Wednesday." Foreman glanced at it.

"Aha," he said, "the silver mine."

"Yes. It contains the full geologist's survey, plus a rundown on the week to week development of the mine. Output, refining throughput, shipments. Stuff I really don't know that much about."

"Has Frank Cook also got this?"

"Yes. His man Topping copied everything earlier this week. I'm sure Mr. Cook has had ample time to study it."

"Well, I'll do the same, Donald, because this time, I'll have to handle things alone."

"Oh?"

"Yes. I want you to get back to Lugano immediately. Or at least by tomorrow. You're boss of that bank, now, and I want you to make that quite clear to everyone right away Monday morning. The first thing you must do is change that name. By the way, have all of those crooks given their resignations?"

"As I understand it, they have been left with a man named Marvin Skinner. In Lugano."

"Well, get them. And get that Skinner out of there. I don't want any of them to ever show their faces in that bank again."

"Yes, sir."

Marjory's nasal voice cut in. "George," she said, "that's enough business. You hear?"

"Yes, Marjory."

"Except for one thing. Debbie is not going to Switzerland. She's staying here in London with me for a while. Isn't that right, dear?"

Debbie nodded.

"You see, George, while you men were working, we've been busy too. Planning. Tonight we're all going out. We've got four tickets to the *Sound of Music*. Isn't that marvelous? And tomorrow night we're going to the Black and White Minstrel Show. You know how I love serious music, George. On Monday, Debbie and I are going shopping, first Harrod's then . . ." And on she droned.

Debbie just sat there, sipping gin. She continued doing so during the intermission at the theatre. And also at the dinner, which followed the show. At Trader Vic's. Marjory Foreman had insisted they eat there, since she knew Vic back home, and also knew how thrilled he would be to hear that they had eaten at his place in London. By the time Debbie got to bed she was bombed. The next morning, Saturday, she didn't even hear her husband leave for the airport. At noon she telephoned Marjory Foreman. She felt awful, she reported. Probably too much excitement. She planned on just cooping herself up for twenty-four hours to recover.

Marjory understood.

"Have a good rest, my dear," she said. "You know how much George and I love you. You just take care of yourself. And when you feel better, just call or leave a message."

During the next hours Debbie did call. But not Marjory. She telephoned at least fifteen times, to one London luxury hotel after the other. Until she finally found Doc Smythe. He arrived an hour later.

They spent twenty-three of the next twenty-four hours in bed; the other hour they ate: a huge platter of Scottish smoked salmon, two dozen snails, accompanied by a magnum of Veuve Cliquot. Room service protested that it would be next to impossible to cook snails at ten on Sunday morning. But the promise of a dollar a snail gratuity produced almost instant garlic. At noon Debbie and Doc went back to bed, after she had left a telephone message for Marjory, not to expect to see her until Monday.

Albert Fiore also spent the entire weekend in his hotel room. With an electronic calculator.

18

The next day, Monday, May 16, 1968, will be remembered by a lot of silver speculators. By some
fondly, but by most with more than a slight shudder.
For that was the day when silver rose to the highest
level thus far in the twentieth century: $2.64 an
ounce. And if you would have taken a poll of investors, whether in New York, Chicago, London, or
Zurich—in fact, anywhere where the smart money
boys either lived or operated—you would have ended
up with a remarkable consensus: the price could only
go in one direction in the future. Up!

At this juncture, the smart money boys were not
alone. They had been joined by half the crackpots in
the United States, as well as a few from abroad, all
trying to make a fortune in silver. And they were
succeeding!

Like Albert had predicted, after the market slump
in January and February, when the price had retreated
to $2.00 an ounce, a revival had set in. A new bull
market got under way. Back to $2.10, then $2.20, up
to $2.35, then $2.50. A new high. Wow! The word
spread: Don't fool around in the stock market. Go
where the action is. Commodities! Buy a silver futures
contract for 10,000 ounces. At $2.00 an ounce, it
represented $20,000 worth of action. And all yours!
Well, not exactly. Because the smart investor buys on
margin. Just put down 10% with your friendly broker,

just $2,000, and the 10,000 ounces are still more or less, all yours. But it is not like a charge account at Sears, or Diners Club. Here you get the real thing—precious metal! Not a crummy washing machine that wears out. Or a fleeting vacation for two in rainy Bermuda. No. Silver bullion. It lasts forever. And talk about performance! Those 10,000 ounces you bought in February at $2.00 an ounce are worth $25,000 in May at $2.50 an ounce. You just got yourself a $5,000 profit in two months on a lousy $2,000 investment. That's 150% in two months. That's 75% a month. That's 18¾% a week; that's 2.68% a day! By Christmas you may be rich. All silver had to do was to go up to $3.00 an ounce.

If it went to $5.00 you'd be filthy rich. At $10 an ounce you could retire!

How could one lose? Because the experts all were saying: the world's running out of silver. Consumption was growing; production was stagnant; stockpiles were dwindling. The price *had* to go up.

Of such are American dreams made. Because the entire essence of America is the hope to first make money—then make money with money—then make lots of money with lots of money. The Germans, the Japanese, the Swiss are, of course, not very far behind in this regard these days. But in the beginning you first have to have that big break. Saving will get you nowhere. Mutual funds are too slow—you might just as well buy life insurance. Stocks? You win some, you lose some, and that's about all. Bonds? Forget it! What is necessary is that first big hit. The one that converts the thousands into ten thousands into hundred thousands. Then, hell, once you're working with digits like that, easy street is just around the corner.

That's the dream of the fellows who follow the ponies, and those who play the numbers. And those who rob banks. But that's all for the working classes. The educated man uses his brains, capitalizes on his education, takes advantage of his connections, studies his charts, researches his fundamentals, calls his broker, and goes on margin. In the commodities market. With soybeans, wheat, frozen orange juice, plywoods, pork bellies. One works with the exotica of the investment world. *That* is not for peons. Oh, no. It is for dentists, airline pilots, IBM salesmen, the men of distinction who own McDonald's franchises.

And in the spring of 1968 the word was out. Buy silver futures today, and tomorrow will be yours. Teeth decayed, airline schedules were disrupted, computers went haywire, hamburgers went without onions, as men throughout America became mesmerized with the silver price. Up two points! That's another two thousand in the bank. Limit up! That's ten points, ten more cents an ounce, ten thousand more profit. All in one day! So buy another contract with the profits. And yet another. On margin. It was a chance in a lifetime to really score. And after that, the easy life.

All that had to happen was that the price of silver kept going up. Which it did.

For one more day. Then it got zapped.

The beginning of the end of the Great Silver Bull Market occurred in London on the morning of May 16, at 9 A.M. sharp. Albert Fiore, accompanied by Doc Smythe, were the first customers of Winthrop's

Bank. Their request was unusual. They wanted to withdraw sixty million dollars. Immediately. They had to wait until 10:15 for Sir Robert Winthrop to arrive. Only he could handle something like this. Upsmanship is the name of the game in merchant banking. So when the request was repeated his response was an unhesitating, "No problem." Of course, it was not taken out in cash. Instead telegraphic transfers were made to a dozen different banking institutions around the world: to the Bahamas, the Cayman Islands, Liechtenstein, Luxembourg, Liberia, Beirut, Singapore, Hong Kong. What with time zones and banks being as slow as they are, Albert could not start spending any of this money, which, technically, belonged to his father, although it was a joint account, until the next day. But he and Doc could lay the ground work. They did by visiting four commodity brokerage houses. All of these operated in both London and New York. One had a direct line with Chicago, another specialized in the exotic markets of the Near and Far East. They all had one thing in common: none worked with Frank Cook or any of his organizations.

The next day, May 17, was sunny and warm, a day when it felt really good to be alive and well in England. At eleven, Doc Smythe and Albert Fiore took a taxi from the Carlton Tower to the City of London. Their destination was Whittington Avenue. At first they had the driver puzzled, something most difficult to accomplish with cabbies in London. Then he remembered: it was that short street that led off Cornhill to the Leadenborough produce market.

It turned out to be a picturesque corner of London, with its narrow passage, open-air stalls, and old-fashioned shops, among them: A. Cook Purveyor of Choice Fruits and Vegetables; Filters High Class Butchers; Ashdown Oysters; and The Lamb Tavern. Most peculiarly, right in the middle of all this, mounted on a high pole, is a wooden plaque citing the Bye-laws, Rules, Orders and Regulations of the Leadenhall Market, number 20 of which reads:

It shall be the duty of the Clerk of the Market to remove or cause to be removed from the market any person whom he shall find engaged in betting or whom he shall have reason to believe frequents the said market for the purpose of betting, or to be a reputed thief, or an idle or disorderly person, or a rogue and vagabond, and any such person resisting his removal shall be liable to a penalty not exceeding £5.

This is peculiar since the London Metal Exchange is situated not more than twenty yards away, a place where some of the most sophisticated rogues on earth practice their art of gambling on a scale which would make even the elder statesmen among croupiers in Las Vegas cringe in fear. Millions upon millions of pounds are "placed" daily, on bets that the prices of world metals—copper, tin, lead, zinc, and silver—will go up, if the bettor is a bull, or down, if the bettor is a bear. The biggest action in this May of 1968 was, of course in silver. And almost all the bettors were bulls.

The LME, as it is fondly known to gamblers world-wide, prides itself on being located on the site of the old Roman Forum. It has no sign above its entrance, just a simple metal plaque beside the modest doorway. Visitors are only allowed in with the permission of the secretariat, provided they are sponsored by one of the members of the exchange.

The arrangements which made it possible for Doc and Albert to attend that day had been done so discreetly that no sponsor was put into the register. They were simply guests of the house. Silver is traded between the hours of 12:05 and 12:10 in the first morning session, then again between 13:00 and 13:05. The buyers and sellers scream offers at each other in a completely demented fashion during these five minutes, and out of it emerges a set price at which silver changes hands—the so-called silver fixing, which is determined by a committee of three members who seek to match up all the buy and sell orders at a "fair" price. Whatever happens in the morning in the LME in London sets the price pattern that is followed around the world during the next 24 hours—first in New York, Chicago, San Francisco, then Hong Kong and beyond.

During the first session, the silver price leaped up a final time. One broker—known by everyone on the ring to be the representative of the Frank Cook group—was the major cause. He was buying all the silver in sight, it seemed. The price hit $2.70. The experts concurred that the next stop on the way up would be at least $3.00 an ounce.

But at the 13:00 session, four huge sellers appeared. They weren't selling physical silver. They were selling silver for future delivery—well, well into the future. In the afternoon sessions—at 15:55 and again at 16:30 it was the same story. Frank Cook's broker was the buyer; those same four brokers were the sellers. The price stalled. It never went beyond that $2.70 mark.

The next day, it, in fact, retreated to $2.60 an ounce in the first fixing.

Doc and Albert were there again to watch the action, standing quietly in the far corner of the trading room. Just after the bell had rung at 12:05, announcing the beginning of the first round of trading, another guest arrived on the floor: Mr. Nicholas Topping. He took a beeline toward Doc.

"What the fuck are you guys doing here?" he demanded.

"The language!" replied Doc.

"You heard," stated Topping, almost shaking with anger.

"Heard what?"

"Come on, don't give me that stuff again, Doc."

"Look, Topping, I'm not giving you anything. What happened?"

"That son-of-a-bitch is pulling a fast one."

"Which son-of-a-bitch," inquired Doc, delicately.

"The fucking Chairman of that fucking California bank."

"What'd he do?"

"We had agreed to finalize the purchase of that silver property this morning. At ten. Right?"

"If you say so, Nickie."

"He backed off. He wants double the price agreed to with Mr. Cook. *Double!*"

"Too bad."

"Too bad! You know damn well it's more than just too bad. We've got our necks stuck way out in this silver market, on the long side and we're acquiring more every day."

"Yes, we heard."

"We also heard something. You bastards started selling yesterday."

"What makes you think that?"

"Want me to tell you the names of the brokers, and exactly how much each has done for you during the past 24 hours?"

"Nick, the lack of discretion in professional circles in England these days is appalling. I'm disgusted."

"But what has us puzzled is this: How could you have known?"

"Known what?"

"That Foreman and that California bank were going to pull shit on us."

"We didn't."

"Then why start selling silver like crazy?"

"Because we think the price is going to go down."

"Why?"

"Because an enormous amount of silver is going to be hitting the market during the next months, even years."

"Because you figured that that bank is going to continue to operate that mine in Iran and cash in. Flood the market with silver and leave Frank Cook holding the bag. Right?"

"No. That is not the reason."

"What is?"

"That is for Frank Cook's ears only."

"O.K. When?"

"Tonight."

"What time?"

"Say, eight."

"Where?"

"At his place. It's private."

"I'll pick you up at seven."

"No. I'll have a car bring me out. I know where it is now. This time I won't come alone."

"Albert coming too?"

"Yes. And somebody else."

"No monkey business, Doc."

"Don't worry. But you might tell Mr. Cook something beforehand."

"That is?"

"He might need a partner, even if it is for the first time in his life. I think we might have what they term a complete mutuality of interest."

"I'll tell him."

Albert and Doc stayed on for a while at the Metal Exchange. By the late session they had already managed to accumulate an extremely large number of forward silver contracts. All on the short side. The price had dropped well below $2.50.

Their paper profit by late afternoon, was over a million dollars. At least that's what Albert said back in the hotel after spending ten minutes with his calculator.

The hall porter at the Carlton Tower managed to

arrange for a Silver Cloud to take them out to Buckinghamshire. They left a little late since the third man needed time to change, following his arrival from the airport.

The trip to the Cook estate took an hour. Nick Topping met them at the car and took them directly to the drawing room. Frank Cook did not keep them waiting. Everyone was still standing when the door to his library opened, and he made his entrance. He immediately addressed Doc.

"Mr. Smythe," he said, "perhaps you could make the introductions."

"Certainly. That is Albert Fiore. I believe you know his father."

"Pleased to meet you, Albert."

"And this is Agha Firdausi. He was our partner in Iran."

The Iranian took Frank Cook's hand firmly.

"Please be seated, Mr. Firdausi."

So everyone sat. No drinks were offered.

"Well, Mr. Smythe, first I must confess that I made a mistake. I should have accepted your original offer on that silver mine. I believe Mr. Topping has told you what has ensued in the meantime."

"He has. But you hardly made a mistake."

"No? But now I can only acquire that mine for an outrageous sum. Yet if I do not acquire it, and all that silver is produced and floods the market, we stand to lose a great deal of money. The price may well collapse. So I am damned if I do, and damned if I don't."

"Not necessarily."

"That's most interesting. Perhaps you could amplify as to your reasons."

"I shall. And I do hope you have a sense of humor."

"I'm not noted for it. But proceed anyway."

"You see, Mr. Cook, we have all been subjected to an enormous hoax."

"Hoax?"

"Yes. Because there is no silver mine in Persia. Is not, and never has been."

"My God," exclaimed Cook, his scowl demonstrating that, indeed, he did not find it funny, "I was within a hair of being defrauded of a hundred million dollars! Are you sure?" He actually got out a white silk handkerchief and wiped his forehead.

"Quite sure," replied Doc.

"No silver at all?" Frank Cook was upset. No doubt about it. But there was suddenly a new gleam in his eye. Maybe he would, as usual, luck it out all the way.

"I did not say that, Mr. Cook. All I said was that there is no silver *mine*."

"Once more, please." The gleam went.

"It is quite simple. Our friend Firdausi has pulled off a highly remarkable feat. He was faced with a situation that required a silver mine. So he created one, so to say. And then let us in on the action. Perhaps you should explain, Agha." As he turned toward Firdausi, Doc's expression indicated both fondness and respect.

Agha Firdausi cleared his throat.

"You see," he began, as his eyes moved around his audience, "I am really nothing more than a smuggler.

270

I smuggle gold into India and silver out. I try to sell the gold expensive and buy the silver cheap. At first it was a small business. But then, as the silver price began to rise around the world, more and more Indians wanted to sell. For gold. It is said that as a result of three centuries of hoarding, Indians now possess three billion ounces of silver. That is more than the entire world, even today, can use in twenty or thirty years. If I could not handle the trade, my clients would turn to someone else. And, alas, I was not a rich man. To handle all the new business, I had to have capital. A great deal of capital. You see, first I must purchase the gold. For cash. Then I must pay the men who sail the djerbas between Dubai and India. With cash. Then I must warehouse the silver, against cash in advance. I must constantly pay off the customs people in India. With . . .”

At this point Frank Cook interrupted: “Yes, we get the point. Go on.”

“No bank likes to finance a smuggling operation, even though it can be highly profitable. So I had to invent something that was, as you say, bankable. Therefore I invented the silver mine. It was not illogical. There definitely *should* be a mine near Susa. Archeologists, the Bible, even geologists agree on that. But what should have been was not. So I corrected that situation, you might say. But I did not cheat. I did produce all of the silver I promised to my partners. In fact, much more. Only it has come from India, not Persia, and it does not come from the earth, but from the bottoms of djerbas. You understand?”

“I understand,” replied Frank Cook, “at least I

understand you, Mr. Firdausi. But," and now he turned to Nick Topping, "I certainly do not understand how you could possibly have fallen for this?"

Nick Topping replied firmly: "It's like the man just said, Mr. Cook, it was logical. Not only that. I actually *saw* the silver coming into Dubai. So did that fellow from the California bank—Luckman. How the hell was I to know it wasn't coming from Iran like it was supposed to? You saw those reports I brought from Switzerland—the assays, the geologists' reports, the estimates of ore reserves, the weekly refining throughput figures, the . . ."

"You've made your point, Topping."

"Well, you believed them, didn't you?"

"I did. By the way, who did those reports, Mr. Firdausi?"

"A man by the name of Ron Howard. He's a mining engineer from Rhodesia."

"Where is he now?"

"Oh, he went back to Africa." Which obviously closed that subject where Firdausi was concerned.

"It's still unbelievable," continued Cook, shaking his head, and looking around the room. "Didn't *anyone* actually try to go down into that mine?"

No one, of course, had.

"How long have you known about this, Smythe?"

"Since last Friday morning, Mr. Cook."

"That phone call in my office?"

"Yes."

"From Mr. Firdausi?"

"No. From Albert."

"How did he find out?"

272

"It's complicated. A former colleague of ours telephoned from Dubai."

"My cousin," added Firdausi. "He's from Sicily."

"Why?"

"Why is he from Sicily?"

"No. Why did he tell Albert."

"Because he felt bad. And also because he said that he was afraid of what Doc might do."

Frank Cook nodded: "Doc almost did. I am indebted to your cousin in more than one way, Mr. Firdausi. But we are straying from the subject at hand. Tell me, how much silver are you 'producing' at the moment down there in Dubai?"

"I bring in about 5 million ounces each month. I hope to double the volume this summer. Of course, this requires even more working capital. But my sister and I now have my cousin as our new partner. And my cousin has arranged that these gentlemen," his hand pointed toward Doc, then Albert, "will help us out in that regard if necessary. Albert has proposed a very fine program for future cooperation." Firdausi smiled.

"Yes," said Frank Cook, "I'm sure Albert has. Because obviously Albert plans on wrecking the silver price that I have been building up so carefully during the past months."

"That is not correct, Mr. Cook," replied Albert. "Otherwise we would not be here talking to you this evening."

"Touché. Why are you here?"

"To insure that our plans in the silver market will be successful."

"And what are your plans?"

"We plan to go short in the futures market. Very short: 250 million ounces. That will involve a cash investment of around $60 million in margin."

"You plan to sell short now at $2.50 an ounce, and cover sometime next year, or later on, at half that price."

"We are not quite that optimistic. We think our profit should average around one dollar an ounce. Which will be quite sufficient."

"But you still have not answered my question. Logically the last person on earth you should want to tell all this to is me. As you know full well, it is I, and my organization, that have been major buyers of silver. As you know, commodities futures are a zero-sum type game. For every winner there's a loser. You should have been happy to have a potential loser like myself around for as long as possible."

"Of course. But we knew that you would not stay on the losing side for long. It must inevitably come out—soon—that that silver mine never existed. In fact, you would probably have been the first to hear anyway."

"My God," interrupted Cook, "this means that the First National Bank of California is stuck . . ."

Now Albert interrupted, "Yes, Mr. Cook. But let us discuss that aspect later. Now, we calculated that when this news came to you, it would take only a very short time before your people came up with the truth. About Firdausi's operation on the Gulf. And you would immediately realize that if it appears that a vast new silver source has opened up in India, that the price would collapse. Then you would have also gone massively short in the market, trying to cut your losses."

"Your line of reasoning is correct."

"That is exactly why we are here. To prevent such a thing from happening. Because if two groups like ourselves go short at the same time, we would wreck the price. We could never build up a position anywhere resembling 250 million ounces. Nor could you. It must be done gradually, over months, hopefully even years. Because as you correctly pointed out, commodities are a zero-sum game. We must insure that we have enough losers. And that will require that we —our group, which controls the silver from Dubai— and your group, Mr. Cook, which is the most powerful organization in the silver industry, work together."

"How?"

"We must play on the psychology of silver investors like a violin. Right now, we must start selling some of that silver from the warehouses in Dubai. But without revealing the source. A small panic will ensue. All of a sudden investors will start to believe that perhaps the world is not running out of that metal. That somewhere somebody has immense amounts of the stuff. Then we must stop. You must stop. We must again create the impression of a growing scarcity. That will bring the investors back, trying to recoup their losses of the prior weeks or months. Buying even more silver futures—on the long side. We—your group and ours, Mr. Cook—will match every one of their purchases with one of our short sales. Then we panic them again. Et cetera. Et cetera."

Albert continued.

"But it is utterly imperative for our mutual success that we completely coordinate two things: how much physical silver we allow to come to the market in any given week, and how heavily we engage in short selling in the futures market. We can succeed. Because almost no investor in any commodity market ever even sees the physical material he is dealing in. We not only see it, we can control a large part of physical silver. We can create one of the most massive and *longest* bear markets of the century, Mr. Cook. And we both can make a quarter of a billion dollars in the process."

"It is beautiful, Albert. But not perfect. What if we fail? What if the silver you throw on the market from Dubai does *not* depress the price for long. What if I try to help along, and sell equal amounts from my warehouses and even that does not work. Then we may not make, but could lose a dollar on every ounce of silver we promise to deliver in the future. We could create a classic bear trap for ourselves and get wiped out."

"That is a possibility, Mr. Cook. No plan is perfect. But we are willing to take that risk if you are. Doc has assured me that you are the type of man to whom a thing like this would appeal."

For at least two minutes the room fell into silence. All eyes were on Frank Cook. Finally he spoke.

"Doc was right. It does appeal to me. And every

silver user on earth will—unwittingly—cooperate. Every industrial firm on earth that employs silver wants lower prices. They want much lower prices. And if—at the right time—all of us psych the crazy small investor that is behind this bull market, create the illusion that the world is about to become awash in silver, then by God it will work and for sure. At least for a couple of years. I will talk to every man I know in the industry about this. And I know most of them. That, my friends, will guarantee success."

"Do you now understand why we came to you, Mr. Cook?" asked Albert. Without waiting for an answer he went on. "It's really because of what Doc figured out during the past few weeks. He said that we and big business were really meant to be part of one large happy family. Our objectives are the same. Our methods essentially the same. We think alike. There is no sense that we fight each other. Because—well, you can finish, Doc."

Doc did. "Mr. Cook. We would be honored if you could consider us as your first partners."

Without the slightest hesitation Frank Cook rose, went to Doc, and grasped his hand.

"Doc, the honor will be all mine."

Which clinched the fate of all those dentists, airline pilots, insurance salesmen, and greedy widows who thought they were going to make a fortune in silver futures.

But there were other fates at stake that evening also: those of the Chairman of the Board of the First National Bank of California, George Foreman, and of the newly appointed head of their Lugano branch,

Donald Luckman. The phone call that Foreman received from Frank Cook later that evening left him puzzled as he had never been in his life. And as worried. After he hung up, his wife looked at him in shock.

"George," she said, "for God's sake sit down. What's wrong?"

"That deal I've been negotiating with Frank Cook. It's off."

"Maybe he's just . . ."

"Marjory, shut up. And stay that way."

He picked up the phone and dialed Room 1217.

"Debbie?"

"Yes."

"Where's your husband staying in Lugano?"

She told him. Then asked, "Is there something wrong?"

"No, no. I just want to talk to him," was George Foreman's reply, and he hung up.

He had her husband on the phone within two minutes.

"I'm glad you called," were Donald Luckman's first words. "Everything is going on schedule. All the resignations have been made effective. I've informed the bank authorities here of our ownership of the bank, and the name change is . . ."

"Luckman, shut up and listen. I want you to get your ass over to that place in Iran. There's something wrong there."

"What do you mean?"

"I mean I think we've been had. In a monumental

fashion. I want you to get down there and find out if that silver mine really exists. Immediately!"

"You must be joking!"

"I've never been more serious."

"But I've never been there."

"Exactly. But I assume you at least know where it is."

"Of course."

"Then go."

"There's bound to be a language problem."

"I'll arrange for someone to help you out. Just cable me the flight number and your arrival time at Abadan. I'll take care of the rest. And listen, Luckman, I want to hear from you the minute you find out what's going on down there. You hear?"

Another phone call followed. To the residence of the United States Ambassador in London. He took it immediately. George Foreman regularly ranked among the top fifty contributors to the party. Yes, they had a consul in Khuzistan. Stationed in Khurramshahr. Of course he'd help out. Just let him know. His man would be met at the airport in Abadan. No trouble, George. That's what we're here for.

A third call went to San Francisco. To the home of the top legal man of the First National Bank of California, who, fortunately, was also a member of the bank's International Committee and thus also on the hook. It was very brief.

"Sid," said Foreman, "we've got trouble over here."

"What kind?"

"I don't want to discuss it on the phone. I want you to come over to London right away."

279

"All right. Where are you?"

"At the Hilton. I'll fix up rooms."

"Rooms?"

"Yes. I want you to bring some other people along. An S.E.C. specialist. A tax specialist. Some man from your department who's fully acquainted with our bonding of employees. And I want you to line up legal counsel here in London, as well as in Switzerland."

"Jeezus, George. What have you gotten yourself into?"

"I told you, Sid. I don't want to discuss it on the phone. Just do what I say."

"O.K. George."

Two days later the worst had been confirmed from Iran. The Firdausi property had tomatoes, strawberries, alfalfa, you name it. But no silver. Worse: No one, anywhere, knew of any mining operation. What now? Donald Luckman was instructed to return to Lugano. He would hear further.

By this time the London Hilton had more lawyers in it than bell hops: two from San Francisco, one from New York, one from Washington, two from London, one from Paris, two from Geneva.

They barely all fitted into George Foreman's suite. Foreman summarized the situation, as all sat in total silence, something that is not easy for one lawyer to do for long, much less nine.

The English solicitor was the first to speak out.

"As I understand it, then, Mr. Foreman, these Americans who sold you the Swiss bank represented to you that the Swiss bank owned a very valuable silver mine in Iran. And there is no such mine."

"That is correct."

"Well, this should be quite simple. We merely inform the authorities here, have the men arrested, and block the funds you paid out. You said that the entire arrangement was done at Winthrop's?"

"Yes."

"We will, of course, need the documents in which all the representations were made in regard to that silver mine, especially the value at which it was given in the Swiss bank's balance sheet and after that, it should prove quite simple."

"But there lies a problem."

"Explain, Mr. Foreman."

"The basis for the entire deal was the audit report made on the Swiss bank by my employee, Donald Luckman."

"Yes."

"No mention is made of any silver mine."

That, to put it mildly, caused some raised eyebrows. How could that be?

George Foreman said he could not explain it himself. He had never really read that audit report carefully. He had depended almost completely upon the oral statements of that fellow Luckman. No reason to mistrust him. What was there in place of the silver mine? Some stuff about oil storage facilities. Which also did not exist, obviously.

"So," said the solicitor, "we do have evidence that the balance sheet of the Swiss bank was deliberately falsified."

"No," replied Foreman, "we have only evidence that Luckman's report on the balance sheet of the bank was incorrect."

"What do you mean?"

"I had the definite, very definite, impression that the people who formerly owned that bank, and sold it to me, were also convinced that there was a very valuable silver mine in Iran, and that it belonged 100% to their bank. I'm sure the *true* records of that bank will reflect this."

"But surely," interjected the lawyer from New York, "they must have noticed that no mention of it was made in Luckman's audit report."

George Foreman shrugged, and then expressed the opinion that it would be most difficult to proceed against the former owners of the Swiss bank. He felt that they all were taking the wrong approach. Obviously fraud was involved. But who was responsible? He, George Foreman, had given the matter a great deal of thought. There was—there could be—only one logical answer: he had been betrayed by his own employee, Donald Luckman. Luckman must have been operating in collusion with the people in Iran. He must have found out, somehow, about the hoax, and made a deal to conceal it long enough to make sure the Iranians were paid off for their share of that non-existent mine, by the former owners of the bank. He also made sure it remained concealed until such time as the First National Bank of California had bought that Swiss bank. Probably the Italian prince that was Chairman of the Swiss bank had also been involved in the conspiracy. But he, along with all the other former executives of the bank, was no longer in Switzerland. And it would be very difficult to get them back, he assumed. The lawyer from Geneva confirmed this. It was almost impossible to extradite people on suspicion of fraud. Every country had a different definition of that crime. So, concluded Foreman, one had to be realistic. Fraud could be proven. Against Luckman. Did everyone in the room concur? They did. Good. That would mean that they could collect at least $15 million insurance. Was that right? The insurance lawyer from San Francisco said he thought so. And probably the remaining loss could be charged off as a taxable expense. Or? The tax lawyer from New York was sure it could be, which would mean that Uncle Sam would essentially pick up 50% of the bill. So although George Foreman had shelled out $60 million, when all was said and done, the write-off which the First National Bank of California would ultimately have to make would probably be no more than $25 million. A lot of money, but it could have been worse. What about the bank in Lugano? After such a fiasco, the only logical thing to do was close it up. Liquidate it. That would probably mean another $10 million additional loss. Better that, suggested the lawyer from Geneva, than getting involved in a major scandal with the Swiss banking authorities, and face bad publicity around the world for God knows how long. He could arrange that the Swiss Banking Commission cooperated in full—provided the First National Bank of California guaranteed that no depositors would lose any money. And provided that the guilty man—Donald Luckman—be properly punished for his criminal activity in Switzerland. This would mean that Mr. Foreman would have to prefer formal charges against him. Was Mr. Foreman prepared to do so? Foreman was.

And the next day he did. Through his Geneva lawyer. Donald Luckman had been on Swiss soil no more than five minutes after returning from the Near East when he was picked up by the police. That same day, the doors to the Bank of Sicily and America in Lugano were sealed. The Swiss bank secrecy laws were called into force, and George Foreman began preparations for his return to California, surrounded by his battery of lawyers.

The only person on earth who knew the truth, and wanted to tell it, was Debbie Luckman. The day after her husband's arrest—the same day that the Foremans were scheduled to return to the United States—after frantically telephoning every ten minutes, she finally got hold of George Foreman. He listened for two minutes to her garbled plea for help. Then he said: "I'm afraid it's out of my hands, Mrs. Luckman. There's no sense in your trying to contact me again."

Marjory was standing beside the phone while he took the call. After he had hung up she made her first, and last, comment on the entire affair: "I never did like them, you know. She was the one that probably pushed him into it."

Debbie's last resort was Doc Smythe. He came to the Hilton, and when he left, Debbie left with him.

But there was nothing, of course, that either could do to help Donald.

The Swiss authorities spent two years investigating the matter, and in the end sentenced Donald Luckman to ten years at hard labor. He had, after all, engineered a monumental fraud, involving tens of millions of dollars. Which was bad enough. But the fact that he had perpetrated it against a bank—a Swiss bank—was unforgivable. So he got the maximum the law allowed.

Especially damning for Luckman were his weird attempts to defend himself. First, he claimed that he had only followed the orders of his Chairman. Of course, Luckman could not produce one document to prove this allegation. Anyway, the Swiss knew full well that a man of the format of George Foreman would never involve himself in such a thing. Three of Switzerland's leading bankers, when discreetly approached on the subject, all testified to this. So that line of investigation was dropped almost immediately. Then Luckman insisted that the billionaire, Frank Cook, and one of his employees, Nicholas Topping, had been behind the entire affair. The Swiss, after exhaustive investigation, found no evidence whatsoever—not a shred of paper —that either party had had the slightest thing to do with either the bank, or that fictitious mine. When Luckman claimed that one of the bank's former executives, a Mr. Marvin Skinner, was a professional counterfeiter, and that he was the one who had manufactured the phoney documentation Luckman had employed in his audit report, the Swiss had no choice but to also investigate that. It was determined that, indeed, a Mr. Marvin Skinner did exist. He lived in a place called Penn, about thirty miles northwest of London, where he bred dogs. Alsatians. Both his reputation, and that of his dogs, the English police said, were beyond reproach. After that the Swiss arranged for Luckman to be submitted to extensive psychological examination. The results were, unfortunately, inconclusive.

The trial itself was very brief. Since bank secrecy was involved, it was, of course, held *in camera*. No witnesses from abroad were present, since none were called. It did irritate the Swiss considerably that they were unsuccessful in their attempts to track down Luckman's co-conspirators: that Iranian and that Italian prince. But both had disappeared. So the matter was dropped.

The bank itself was liquidated in a very slow, though proper, manner. All in all, it took around three years. One of the bank's major assets, a large agricultural property in Iran, was sold off to Middle Eastern interests, represented by a bank in Kuwait, for an exceptionally good price. But the unexpected gain from that source was more than offset by the unexpected losses which turned up in the commodity department. The reason was that the Swiss bank had held a rather large number of silver futures contracts for its own account. The liquidators decided to hang on to them for a while, even roll them over, because —as they later argued when criticized by the Bank Commission—they had felt that silver was a solid investment. Everyone, but everyone, they had consulted, had expected the price to go up. But for some inexplicable reason, it had done just the opposite. In the end they had been forced to cover their longs right at the bottom of the most spectacular bear market in the history of silver—on October 22, 1971, when the price hit $1.29 an ounce.

Part 3

(1976)

Epilogue

Every year, on October 22nd, Frank Cook put on a little luncheon at the Atheneum Club in London in commemoration of the day the silver bears had achieved total victory. At the first such affair Agha Firdausi and the prince had been in attendance. But after that, no longer. The reason was that their silver operation on the Gulf ceased to exist. For, as had been predicted by Albert, the gold-silver trade between India and Dubai eventually dried up. During the good old days in 1968, and even 1969, when the price of silver had been $2 an ounce or more, and the price of gold had stayed between $35 and $40 an ounce, the Indians could hardly get rid of enough silver. After all, for each ounce of gold they only had to give up 17 or 18 ounces of silver. But then the gold price soared—to $170 an ounce and above—while the price of silver slumped ever further. By the early 1970's it took 60, sometimes 70, ounces of silver to get an ounce of gold in return. That killed it. Of course, the London silver consortium had covered all their shorts well before this point. And had, naturally, then gone long. Because they knew full well that the silver shortage—which had been there all along—would now appear in full force. And it did. The morning silver fixing in London on this anniversary day was $6.25 an ounce! The London consortium was ahead by well over a half billion dollars by this stage.

Doc, Albert, Marvin, and Frank Cook, however, ate frugally. At the Atheneum Club it was difficult to do otherwise, since a large number of its members were Bishops of the Church of England who considered extravagance in any form improper, but especially frowned on public displays of gluttony. So it had been, as usual, lamb chops, with three side dishes of soggy vegetables. The fact that it was served on long wooden tables did not help. One of Frank Cook's rules was that no business be discussed over lunch. That had to wait until coffee and cognac was served in the library on the second floor.

Nick Topping, perhaps deliberately, arrived too late for lunch, but in time for cognac. His was a pensive look as he entered the upstairs room, and took a seat beside Doc. He made his usual obeisance toward Mr. Cook, accepted a cognac, and then started talking to Doc.

"How's it going?" was his opener.

"Fine. How were things over at the Metal Exchange this morning?"

"Quiet. Where's Debbie?"

"She's having lunch with a friend. At Fortnum and Masons."

"Her friend anyone I should know?"

"In fact, yes. It's Shireen Siracusa."

"I guessed as much."

"How?"

"Because of the latest gossip on silver."

Now everyone around the coffee table, even Frank Cook who had been dozing, lent at least a partial ear.

"You see," continued Topping, "there's a new story

that's making the rounds at the Metal Exchange today. Want to hear it?"

Of course they wanted to hear it.

"It seems there is this Sicilian prince. He's the partner of a royal, or some such thing, from Iran. He, the Sicilian, is married to the Iranian's sister, who is, naturally, a dark beauty. They are in town this week, looking for a partner who will provide them with a little venture capital. The figure of fifty million pounds is being mentioned."

Now Topping had the full attention of everyone.

"Why, you ask, does he need this capital? I will tell you. It seems that a few years ago these people bought a large agricultural property in Iran—from a Swiss bank that had been put into forced liquidation. And guess what? On that property they have made one of the richest silver strikes of the century. At a location called Choga Zambil. It's in Khuzistan, right next door to a place called Susa. Now here comes the amazing thing. If you look up Susa in the Bible, you will find out that it was loaded, really loaded, with silver. You can read it in the Book of Esther—'the beds were made out of gold and silver.' Right? But where did the silver come from? Answer: Choga Zambil. Now according to the boys down at the exchange, it could amount to as much as 100 million ounces, and . . ."

No one said a word until Topping's tale was completed. And then a spirited discussion followed. Because although no one, it was agreed, had ever seen that silver mine in Persia, no one had ever proven that it wasn't there. And if it was, hell, all that silver coming onto the market could wreck the price!

The only one who refused to be drawn into the speculation was Albert. Why? Just before the party broke up, he explained. He'd only met Agha Firdausi three times, but he had learned of his favorite piece of poetry—over drinks in Teheran a few years back. It was not from the Scriptures. Rather from Omar Khayyám. Although written in the twelfth century Albert considered it enlightening:

Take the cash. And leave the sound of distant drums.

All agreed. It was enlightening. Perhaps even pertinent. Omar Khayyám was no doubt right.

But could the Bible be wrong?